TREAS

Treasure Hunt

Catriona Beck

Publisher's message

This novel creates an imaginary sexual world. In the real world,
readers are advised to practise safe sex.

First published in 1998 by
HEADLINE BOOK PUBLISHING

A HEADLINE LIAISON paperback

10 9 8 7 6 5 4 3 2 1

ISBN 0 7472 5916 X

Typeset by Avon Dataset Ltd, Bidford-on-Avon, Warks

Printed and bound in Great Britain by
Mackays of Chatham plc, Chatham, Kent

HEADLINE BOOK PUBLISHING
A division of Hodder Headline PLC
338 Euston Road
London NW1 3BH

Treasure Hunt

One

Chrissy Fielding shifted position on the bar stool and turned once again towards the door, checking her watch. No doubt about it – she had been stood up. Not that it really mattered; she grinned slightly to herself. Any night out, even one drinking alone in a hotel bar, was preferable to another quiet night alone in her flat. The barman caught her grin and smiled back at her. Impulsively Chrissy winked, and for a hopeful moment it looked as if he would come over and chat, but an old man at the far end of the bar held up an empty glass and, with a shrug at Chrissy, he turned to attend to his customer.

Chrissy would not have minded speaking to him. In fact, she was so bored now that she would have talked to anyone. The barman would have been the first attractive man she had spoken to in days.

Deciding that she was not going home just yet, she looked around the room with interest. Three men in business suits sat round a table in the corner, no doubt guests of the hotel. One of them was eyeing her speculatively, but she let her gaze slip away, giving him no encouragement. Too old; too fat; too married. Four students talking animatedly at one table, a middle-aged couple barely talking to another – why on earth did people go to pubs, if they had nothing to say to each other? – and of course, the old man who still held the barman's attention. Not exactly a lively bunch. She tossed her fair glossy hair restlessly. If only something interesting would happen.

The door from the lobby swung open and a young man entered. Now he definitely looked worth talking to. In jogging pants and polo shirt, he had obviously just come from a hard session at the gym. There were damp patches on his chest and underarms, and his fair hair clung to his forehead, but he looked tanned and fit and handsome – and totally out of place in this lifeless room. Chrissy looked down at her drink. If she waited till this newcomer was served she could order another; once she got the barman talking she had no doubt that she could keep his attention. Then the evening would not be a total washout.

Absorbed in her thoughts, she jumped slightly when the newcomer came up behind her and dropped his sports bag with a thud at her feet.

'Thank God you're still here. I thought I'd missed you.' His voice was smooth and cultured and he grinned happily at Chrissy

She couldn't help smiling back.

'I'm really sorry I'm late,' he said. 'I got stuck in court and then I had to meet a client for a game of squash – couldn't get out of it. I hope you're not too mad. I've been looking forward to this all day.'

'I'm sorry, I think—'

'You look great. I think this is a fantastic idea. I was really knocked out when you phoned. You look absolutely stunning.'

'Thank you. Listen, I—'

'Do you mind if I have a drink before we start? Would you like another?'

'No, thank you, I—'

'I really need one. Do you mind? I think I'm dehydrated.' He ordered a long cold drink which he drained thirstily. She watched with amusement; his entrance had certainly livened things up.

He was an extremely handsome man, and Chrissy felt a pang of regret that she was not the person he had come to meet. His personality was overwhelming, like a large boisterous dog. And he never stopped talking. It was obvious that he had mistaken her for someone else and it was time to put him right.

'I'm sorry, but—'

'OK, ready when you are. Shall we go? I can't wait.' He dropped a ten-pound note on the bar, picked up his bag and waited expectantly for her. Chrissy's mind was racing. He was attractive and she had an inkling that what he had in mind would be very interesting. However, she made one more effort to put him straight.

2

'You seem to—'

'Talk too much? I know. I haven't changed. But you have. Did I say you look wonderful?' He eyed her slim body appreciatively, his eyes lingering for a moment on her large breasts. 'And grown a bit too, if I remember correctly.'

She trembled under his admiring gaze. It was a long time since a good-looking man had looked at her like that, and she realised how much she had missed it.

He was propelling her along as he spoke and they stopped beside the lifts. After pushing the buttons, he pulled a room key out of his pocket and twirled it impatiently. So that was it. She had thought as much; he believed that she was a prostitute. Presumably one he had met some time in the past. What was she going to do? She could still explain his mistake and go back to her seat, but she was reluctant to do so; the thought of another evening alone was not appealing.

One of the lifts was descending. She had twenty seconds to decide whether or not to go to a hotel bedroom with a very attractive man for sex. Decision time.

'OK,' she told herself. 'If the lift is empty then I'll go with him. If my mother's inside, then I'll slap his face and call for the manager.'

With a ping the doors opened. It was empty. He was still talking as the doors swished closed. 'This is fantastic,' he assured her. 'Things are really going to liven up, now that you're back!' Chrissy was listening with half an ear, her mind in turmoil. What was she going to do? She knew what she wanted to do, all right. Her companion was attractive and, in the confined space of the lift, the clean masculine smell of his sweaty body filled her nostrils. She had not had a man in a long time and she was very tempted to go through with this. What harm could it do? No-one would get hurt.

He wanted a woman. She, she suddenly realised, wanted a man. This was almost certainly the cause of her restlessness, these past few days. It would be a problem if and when he offered her money as he was bound to do, but she would cross that bridge when she came to it. With a start Chrissy realised that she had already decided to go ahead and sleep with him.

'Was this your idea or Portia's? Yours, I expect. She never

3

did have much imagination, the bitch, though I don't suppose Bas would agree with me, the poor downtrodden bastard. Still, each to his own, I always say. Though she won't get me on her Treasure Hunt, that's for sure! I value my balls too much!' He laughed loudly at his own joke. 'Here we are.'

Chrissy, who hadn't a clue what he was talking about, smiled inanely and allowed herself to be led into the bedroom.

'I'll just have a shower first, if that's OK with you. I must smell like a billy goat.' Chrissy would have told him that he smelled just fine but had decided to keep her mouth shut in case she put her foot in it. It was easy to keep quiet, as even from the shower he kept up a constant, one-sided conversation.

'Met Tom at the squash club. Remember him?' he called over the sound of splashing water. 'He asked me to ask you to bear him in mind, if you know what I mean.'

'Mm,' answered Chrissy non-committally, wondering what the etiquette was in these situations. She looked around the room; it was fairly basic but clean, and the bed was turned down invitingly. Catching sight of herself in the mirror on the wardrobe door, she paused for a moment to examine her reflection.

Her hair was freshly washed, hanging loose around her shoulders, warm gold highlights catching the light. The simple style was still too new to be familiar and Chrissy took a second to appreciate it, loving the way it moved softly when she shook her head. She did this now, before continuing her scrutiny. Hazel eyes, shining with excitement, watched from a face almost bare of make-up.

Somehow, a quick farewell drink with her friend Karen had not seemed to merit making too much of an effort and anyway, she preferred it that way. She knew she had a good body, long and lean and fit, but in her jeans and T-shirt she certainly did not look like a lady of the night. Looking at herself, Chrissy was perplexed. It did not make sense that she had been mistaken for a professional. Maybe she was reading the situation wrong? Now if she still had the brassy curls and abundant make-up that Marc had preferred . . .

Marc. Despite herself, a vision of his gorgeous face arose in her mind, his thick brows drawn in the frown of concerned

4

disapproval that she had grown to dread over the years. Quickly she pushed the thought of him aside, but the damage had been done. She fought to control the familiar feeling of rising panic. Again her eyes were drawn to her reflection and this time, instead of the happy, attractive, positive young woman she had seen moments before, she saw an ordinary, dull-looking woman in a too tight T-shirt. Now her nerve failed her and she turned, her face flushing with embarrassment as she searched for the door. How could she have thought that the man in the shower found her attractive? Wasn't she just flattering herself a little too much to think that he had invited her to his room for sex?

But by the door she paused, drawing some deep breaths into her lungs. Marc was in the past. His opinion, his approval did not matter. He had no control over her life; he never should have done. The words, a familiar mantra over the past six months, had a soothing effect; gradually her breathing returned to normal, the panic attack receding. Chrissy was pleased with herself. The attack had lasted only a few seconds and once again she was in control. But standing with her hand on the door handle, she was once again faced with the dilemma of what she was going to do in the present situation.

Just then the door to the small bathroom opened and her new friend emerged in a cloud of steam, drying his hair vigorously with a towel. The rest of his body was naked, still damp from the shower; moisture clung in droplets to his thick chest hair. Like a magnet, Chrissy's gaze was drawn downwards over his flat stomach to where his penis, already semi-erect, rose thickly from his damp blond curls.

Licking her lips nervously, she could not tear her eyes away. How long was it since she had last seen a naked man? As if in response to her hungry gaze, his cock gave a jump and seemed to swell and grow as she stared. It was hard to resist the urge to reach over and stroke it to full size.

Tossing the towel aside he stared in surprise at where she stood, poised, fully clothed by the door.

'What's wrong?' he asked anxiously. 'Haven't changed your mind, have you?'

Her mouth too dry to speak and her eyes fixed on his growing cock, Chrissy could only shake her head. She was nervous still, not sure if she could pull this off; though heaven only knew how much she wanted to.

'Let me give you a hand then.' He reached eagerly for her, but she stepped back, not quite ready for that.

'No, I'll do it.' Swiftly, before she could change her mind, she pulled the T-shirt over her head and slipped out of the jeans. She stood before him in her white bra and knickers, which were more functional than seductive, and hesitated. Somehow, removing her bra in front of a total stranger was beyond her.

'Let me.' Moving behind her, he cupped her breasts in his large hands, circling her nipples through the soft fabric. Any doubts Chrissy was harbouring disappeared as he nuzzled her with his lips, his breath softly blowing the tiny hairs at the back of her neck, sending shivers racing along her spine.

Leaning back against him, her eyes closed, she rubbed her bare shoulders over his damp chest. When his fingers slipped inside her bra, she gasped audibly. The nipple rose and hardened, while his other hand pushed under the elastic of her knickers, probing the tender furrow between her legs. Despite her nervousness Chrissy moaned at these twin sensations, tiny ripples of delight chasing through her body. It was a long time since a man had touched her like that and it felt so good.

She could feel his cock, now fully erect, pressing urgently into her buttocks, and she wriggled slightly against him, causing him to moan in turn at the delicious friction. He unhooked her bra, then turned her round to face him so he could admire her breasts.

'God, Clarissa, you have changed. I'm sure I would have remembered tits like these.' Staring enraptured at her firm, round breasts, he missed the sudden flash of panic in her eyes. But Chrissy's fear of discovery vanished in a wave of pleasure as he lowered his mouth to her breasts and began to suckle first one nipple, then the other. Each tug of his lips sent waves of pleasure shooting into her womb and she arched backwards, supported by his strong arm. Easing her down onto the bed, he knelt above her, nudging her thighs apart with his knees.

'Is there anything in particular I need to do? Wait; I'm the first, aren't I? That means I get to do anything I like.'

Still playing happily with her breasts, he did not notice her confusion.

Surely she was not supposed to play the part of the reluctant virgin? This was getting harder by the minute!

He must have detected the sudden tension in her, because he paused and glanced up at her face. 'Sorry, I'm talking too much. I'll stop.'

The rosy crest of her nipple was once more enclosed by his lips, practised and confident, and she relaxed, lost in the sensation. Steeling herself, Chrissy reached for his cock, circling the thick shaft with her fingers and sliding the loose silky skin over the sensitive glans until his breath grew short and he moaned in her ear. Catching her hand in his, he slowed her motion.

'Remember, I've been looking forward to this all day – just let me play a while or I'll get over-excited.'

Slipping her panties down her smooth thighs, he ran his hands over her naked curves. Her legs parted slightly and he allowed his gaze to linger over the glistening line of flesh visible through her thick blonde public hair. Chrissy was embarrassed by how ready she was for him, how wet, as the musky scent of her arousal reached her own nostrils. But he could not tear his attention away from his main interest for too long – her magnificent ripe breasts. Tenderly he caressed them, his tanned brown hands contrasting with her own milky skin.

She moaned and writhed as he teased her swollen nipples, all thought of guilt and conscience abandoned when he rolled them between his fingers, making them burn and ache with exquisite pleasure. Lifting the luscious globes, he pushed them together, and she gasped as he pressed his face into their softness. When his teeth scraped over her sensitised nipples she bucked her hips with excitement, drawing his attention to her neglected pussy.

Forgetting that she was supposed to be playing the shy retiring virgin, Chrissy took one of his hands and pressed it between her legs, conveying the sense of her urgency, though still careful not to speak. Her arousal was obvious as he sank two fingers deep into her welcoming softness, and they both groaned, their passion rising out of control.

'Just a minute,' he murmured, and slid off the bed, opening a zippered compartment on his holdall. Removing a condom, he

7

tore the packet open before rolling the thin rubber down his rigid length. Chrissy watched without a word as he moved back on top of her, his cock instinctively finding her desperate opening. Pausing only a second or two to move along the slick lips of her sex, lubricating his shaft with her own slippery juices, he thrust himself into her, forcing a gasp of pleasure from her as she opened eagerly to accommodate him, gripping his thick cock snugly.

He began a hard, steady rhythm, drawing Chrissy with him on a wave of pleasure. Already she could feel her orgasm building; it had been too long since she had had a man inside her. Her hips rose up to meet him with every thrust, her hands cupping the taut muscles of his buttocks, pulling him closer, their public bones grinding together deliciously with every movement. As the pressure built inside her very core, she dug her fingers into his flesh, parting the cheeks of his buttocks; she teased the sensitive skin of his anus with her long nails, making him gasp and increase his hard rhythm.

With a cry of release, Chrissy came, her body shuddering convulsively. Her partner groaned loudly, his own orgasm rushing through him and he arched his body upwards as his seed spurted deep inside her, prevented from flooding her body only by the thin layer of latex. Exhausted and drained, he collapsed on top of her and they lay entwined in a tangle of sweaty limbs.

Covering her face in fluttering kisses, he murmured in her ear, 'You really are the best. I can't believe we never got it together before. Do you think that when this is over – you know, the Hunt – we could get together again, just the two of us?'

'Mm,' Chrissy responded vaguely. This was when he would discover that she was a fake. Suffused with the afterglow of a wonderful orgasm, she could not get too uptight about the fear of discovery now; though she realised it was not going to be easy to bluff her way out of this. But it could wait until he confronted her directly – she could not see that she had done anything really wrong. It was his fault, anyway. He talked far too much. He should have given her a chance to explain.

Having justified her actions she stretched languorously, enjoying his continuing caresses. But she sat up abruptly at his next words.

'It'll be Will tomorrow, if that's still OK. Lucky bastard. I won't be seeing him so I'll leave the key with you. We took the room for two nights, didn't we?' He stood up reluctantly. 'I've got to go back to the office now; can you believe it? If we lose this case tomorrow I'll be out on my ear.' He laughed loudly as if this was extremely funny, and dressed quickly, glancing down at her.

When she did not move to get off the bed he asked, 'Are you going to stay here all night?' He looked around the small hotel room doubtfully, then back at Chrissy. She shook her head. He kissed her briefly, his mind already at the office, but at the door he hesitated and glanced back, grinning. 'You know it's hard to believe that all this is for charity.' And he was gone.

Chrissy lay back on the bed and stared at the ceiling, stunned. Charity? What the hell did he mean by that? You could not sleep with someone for charity, could you? It gave a whole new meaning to Bob-a-Job week. She giggled, despite herself.

She would have liked to linger for a while on the bed, trying to get her thoughts straight, but she began to feel nervous. She was not used to hotel rooms; and what if he came back? Or what if he had met the woman he was supposed to meet, in the lobby, and they were even now making their way back up the stairs to denounce her?

In a sudden panic, Chrissy grabbed her clothes and dressed quickly. The key was lying on the covers where he had tossed it and she hesitated. Should she take it? Of course she would not be back tomorrow; that would be stupid. But on impulse she stuffed it in her pocket. The room was paid for two nights he had said. Just because she took the key did not mean that she planned to use it.

Rushing out of the hotel, she did not risk going in to the bar for another drink, though she badly needed one. When she got home, the red light on her answer-machine was blinking and she switched it on, knowing the message would be from Karen.

'Hi Chrissy. I'm sorry I stood you up tonight, but our plans have been moved forward. Apparently there's bad weather on the way so they want us and the equipment there a few days early; you know what the weather can be like on the Orkneys, even in summer. So we are having to leave tonight to get tomorrow's ferry. I'm really sorry; I hope you didn't wait too long. I'll speak to you soon, OK? Bye.'

Karen was Chrissy's best friend, a final year archaeology student who was working on a dig in the Orkneys all summer. Quickly Chrissy dialled her number, hoping to catch her before she left, but all she got was an answer-machine. Pity. She was bursting to tell someone about her evening, but it looked as if she would have to wait. And it was such a long time since Chrissy had done anything worth telling! Still smiling smugly to herself, she prepared for bed.

Two

Next morning, Chrissy woke slowly in her own bed. The sun streaming through her attic windows shone directly on her face and she did not open her eyes for a few moments, enjoying the warmth. The fact that the sun actually reached her bed told her that it was already mid-morning; she had overslept, but no matter. She had the whole day to herself.

Pushing the duvet down, Chrissy indulged in a long slow stretch as the sunlight danced across her naked skin. At the height of her stretch a slight unaccustomed tenderness between her legs brought her up abruptly and memories of the previous evening's activities came flooding back. She flushed with embarrassment, but also with the thrill of it. Hugging herself close, she could not believe what she had done. It was the most exciting sex she had had for a long time – a once in a lifetime experience. Chrissy felt absurdly pleased to have carried it off and also slightly shocked that she had had the nerve.

Gently she explored her inner thighs, stroking their softness with her fingers. It was a shame to have let those muscles get so out of condition. After Marc ... Well, after Marc she hadn't seemed to feel like sex for a long time. But now she made a positive mental note not to allow her sex to become so neglected again.

Opening her eyes, she squinted slightly against the brightness. The room was a large airy loft, with wonderful views from the two windows set in the sloping ceilings. Chrissy loved it and had been lucky to find it; the rest of the house was in the middle of an extensive conversion and hers was the only habitable floor. Far below, she could hear the workmen calling to each other. She moved her long limbs to absorb the sunlight now spreading across the bed.

11

Running her hands over her sun-warmed skin, she met the gentle swell of her breasts and began to knead and massage each in turn, pulling and stretching the delicate nipples. Moaning softly in pleasure, she focused her mind once again on the previous night's sex. What a thrill it had been to make love to a man whose name she did not even know.

She kept up her slow, sensual massage for a long time, listening to the distant laughter of the workmen. Her breasts were large and she could lift them up to her lips and flick her tongue over the rising nipples, keeping them hard. Shivering, she remembered how much he had admired them, the way he had worshipped them with his mouth.

Eventually, the attention she was lavishing on her breasts drew tingling responses deep within her womb. Pleasure flowed through her body, and her breathing grew shallow. With no sense of urgency, she allowed one hand to slide down once more to caress the tender skin of her thighs. Thrills of pleasure shot through her, but she took her time as she let the hand settle for a moment on her mound, twirling and pulling the curls, prolonging her pleasure. Finally, the excitement becoming too much, she let her legs fall apart, exposing her inner lips to the gently probing sunlight and her own exploring fingers.

Kicking off the rest of the covers, Chrissy stretched her legs as far apart as she could, twining her pubic curls around her fingers to tug her labia gently apart. The warmth of the sun felt good on her sex, but memories of the previous night began to crowd into her mind: the sight of the stranger, naked and damp as he emerged from the shower; the feel of his mouth as he nuzzled her breast; and the tight knot of tension in her belly as she watched his cock swell with desire.

Suddenly her need grew more urgent. Her fingers, coated in her own silky moisture, sought and found the exact tiny spot that was the centre of her pleasure. Increasing the speed and pressure of her rubbing she began to move her hips in a steady rhythm. Thrusting her hand faster and faster, fingers flying over the slippery bud, her head thrashed on the pillow. Her moans grew louder, but there was no-one to hear; she felt her orgasm building, until finally it burst over her and she turned her head into the pillow to muffle her cry. Her thighs were clenched tightly round her hand; her body trembled with the aftershocks of an orgasm so powerful she could feel the blood pounding in her ears.

Gasping breath into her straining lungs, she pushed her hair back off her face and grinned. Whatever else the stranger last night had done, he had re-awoken a sexuality that had lain dormant for far too long.

The barman recognised Chrissy as she made her way to the same stool she had perched on the previous evening.

'Hi. Same as usual?'

She smiled at the idea of having a 'usual' after only one night, but nodded.

'On your own tonight, then?'

'Yes. Just in for a quiet drink.' Her jaw tilted in an unconsciously defensive gesture, trying to mask her nervousness. What on earth was she doing here?

He introduced himself as Harry as he gave her her drink. In his mid-thirties, with black curling hair, he really was an attractive man. 'Always like to get to know my regulars.' His blue eyes twinkled as he spoke, and he leaned on the bar after serving her. 'You're new around here, aren't you? I haven't seen you before.'

Chrissy nodded, glad to have someone to talk to. Her stomach was turning somersaults and her eyes flicked nervously to the door each time it opened. Her mouth was dry and she lifted her glass gratefully to her lips. She did not know why she had come. 'Yes, I only moved here a few weeks ago. I've been accepted as a mature student to start at the university in September. How to make you feel old at twenty-nine.' To her own ears, her laughter sounded forced and she made a conscious effort to calm down. 'I thought I'd arrive a few months early and get myself a job for the summer. I've been for an interview today.' With her hand she indicated her smart appearance and carefully made-up face. Harry eyed her calf-length suede skirt, split to mid-thigh at one side and exposing an exciting amount of bare skin.

'Very nice.' He nodded approvingly. 'I hope you got the job?'

'No.' She waved her hand dismissively. 'I'm not desperate enough to want to spend the summer stuffing letters into

13

envelopes. Not yet. I can afford to hold out for something more interesting.' Why was she talking so much?

'Good for you. Damn, I'll have to go.' Some customers further down the bar were getting restless, waiting to be served. 'I'll maybe see you later?'

Chrissy nodded and continued to fiddle with her drink. Just last night a five minute conversation with Harry would have been the highlight of her evening. But now, nice though he was, she needed time to think. The room was beginning to fill up, but so far she had not seen anyone who might be 'Will'. She wondered what he would do when he could not find 'Clarissa', or if he would even turn up. The room key weighed heavily in her pocket.

'So you did come. I didn't think you would, somehow.'

Chrissy jumped and, turning, found herself face to face with a tall fair-haired woman who was staring at her with frank curiosity. With a shock Chrissy realised that the woman, though slightly older than herself, could have been her sister. Her heart sank, and she blushed to the roots of her hair. This could only be Clarissa. Oh God, now there was going to be a huge scene.

'Ah, so you recognise me,' said the woman, pleased. 'That makes it easier. I'm Clarissa Asquith and I am curious to know why you pretended to be me last night and fucked Philip Woodward.' Her voice, though not unfriendly, was loud and carrying and she had managed to draw the attention of several people – including Harry, who was gazing from her to Chrissy in open-mouthed astonishment.

Seeing Chrissy's face flush with shock and embarrassment, Clarissa hurried on, in a loudly misguided attempt to placate her. 'Not that I'm complaining – don't get me wrong. Phil phoned today to thank me; said I was a fabulous lay, best tits he's seen in a long time. Now Phil may have the reputation of being none too bright, but even he knows when he has fucked someone and it certainly was not me.'

'I'm sorry, I don't—' Chrissy looked around wildly for escape, desperate to stop this tirade before the whole room was listening, but Clarissa was not to be silenced.

'Truth is, I'd forgotten all about our little tryst. So then I got to wondering if you would have the nerve to come back tonight

14

and try it with Will – he's going to be late by the way, that's why Phil phoned – and I thought I'd come and have a look at you for myself. And here we are.' She smiled widely. 'You do look awfully like me, you know; I can understand why Phil made the mistake. Shall I buy you a drink and explain? You did me a favour; I'm not at all cross.' She had watched Chrissy carefully while she was speaking, and was amused by her confusion.

'I think we both need a drink.' She beckoned to the barman who was there in a flash. 'I will have a very large vodka, please.' She looked quizzically at Chrissy. 'And the same for my friend. I think she needs it.'

While Clarissa paid for the drinks and flirted with Harry, Chrissy gazed openly at her. She supposed she could see a certain physical resemblance between herself and the other woman. They were of a similar height and colouring, though her hair and make-up were far more stylish and professional than Chrissy's own. She wore a blue dress in a shimmery material which accentuated every curve of her slim body. Chrissy would not have been seen dead in the dress, but she could only guess at how much it must have cost and felt dowdy by comparison.

Clarissa was now peering suspiciously at a bar stool. She brushed it carefully with her hand before sliding her elegant bottom on to the worn velvet. 'Now please tell me your name and why you slept with Phil. You mustn't worry; he's not my boyfriend or anything.'

Chrissy, still scarlet and on edge, gradually allowed herself to relax. It didn't look as if there was going to be an unpleasant scene after all. Clarissa actually seemed quite friendly, and she found herself very curious about the situation.

She wasn't the only one. Aware that several people were still trying to eavesdrop, Chrissy spoke quietly. 'Well, he just sort of assumed I was you. It all happened so quickly . . . and I was bored, and . . .' She tailed off, further embarrassed by how lame her excuse sounded, but Clarissa seemed satisfied.

'Wonderful. I was hoping you would say something like that. Do you often sleep with strangers because you are bored?' There was no trace of sarcasm in her words; just genuine interest and excitement.

'No, of course not,' hissed Chrissy. 'Would you please keep your voice down?'

'What? Oh, sorry. Look, there isn't much time before Will comes. It's all a bit awkward. He thinks he's going to have sex with me tonight, poor lamb, but I'd really rather not, and I was wondering if you would consider being me again. I know it's a lot to ask when you don't even know me, but I hear he's rather sweet. I'm sure you would enjoy it.'

'What?' Now it was Chrissy's turn to be loud.

'Oh dear, this is going to be very difficult to explain and there isn't much time before he comes.' Clarissa peered at her wristwatch.

'I think you had better try, don't you?' Chrissy was recovering her composure.

'All right, but I'm not very good at explanations,' Clarissa warned. 'It's all to do with a Treasure Hunt. Are you familiar with them?'

'You mean when everyone gets a list of objects to collect and the person who finds the most gets a prize?'

'Exactly! Ours is a tiny bit different, but quite simple. Everyone taking part has a Treasure Hunt card – I brought it with me for you to see.' She rummaged in her bag before handing a large piece of card, folded neatly into three, to Chrissy. 'You can see that it is broken down into categories. Occupations, places, type of activity, that sort of thing. Between now and the end of the month I've got to sleep with as many men as possible on the card, in as many ways and combinations as possible. We get a tick for everything we do. The one with the most ticks wins. It's simple.'

Chrissy could not believe what she had just heard, but Clarissa, not realising she had dropped a bombshell, hurried on earnestly. 'You can see how much fun it will be. Everyone at Portia's party thought it was a wonderful idea.'

'So where do I fit in?'

'Well, I agreed to do it, but now I can't, and I was hoping you'd stand in for me. You do look very like me, you know.'

Chrissy looked at her in disbelief. 'But if they're your friends, they'll know straight away that I'm not you.'

Clarissa shook her head emphatically. 'No. Not in Edinburgh, they won't. I've been in the States for a long time, and in London before that. Some of them haven't seen me for years. And you fooled Philip, didn't you? I don't expect you to sleep with millions of men, or anything. Not unless you want to, of course. You don't have to win the Treasure Hunt for me – just be seen around. As me.'

'But why?' This whole conversation was so odd that Chrissy felt she must be dreaming. 'Why can't you do it yourself?'

For the first time Clarissa became evasive. She did not quite meet Chrissy's eye when she spoke. 'This is going to sound really feeble, but I've met someone. A man. He's different from anyone else I've ever met, and he doesn't know anything about me, or the "games" I sometimes get involved in. He doesn't know any of my friends, either. He's very sweet, and I think he would be shocked if he found out.'

Chrissy said nothing, waiting for Clarissa to continue.

'In fact, I know he would be shocked. I really like him, and I think he likes me. What I want is for him to get to know me better, before he hears any rumours about me. Even if I backed out of the Treasure Hunt now, there would be such a fuss that he would be sure to hear. Portia can be such a cow, you honestly have no idea. She wouldn't rest until she had unearthed the truth and done her best to spoil things for me. And somehow I don't fancy the Hunt as much as I did when we planned it. I'd rather be with John. I thought, if you would take my place, John and I could go off for a few days, just the two of us, and spend some time getting to know each other. And then, when the truth about my past eventually comes out, then maybe he won't judge me too harshly. People can change, can't they?'

It did sound corny, but she seemed sincere and Chrissy believed her. She asked the obvious question. 'Why? Why would I do it?'

Clarissa raised her eyes and looked straight at her. She had clearly given this a great deal of thought.

'For a week,' she said, carefully, 'you could have unlimited, anonymous, uncomplicated sex. You could act out your dreams, your most hidden fantasies and no one need ever know. Because you would not be yourself – you would be me.'

Chrissy was silent for a long time. Absently she toyed with

the Treasure Hunt card while she allowed Clarissa's words to sink in. Then she found her voice. 'You do this sort of thing for fun?'

'Oh no!' It was Clarissa's turn to be shocked. 'For charity. The loser has to give £10,000 to charity. We've signed an agreement.'

Chrissy's jaw dropped. She gazed at Clarissa in astonishment, then picked up her drink and took a long swallow. £10,000 to charity for a game! This had to the most bizarre story she had ever heard.

'How many people are doing it?' She couldn't believe she was actually considering this preposterous idea.

'Oh, only two. Portia and myself. I don't really think anyone else can afford it. Does this mean you will do it?' Clarissa held her breath.

Chrissy thought of the interview she had had that day, and her prospects of finding an interesting job. She thought of how wonderful it had felt to have a man inside her again, but knew she did not want to get involved in a relationship just yet. Maybe not ever. This was very, very tempting. Sex with lots of men with no strings attached. All the pleasure, and none of the responsibility. She wondered if she had the nerve to pull it off. She took a deep breath. 'OK. I'll give it a bash. It does sound quite exciting.'

Clarissa was relieved. 'Great! You'll have a wonderful time, I promise you. There are just a few things I should tell you, before Will comes.' She rummaged through her bag again, becoming very business-like now that Chrissy had agreed to her request and handed Chrissy a bunch of keys. 'Here are the keys to my house. John and I are going away, so you may as well live there; it will be easier for people to get hold of you.' She handed over a card with her address printed on it.

'Watch out for Portia. Portia de Havilland. She really is a bitch, but with a bit of luck you won't have to see her. She hates Edinburgh. I'll be back in time for the Hunt Ball on the 31st of July. I'll go to the Ball, and then just sort of gradually drop out of sight afterwards. I'm really rather looking forward to a quiet life for a change.

'You and Portia each have a referee, just to make sure that

you do actually sleep with everyone you are supposed to. Portia has that weasily little sod Bas to keep an eye on her. You've got Ross Sinclair. He is seriously gorgeous, though, to be honest, a bit dull. Supposed to have the biggest cock in Edinburgh, but he keeps it well tucked into his trousers. He works for Down and Out, the charity we are giving the cash to, so he has agreed to act as my minder, though he doesn't approve one little bit. I'll arrange for Ross to contact you at my house tomorrow and he will help you with any difficult situations, I'm sure. And don't bother about trying too hard to win. Portia always wins. She arranges it that way. Now I'd better go, before Will comes.'

'Wait! What about Will?' Chrissy called after her.

'He won't be a problem. I've only met him once, ten years ago. Phil set it up. He's six foot two with brown hair; painfully shy, apparently. Have fun!' And she was gone, in a cloud of Diorissimo.

Chrissy was left alone at the bar, her eyes sparkling, a band of excitement tightening across her chest which made breathing difficult. What on earth had got into her? She could not believe what she had just done. Before she had time to organise her thoughts or change her mind, the door swung open again and she knew immediately that the man who came in was Will. He was tall and broad-shouldered, slightly over-dressed in a beautifully cut dark suit. Nervously his eyes searched the room until they lit upon Chrissy. Recognition showed on his face and, for a moment. Chrissy thought she saw a flash of panic in his eyes as he made his way over, his fingers pulling uncomfortably at his shirt collar, as though he were unused to wearing a tie. Formally he shook hands.

'Hello. I'm William Barnes. You must be Clarissa.' His eyes did not quite meet hers, through shyness, but his voice was a pleasant surprise – deep and resonant. 'I'm afraid I wouldn't have recognised you after all these years if Phil hadn't described you.'

'I hope he was flattering.' Chrissy smiled self-consciously.

'Oh yes, he was. Very flattering.' Will still had not quite raised his eyes to hers.

In the ensuing silence Chrissy struggled for something to say, but could think of nothing. Ever since she had heard herself agree to Clarissa's proposal she had been aware of a tension building inside her. Her body wanted sex with an intensity that astounded her, and the thought that in a few minutes she could be lying naked beside this man made breathing difficult and conversation impossible.

When the silence became unbearable, Will spoke again in a deep, sexy voice. 'I'm sorry I was late. One of my mother's hunters had colic and I couldn't leave until I knew he was going to pull through.'

'That's OK, I got your message. Is he all right?' Her voice sounded throaty, making him glance quickly at her.

'Yes. Fine.' He lapsed into silence.

Now what? Chrissy wondered. Obviously Will was not one of the great conversationalists of the world; she was finding the rising tension almost unbearable. 'Do you think we should just—' She indicated the doorway he had come in and found herself blushing.

'Yes, please.' The relief in his voice was palpable and for the first time he looked directly at her and flashed her a beautiful smile. 'I'm not very good in crowds,' he explained. The smile transformed his whole appearance and she realised that he was a seriously handsome man. They grinned at each other and he helped her off the stool before making self-consciously for the lifts.

Neither of them spoke again until Chrissy had drawn the key from her pocket and opened the bedroom door. Number 23. Same as last night. Someone had been in and straightened the covers, but apart from that the room looked the same.

Will stood just inside the door, silent and self-conscious. Gently Chrissy touched his hand, which was large and callused.

'Look, we don't have to go through with this, you know. It's supposed to be just a bit of fun. We can go back downstairs if you like.'

'No, please. I want to do it.' He shrugged helplessly, looking at the floor. 'It's just that I'm not very good at this sort of thing. I haven't—sometimes I—What I mean is, I don't really know many women,' he finished lamely.

'That's OK. Shall we play it by ear? Why don't you sit down?'

She walked over to the bed and patted the cover. Will sat rigid, unable to relax and for a moment she stood by his side, at a loss how to proceed. Last night all she'd had to do was lie back, keep quiet and let Phil take the lead. But it looked as if she was going to have to work a lot harder tonight. But how should she do it? It was a long time since Chrissy had tried to initiate sex. Marc had had very fixed ideas about a woman's role in loveplay.

It looked as if Will expected Chrissy to take complete control and suddenly the idea excited her very much. As she looked at him now, she noticed him shift position slightly to accommodate an impressvie bulge in his trousers and felt a coil of excitement tighten in her stomach.

Leaning over, she whispered in his ear and he jumped as her lips brushed him. 'Why don't you take your jacket off?'

He did so and hung it carefully on a hanger. Chrissy had to stifle a smile at his stalling tactics. She knew what she was going to do now and couldn't wait to get started, before she lost her nerve.

'Right. Will you sit down and just watch me? You don't have to do anything,' she added encouragingly.

Standing up, she moved a few feet away from him, still not entirely at ease herself. She had always wanted to do a strip-tease and now was her chance. Sometimes she thought there was a lot of the exhibitionist in her. Once she had even tried it for Marc.

He had been working hard for some time, lots of late nights at the office, and as a result he had often been too tired to make love. So Chrissy had planned a surprise for him. All day she had worked on her preparations, choosing her clothes with great care. The exquisite ivory silk underwear, she had bought herself with the money Marc had given her on Valentine's Day. Her outer garments had been chosen with just as much care: lots of layers that she could peel off seductively. Even the room had been prepared carefully: scented candles burning, soft music playing, everything designed to tease him beyond endurance.

That had been the plan. The reality had been that Marc had opened one sleepy eye and murmured, 'Frankly, love, you might give a bit of thought to losing a few pounds if you're going to wear that outfit. Do you mind opening a window? That awful

21

smell is giving me a headache. Why don't you come to bed? I'm exhausted.'

Chrissy's ears burned with remembered humiliation. But she refused to think of him now. Now it was Will sitting in front of her and she had no doubt that she had his full attention. Slowly, she began to undo the buttons of her white linen blouse. Very, very slowly. Will's face blushed scarlet and his eyes slid away though she could see a sheen of sweat on his forehead.

'Look at me, Will,' she commanded softly. He did so and she gasped at the promise of passion she saw there. His dark eyes burned with a hunger that sent shivers of excitement crawling down her spine. Forcing herself not to hurry though her fingers now trembled, she lowered the blouse off her shoulders and let it drop to the floor. Standing before him in her white bra, her full breasts barely contained by the lacy material, she saw his eyes widen with lust and could not resist pushing the cups down to show him her hardening nipples.

As the cool air in the room hit the puckered skin they rose up eagerly and she moaned, circling them with her palms, feeling them swell pebble-hard. Lost in the sensation, she had forgotten Will for a moment but his sudden sharp intake of breath brought her back and she gazed seductively at him through long lashes, her fingers still stroking her nipples. Yes, there definitely was a streak of the exhibitionist in her!

'What do you think, Will?' she teased, finally unfastening her bra and cupping her breasts in her hands, offering them to him without stepping closer. 'Do you like them?' Will was breathing fast, his cock now pushing very visibly against his trousers; he nodded, but still made no move towards her.

Chrissy realised that she was teasing herself as much as Will. A fast, damp pulse was beginning to beat between her legs as she undid the side fastening of her skirt and dropped it to the floor. Stepping out of it, she stood for a moment in her skimpy white knickers before moving to stand in front of him, so close she could feel his hot breath on her skin and the leashed passion which throbbed through his body.

But still, frustratingly, though he clenched and unclenched his fists nervously, he made no move to touch her. Always in the past, even before Marc, she had been attracted to stronger, more forceful men. This was a novel experience for her, and she was revelling in it.

Shivering, she could feel the erotic tension in the room and smell the musky odour of her own excitement. Leaning forward slightly, she rubbed her hard nipples against him, moaning as they rasped against the rough skin of his face. Finally, teased beyond endurance, Will grabbed her and pulled her into his arms, burying his face in her full soft breasts and kissing them hungrily. Chrissy ran her fingers through his thick curly hair, her breasts aglow as his lips brushed tentatively against her aching nipples. As she encouraged him, cradling his head against her, he nibbled and bit her hard, sucking her far into his mouth, gorging himself on the soft flesh.

At first his hands spanned her slim waist, then his fingers moved down under her panties to knead the firm flesh of her buttocks. A burning heat was rising within her, and eagerly Chrissy began to tug at his tie and the buttons of his shirt, desperate to feel his naked skin against her.

In her excitement she fumbled clumsily and Will, equally impatient, stood up and pulled the shirt over his head in a smooth and very masculine gesture. He immediately drew her back into his arms and Chrissy had only a moment to savour the sight of his broad bronzed shoulders and flat stomach before she was engulfed once more by his surprising strength, her soft breasts flattened against his hard muscular chest. He nuzzled her neck and she raised her head up to be kissed, one part of her mind wondering where his shyness had vanished to, before she lost herself once more to the moment, allowing him to claim her mouth with hungry lips.

Desire was pulsing insistently between Chrissy's legs and though she was enjoying the kiss, she knew she wanted more. She could feel the heat of Will's arousal transmitting itself through the straining bulge in his trousers, feel his readiness pressing into her belly as she moved against his erection, and reached for his zip.

His body tensed and, looking up, she saw that he was blushing again. Never before had she met a man who blushed so much. Involuntarily he stepped back and Chrissy used his momentum to push him over onto the bed, straddling him with her knees on either side of his hips. For the first time she could explore his powerful body properly, and she did so, admiring the well-defined muscles, honed, she suspected, through hard physical work rather than hours in a gym.

He moaned at every touch of her fingers on his skin, his liquid brown eyes flicking from her face to her quivering breasts, allowing himself to relax once more, happy to let her take control. Her eyes burned hotly as they followed the line of the rough hair on his chest to where it arrowed downwards, disappearing into the waistband of his trousers. The tautness of his stomach was drawn in involuntarily, and he groaned as her fingers deftly unfastened his trousers.

Before she had even got the zip halfway down, his cock sprang free, bouncing gently against her palm. It stood straight up, engorged and needy, and she took him in her hand, running her fingers up his length and savouring the underlying hardness beneath the silky, soft skin.

Chrissy eyed it hungrily. How would he react if she took him in her mouth? Oral sex was yet another of the things Marc had not approved of and Chrissy had missed it dreadfully. Well, not all men were like Marc. She glanced up to find Will watching her and paused only to push her hair back off her face before lowering her mouth onto his swollen tip. Will's whole body tightened and his cock jerked convulsively, his long-drawn-out moan leaving her in no doubt that he did not share Marc's distaste.

Chrissy closed her eyes. Her hair gently brushed his belly as her head bobbed up and down; she savoured the clean, salty taste of him. With each upward stroke she drew him with her, his hips almost rising from the bed and his toes curled in pleasure.

His inhibitions seemed to vanish now as he reached down and held her head in his hands, gasping each time he saw his cock disappear between her lips, fighting the urge to thrust himself deeper. Chrissy grinned, proud of the power she had over him, proud to be in control.

As his breathing grew more ragged, a familiar tingling began to spread upwards through Chrissy until it could not be ignored. Standing up, she removed a condom from her bag and slipped off her panties, allowing him his first tantalising glimpse of her sex as she climbed back astride him, rolling the condom down his straining member. Then she lowered her head and kissed him again, full on the lips, tickling her nipples against the rough hairs of his chest while his cock was pinned deliciously between his belly and her parted labia.

Will held her head with both hands, and kissed her, the last traces of awkwardness vanishing. It was a wonderful kiss, deep and passionate, and Chrissy was reluctant to break it off. But the throbbing between her legs had grown almost to an ache, and she knew that she had to feel him inside her.

Sitting up, she raised her hips till his cock was resting at the very entrance to her body, teasing herself and him one last time. Lifting her hair with both hands, she let the cool air in the room play over her neck, allowing him an unspoilt view of her slender throat and smooth white breasts as they trembled high above him. Will made a small sound at the back of his throat as Chrissy slowly lowered her hips and the head of his cock disappeared into her welcoming depths, deeper, until his whole shaft was enclosed by tight walls, their pubic hair mingling and her firm bottom resting lightly on his balls.

This sight was too much for him. With a growl he pulled her down and rolled her over onto her back in one smooth movement, possessing her for the first time. With her thighs wrapped fervently around his waist they began a steady rhythm, slow at first then harder and faster; her body rose up to meet each thrust, matching his passion with her own. This was so wonderful, so wild and abandoned. She couldn't remember when it had last been like this.

Will's moans became louder in her ear as his orgasm drew closer, until with a great roar he came, pulsing deep inside her with each shuddering thrust. As his orgasm raced through him, Chrissy came too, again and again, her muscles spasming in a pleasure so intense she thought she would die. It was almost with relief that the shuddering finally stopped and she felt Will's weight slump on her.

After a moment, aware that he was crushing her, Will rolled off and lay beside her, his head propped on his elbow.

Self-consciously, they smiled at each other.

'That was wonderful,' said Chrissy, lightly stroking the sweat-damp skin of his chest.

'Yes? I thought so too. Mostly thanks to you,' he grinned sheepishly. 'Thanks for being so patient with me.'

'Patient? I wasn't patient. I couldn't wait to get your clothes off.'

'Yes, well, you know what I mean.' Now that the heat of passion was over, Will was reverting to his old self, and Chrissy could not help feeling a little sorry.

'You don't need to be so shy, Will. You are a lovely man with a gorgeous body. A wonderful lover.'

'It's nice of you to say so.' His tone was not convinced, and he rolled onto his back, staring at the ceiling for a moment in silence. 'You know, you're not at all what I expected.'

'Oh?' Chrissy was immediately wary.

'You're different somehow.'

'In what way?' Should she tell him? She genuinely liked him and hated to lie, but she hesitated. It would be a bit much if she blurted out the truth to the first man she had sex with after agreeing to take part in the Treasure Hunt.

Beside her she felt Will shrug. 'I don't really know. Just different. Nicer, I suppose; more friendly. It's hard to put into words.'

'You're not sorry, are you? About this evening?'

'No way! It's the best night I've had in a long time.'

'Good. Me, too.' No, she had better not say anything. Keep it simple.

Reluctantly they both got up and dressed, travelling down in the lift in silence. Only now it was a comfortable silence. In the lobby they paused and looked at each other.

'Do you think, when this is over, you know, the Treasure Hunt, do you think we could maybe see each other again sometime?' Will asked hesitantly.

Chrissy looked into his hopeful, honest face, and thought she would have liked nothing better. 'I don't know, Will. I don't really . . .'

'That's OK. It was just a thought,' he said quickly, and she could see that he was hurt. But he would be even more hurt if he knew that she had been lying to him all evening. She owed him some kind of explanation. She took his hand in hers, feeling again how hard and callused it was. 'Listen Will, my life is very . . . complicated at the moment. I have to warn you that I'm not looking for a relationship. But I do really like you, and I had a wonderful time tonight. Please believe that.'

He flashed his beautiful smile again. 'OK, we'll leave it at that. But I probably will see you around.'

Chrissy nodded, and watched as he left the hotel. She waited a few minutes then left herself.

Uncomplicated anonymous sex – that was what she had promised herself. And she was right when she had said that she did not want another relationship. It was just a pity that Will had been so nice. Putting aside the pangs of guilt she could ill-afford, she hurried out into the night.

Three

Breakfast next morning was a leisurely affair, partly because Chrissy had such a hearty appetite and partly because she was clearing out the fridge in preparation for her few days away at Clarissa's house. She had given this matter some thought and finally decided to move into Clarissa's. She was going to keep every part of the Treasure Hunt completely separate from her real life.

Over a third cup of coffee she smoothed the Treasure Hunt card on the table, placing it alongside Clarissa's house keys and the sheet of paper with the address. It was an ordinary piece of white card, folded in three to open up rather like a menu, but it made riveting reading and Chrissy choked on her coffee more than once as her eyes skimmed down the list. Suddenly it seemed too hot in the little kitchen area, stifling, and she loosened the knot on her bathrobe slightly, though it did little to ease her breathing.

When the phone rang she snatched it up, her eyes still on the card. 'Hello?' Even to her own ears she sounded rather breathless.

'Chrissy? Not interrupting anything, am I?'

'Karen!' Chrissy was delighted. 'Yes, you've interrupted my breakfast. Where have you been? It took you long enough to phone back.'

'I told you, I'm in the Orkneys. I've only just checked my messages. Now what is this exciting news that I absolutely will not believe? Have you got a job?'

'Not quite. Listen.' So Chrissy told her. About her experience with Phil, her meeting with Clarissa, and about Will.

There was silence on the other end of the line.

'Hello? Hello? Karen? Are you still there?'

'I'm still here.' The voice was so faint that Chrissy could barely make it out. Then stronger. 'I'm still here, but I don't believe what I just heard. Please tell me you've made it up, Chrissy. This is too off the wall; not like you at all.'

'Of course I haven't made it up.' Chrissy was affronted.

'But it's only two days since I saw you. What happened to "I'm fed up with men, I'm going to devote the next few years to my career"?' Karen sounded rather plaintive.

'Yes, that's the next few years. I'm talking about the next few days. And I'll tell you something else – I've got the list in my hand, and you would not believe some of the things on here.'

'What things?' Karen asked despite herself, just as Chrissy had known she would.

'Are you sure you're interested?'

'Tell me!'

'It's divided into three columns: who, what and where. "Who" isn't too bad: there's a lawyer, a farmer, a sportsman. And a waiter, a tradesman, a groom—'

'Right. Ten a penny on the streets of Edinburgh.' Karen's tone was sarcastic but Chrissy knew her friend's interest was roused.

'Don't you want to hear the rest?'

'Don't you dare stop. Quick, give me some change,' she added over her shoulder as the pips sounded on the phone.

'Ok. Then there is "what". Oral, lesbian, virgin, *menage à trois*, bondage, S&M—'

'Chrissy!' Karen's voice was almost a squeak. 'You wouldn't! Tell me you wouldn't!'

'I might. You never know. And then there is "where". On a train, outdoors, in a public place, in a motorway service station . . . Shall I go on?'

'Oh God, no. I don't think I could cope. Seriously though, Chrissy, do you think this is such a good idea?'

'What do you mean?'

Karen chose her words carefully. 'You know what I mean. You've been through a lot recently. Do you think you're ready for something like this, after . . . after . . .'

'After what?'

'Well, after . . .'

29

Chrissy took pity on her friend. 'After Marc, you mean? It's all right, Karen, I can hear his name without swooning away, you know.'

'Not for a long time, you couldn't,' Karen defended herself.

'You're right, but that was a while ago. I'm well over him now.' Chrissy listened to her own words and for the first time believed that it might actually be true. She softened her tone. 'I'm fine, Karen. Honest. I know what I'm doing.'

'But after what you said about men and unfaithfulness, and lack of commitment,' protested Karen.

'That's why this will be so much fun! There is no commitment on either side, so no-one can get hurt.'

'Well,' Karen conceded, 'it certainly sounds exciting. As long as you are sure you know what you're doing. I just don't want you to get hurt again.'

Chrissy felt a rush of warmth and affection for her friend. Karen had been the person she had run to when she had eventually found the courage to leave Marc: the only person she could have turned to. Over the years they had been together, Marc had systematically alienated all her other friends, till Karen was the only one left. This had been done very subtly, of course, because that was always Marc's way. He had never forbidden her to see anyone – he didn't work like that. Chrissy would have rebelled if he had been so obvious or high-handed.

But all too often when she had arranged to meet her friends, Marc would surprise her with two tickets for a show she really wanted to see, or announce that he had booked a table at their favourite restaurant. He was always so crestfallen when she gently reminded him that she had made other arrangements that she couldn't bear to disappoint him. Her friends had been understanding when she called to put them off at the last minute. Or at least they had been, at first. Eventually however, after too many broken dates, they stopped phoning.

By then Chrissy was already too smitten with Marc, too much in love, to wonder why his romantic surprises had also stopped. Night after night they sat in and watched TV, or she sat in alone while Marc worked late.

But Karen had resisted all his attempts to erode her friendship with Chrissy. When she realised that messages she left were not being passed on, she merely started calling Chrissy at work. She took to turning up unannounced on the doorstep with a bottle of wine some evenings, more often than not finding Chrissy on her own. Marc was furious when he finally came home, taking himself off to bed to sulk. Neither he nor Karen made any attempt to hide the fact that they loathed each other. At first Chrissy had been hurt to realise that her two best friends were making no effort to get on. But eventually she had learned to accept the fact that they just didn't like each other. But she hated it when one criticised the other, and had to ask them both firmly to stop.

So it was to Karen she had run for help when she had finally fled, turning up sobbing and hysterical on Karen's doorstep. Karen had asked no questions, putting the tearful, bedraggled Chrissy to bed, supplying endless tissues and TLC and suppressing her curiosity as to what had finally opened Chrissy's eyes to what a bastard Marc really was. She had listened for hours to Chrissy moan about how much she loved him, how she could never live without him. And eventually, when Chrissy had slowly begun to emerge from the self-pity in which she was wallowing, Karen had been there to help her pick up the pieces, never judging, not once saying 'I told you so'. For that alone Chrissy would always be grateful. She would never put their friendship in jeopardy again.

'Honest, Karen, I know what I'm doing,' she said gently. 'No-one will get hurt. You have to admit, it sounds like fun.'

'We–ell.' Karen was actually delighted. For the first time in goodness knew how long, Chrissy sounded like her old self again.

'Come on, seriously; what do you think?'

'I think,' Karen spoke slowly and carefully, 'I think you are going to have the best bloody summer of your life. Just be very, very careful. And phone me every day! I want to be kept up to date.'

Clarissa's house was in a quiet crescent of Georgian houses in Edinburgh's New Town. Chrissy stood on the doorstep for a few moments, admiring the window boxes and elaborate brass knocker, stalling a little – reluctant to go in now that she was here. Out of politeness she rang the bell, but of course there was no reply. Quickly, before she could change her mind, she opened the door with the key she had been given and slipped inside. It was immediately obvious from the neglected, slightly stale air in the tiled hallway that the house was empty and she let out a sigh of relief – it looked as if Clarissa had already gone.

Putting her small case down on the polished tiles, Chrissy began exploring the rooms on the lower floor. She was rather disappointed with what she found. There was evidence that an interior designer and a contract florist had been at work. But while it was obvious that little expense had been spared, there was no warmth in any of the rooms, no clues to the owner's personality. Well, Clarissa had said that she had been away.

While admiring a portrait of a stern-looking Victorian gentleman, Chrissy noticed the red light of the answer-machine flashing urgently on the sideboard. She walked over to it and her finger hovered above the play button. It was one thing to live in Clarissa's house and sleep with her lovers, but should she listen to her messages as well?

She pressed play.

'Hi. If you are listening to this then you must be Chrissy. This is Clarissa. I'm just phoning to tell you that I eventually managed to get hold of Ross and he has agreed to help, though I must say he was rather sour about it. And I've lined up the two most gorgeous polo players in the world for you tonight, if that is OK; I would almost envy you if it wasn't for John. Anyway, have fun and see you in a week or so. Bye, and thanks again. You're a life-saver.'

So it was still on. There was something deliciously clinical about being told who she would be having sex with in a few hours' time, and Chrissy felt a flutter of excitement deep within her.

The phone rang while she was still by the sideboard, making her jump.

'Hello?' She answered it tentatively.

'Christine Fielding? This is Ross Sinclair. Clarissa Asquith asked me to phone you with arrangements for tonight.' The voice was steady and deep, but the tone was rather curt, not giving her a chance to reply.

'Here is the address. Take it down. I will meet you there tonight at eight o'clock sharp. Don't be late. There, I understand, you are to meet two polo players. Is that correct?'

Chrissy mumbled an affirmative. It was difficult to strike up a conversation in the face of such obvious disapproval.

'Oh, and let's get one thing straight. I don't know what Clarissa has said, but I will tell you now that I am not here to pimp for you. You will arrange your own assignations. I hope that is understood? Goodbye.' The phone clattered down.

He sounded a bundle of laughs, Chrissy thought sourly. He had made absolutely no attempt to hide his distaste, but still there was something about his voice, a deep sensuality that even his hard words could not entirely mask. Tonight's party might be interesting – not only for the polo players. But for now Chrissy put him out of her mind and continued her exploration of the rooms, talking aloud to herself and trying to practice Clarissa's clipped, slightly nasal tone. Three years of amateur dramatics were about to be put to good use.

She explored for a while, amazed at the size of the house and the huge number of clothes and shoes that Clarissa seemed to possess, but she found it difficult to relax. It felt odd being in someone's house with the owner away, but it wasn't just that. Ever since she had agreed to take part in this Treasure Hunt, she had felt sexual tension coiled like a spring inside her, as though her body could not wait for the next encounter. Even Ross Sinclair on the phone had unsettled her more than she liked to admit. Despite his obvious disapproval, the mere sound of his voice gave her goosebumps.

She wandered aimlessly through each room for a while, made a sandwich that she did not finish, then ran herself a bath in Clarissa's over-large and elegant bathroom. Perhaps it would relax her.

Chrissy poured the contents of various fancy bottles into the running water, filling the bath with foam and scenting the air beautifully. She sifted through the contents of the bathroom shelves, filing her nails for a few moments, then fitfully plucking her eyebrows. Her restless eyes lit on a tube of depilatory cream. Undressing quickly, she picked it up and began to smooth it onto her legs. She carried on to her bikini line, her mind on the many gorgeous g-strings she had seen lying in Clarissa's dressers, most of them still wrapped in tissue paper. If she was going to be a *femme fatale* then she may as well look the part.

Not quite knowing what had got into her, she continued spreading the cream way past her bikini line, between her legs and over the hair that covered her sex lips. Working quickly, in case she changed her mind, she smoothed the cream carefully over her entire labia before wiping it off and easing into the bath to rinse herself.

Her lower body was completely covered by the fragrant foam and she could not see her bare pudenda, but she ran her fingers over the smoothness, exciting herself with the strange feel of it. Emerging from the bath a few minutes later, she gasped at the sight of her naked skin in the bathroom mirror. Her pubis was completely smooth and bald and she felt more naked than she ever had in her life. The air played over her sex in a way it never had before, now that it had lost its protective covering. Chrissy felt a tingle of excitement at the feeling of utter nakedness and vulnerability.

The bath had been hot but Chrissy felt hotter still. Naked, she walked through to the bedroom and began to rifle through Clarissa's clothes. She was going to a party.

Ross Sinclair lounged against an Adam fireplace, paying little attention to the conversation going on around him. The only man there in a dinner jacket, he stood out from his more casually dressed companions, though it didn't occur to him to feel awkward or uncomfortable. In fact he would have stood out in any group, whatever he wore – not so much for his dark good looks or his vivid blue eyes, but for the restless, caged tiger quality he had about him.

As soon as this idiotic friend of Clarissa's arrived, he could introduce himself and leave. He had yet another fundraiser to attend this evening. In fact, he realised as he glanced at his watch impatiently, he should be there now.

Watching Chrissy come into the room, Ross recognised her immediately; the resemblance was remarkable. The honey-coloured hair was almost exactly like Clarissa's pampered locks, though he suspected Clarissa owed a lot more to Vidal Sassoon than this woman did. Her hazel eyes were enormous, her face pale, and she slipped through the doorway in a manner he suspected she thought was unobtrusive. If that was her intention, she should have chosen something to wear other than the tight tube minidress in emerald green that seemed to defy gravity, barely containing the most magnificent breasts Ross had ever seen. His eyes lingered appreciatively on the shadow of her cleavage before moving down to take in her long bare legs, thrown into flattering relief by the black stiletto shoes.

Watching her circle slowly round the high-ceilinged room, Ross was surprised to see that she was enjoying herself. She had a good body and knew it, moving with ease and confidence, even amid strangers, hovering on the periphery of conversations and drifting away before she became too involved. Good. At least she was not going to give the game away before this stupid charade had even got underway. There was something about the way she moved, the way those breasts defied nature to stay so snugly within the confines of that impossible dress, that made Ross feel he could watch her all evening.

Suddenly she seemed to become aware of his scrutiny. Slowly she turned and surveyed the room with a slightly puzzled expression, before her eyes settled on him. As she openly returned his look, Ross felt his interest quickening.

He was the most attractive man Chrissy had ever seen. She had felt eyes boring into her from the moment she walked into the room and at first had thought nothing of it – in a dress like this she had been drawing stares all evening. But as she had wandered around, the feeling of being watched had intensified. At first she tried to ignore the tiny prickles of alarm spreading from the nape of her neck, but before long she was compelled to turn and seek out her admirer. She spotted him at once, a dark-haired man in a dinner suit standing about twenty feet away. He was staring at her with open interest and Chrissy knew the sudden spark of desire she recognised in his eyes was reflected in her own.

She remained motionless for a moment, almost mesmerised by the intensity of his gaze, everything else in the room fading into insignificance. Her senses were filled with him, his masculine aura somehow reaching out to her even from across the room. What colour were his eyes, she wondered, blue or grey? It was hard to tell from this distance. Suddenly it seemed vital that she know. Almost unconsciously, she began to drift closer, her feet seeming to move of their own accord. Equally affected, the man continued to stare, his hypnotic eyes never leaving her own. Before he could move towards her though, one of his friends caught his arm.

'Isn't that right?'

'What?' he asked absently, his attention all on Chrissy.

'You probably support them, don't you? They want to ruin me and you support them!' The voice was angry and slightly slurred; a full glass of whisky sloshed in his hand.

'They won't ruin you.' Ross's voice held an almost total lack of interest; his eyes watched Chrissy draw closer.

'How do you know? You never saw the bastards. I earned that money. It's not right that they should take it! How am I supposed to live?'

Chrissy stopped a few feet away, listening. His voice had immediately identified the man in the dinner jacket as Ross Sinclair and she found herself holding her breath as she stood near him, every nerve ending aglow.

'We'll probably have to sell the gatehouse and have Mother move back in with us. Fiona will love that.' The drunk man continued to grumble.

'Consider yourself lucky that you have a gatehouse to sell.' Ross's tone was still bored, but tightly controlled. Obviously he had heard this conversation before. His eyes never left Chrissy. Blue, she saw. His eyes were blue. A clear, brilliant, startling blue.

'Oh yes. I knew you would take that attitude. You and your bloody left-wing councils. Determined to make people who actually work for a living pay for the hordes of scroungers who never lifted a finger for themselves.' The man seemed to realise finally that he did not have his intended audience's full attention, for he now emphasised each word by jabbing a pudgy finger into Ross's shoulder.

There were murmurs of agreement from others in the group and Ross finally turned to the speaker. His fabulous eyes now glittered with irritation.

'For God's sake, Hugo, it's a tax bill. If you had paid the bloody taxes in the first place, you wouldn't be in this mess now.'

Despite herself Chrissy began to pay a little more attention to the conversation.

'And this Child Support Agency,' Hugo continued as if he had not heard. 'Any little tart with a baby can say I'm the father. Have you any idea how much I have to pay a month to that bloody scrubber? If women can't protect themselves from pregnancy in this day and age they should all be sterilised – not bloody well look on me as a meal ticket. I'm going to be ruined!'

Chrissy, all her good intentions to keep a low profile going out the window, turned on the speaker. 'Did I hear right?' she asked, incredulously. 'Are you going to tell me that all this moaning is about getting caught for tax evasion and having to pay for the upkeep of your own child? Why shouldn't you pay? Who do you think you are? What makes you better than the rest of us?'

Hugo turned to her, his face shiny with drink and self-pity. 'Who the hell are you? And who the fuck asked for your opinion?' He blinked rudely at Chrissy, astonished at being interrupted. Before she could speak Ross was there, smoothly introducing them.

'Clarissa Asquith. Don't you remember her, Hugo? Been in the States for a while, haven't you, Clarissa?' His perfectly manicured hand caught her elbow with a firmness she felt was unnecessary, but his touch sent a distracting tingle up her bare arm. As she gasped in a breath, her nostrils were touched by the spicy scent of his aftershave, citrus and cedar wood, with an underlying essence of his masculinity that sent her senses reeling, making her light-headed. But she was too angry to be distracted for long.

'Men like you make me sick,' she snapped at Hugo. 'You think you can do what you like until you get caught and then whine that it's not your fault.' Her eyes sparkled with genuine fury.

'Why, you little . . . . I can see that America hasn't taught you much in the way of manners.'

He stepped closer, breathing whisky fumes into her face.

Instead of backing down, she shook off Ross's hand. She and Hugo glared angrily at each other, while the onlookers shuffled in embarrassment.

'Steady on, Hugo,' a few of them muttered.

Hugo's face was now a vivid shade of purple, but Chrissy wasn't frightened. She had had her fill of bullying men.

Ross gave up trying to lure her away and stepped between them. 'That's enough, Hugo,' he said quietly. 'You've had too much to drink. Why don't you go home? Nigel, I think Hugo wants to go now.' He watched as Hugo was led away by his friends, still complaining loudly, then turned to Chrissy.

'Ross Sinclair,' he smiled, his eyes alight with amusement. 'I won't offer to shake hands because we are supposed to know each other and people are watching. You really know how to make an entrance, don't you?'

'Arrogance like that infuriates me. People who think they are so much better than everyone else, who think the world revolves around them and their selfish needs.' She was still bristling, but not so angry that she was unaware of Ross's proximity. Somehow, just standing so close to him made her heart jump alarmingly and she was glad to see that her presence also seemed to be having an effect on him. Leaning closer, he fixed her with an approving gaze, assaulting her again with his heady, elusive scent.

'You shouldn't pay too much attention. He was very drunk, and a lot of what he was saying was just to wind me up. They like to do that at parties.'

'They?'

'My friends.'

'Some friends.'

He gave a low rough laugh. 'They're not so bad. Hugo's a fool, but he does have a lot of problems.'

'Which he seems to have brought on himself,' she pointed out, not willing to let him off the hook.

'Yes, you're right.' His eyes crinkled in amusement. This hot-headed beauty was not in the least what he had expected. 'You're very uncompromising,' he said admiringly, 'and I'd better warn you, you're acting out of character. I don't think Clarissa Asquith ever held a strong opinion in her life. Hugo has an illegitimate child whom he loves to bits, but if his wife finds out, she will throw him out; she's the one with the money. And he opened their home to the public a few years ago; he's been raking the money in, but he forgot to tell the Inland Revenue about the very lucrative tea-room. I know, I know, he brought it on himself.'

As he spoke he allowed his eyes to roam unhurriedly over her face and down her body, his frank appraisal causing an unmistakable shiver to flow over Chrissy, setting her large breasts aquiver. The rosy blush which had spread over her skin during her angry encounter was beginning to recede, and Ross's eyes settled for a few seconds on the spot where the flush disappeared into the shadow of her cleavage. When he looked up again, his expression had barely changed, but in her heightened state of awareness, Chrissy could detect the tiny, almost imperceptible signals of his quickening interest. The heat of his gaze seemed to lure her, pulling her closer. Flustered, she took a small step back. Ross followed her, as if reluctant to allow any distance between them.

'What's the matter?' he smiled, his eyes teasing. He seemed to know exactly the effect he was having on her, and was enjoying her discomfort.

'Nothing's the matter. Or maybe I'm just a bit nervous,' she babbled. 'This is rather an unusual situation for me.' She couldn't think straight with him so close. Five minutes in the company of this extraordinary man and she was already so hot that she would have sex with him right now on the floor, if he asked.

Thoughts like this made her blush again, and it was as if Ross could read her mind, for the heat in his eyes intensified, his gaze drawing her, almost locking her to him. But the thought also reminded her of why she was at the party. The polo players! She had forgotten them completely. The thought of having sex with anyone other than Ross at this moment was completely out of the question. For a brief second she considered asking him to leave with her before the others arrived. But no. That would be rude. She should see them herself and come up with an excuse. Any excuse. Clearing her throat, she asked, 'Are the polo players here yet?'

For a second Ross froze, looking puzzled. Then a remarkable transformation seemed to take place. Where a moment before he had been relaxed and smiling, leaning towards her, now he drew himself upright. Something chilling entered his expression and his eyes, till then a warm inviting blue, turned grey and flat. 'You're not really going through with this performance, are you?' he asked coldly.

'What?' Chrissy was confused. She had never seen anyone's mood change so quickly, so completely. 'It . . . it's why I came. I . . . I should speak to them. They're expecting to meet me.'

'Well if they're expecting to meet you, then I'd better not stand in your way.' Ross's sarcastic tone hid bitter disappointment. He too had forgotten why Chrissy was here, forgotten all about this absurd arrangement with Clarissa. He had been so carried away with the pleasure of speaking to a woman who, as well as being beautiful, actually had a mind of her own. A woman who had some principles she felt worth defending. Never before had he been so instantly attracted to anyone. His cock had leapt to rigid attention the moment he laid eyes on her – a reaction he hadn't had to contend with since he was a teenager. Even now, when he had been sharply reminded of the kind of woman she really was, his erection refused to subside, responding to those deceptively honest eyes and those achingly sweet breasts.

Chrissy stared at him. It wasn't difficult to see that he was very angry, his rage no less potent for being tightly controlled. What bothered her was why he was quite so angry. The mention of the polo players had done it. If the very idea of the Treasure Hunt annoyed him so much, why on earth had he agreed to help Clarissa? Always preferring the direct approach, she opened her mouth to ask him, but his next words silenced her, chilling her in a way that he could not possibly know.

'Surely you're not going ahead with this.'

He continued talking, and though Chrissy kept staring at him, as if she was listening, his words washed over her and through her, and she could not make out a single discernible sound. Only his first three words echoed loudly, round and around in her head. *Surely you're not . . . Surely you're not . . .* How many times had she heard those words from Marc? Little words, spoken softly, always with loving concern and a smile. Surely

40

you're not . . . going to wear that dress, that colour, that lipstick, your hair like that. Repeated again and again, draining her confidence, questioning her judgement, till eventually she did not know what she liked, what suited her. It had been simpler to go along with what Marc wanted, easier to laugh and agree that he knew best, rather than face his sulks, the unbearable withdrawal of his affection.

But not now. Though those words entered her heart and still chilled her, no longer would she have to go along with any man's suggestions about how she should behave and what she should do. The only outward sign of her anger as she waited for Ross to stop talking were the two fiery discs of colour which reappeared on her cheeks.

Ross was uneasy. He had seen a glimmer of something that could have been alarm in Chrissy's eyes while he tried to persuade her to give up the Treasure Hunt and wondered briefly what he had said to cause it. Now he had the uncomfortable feeling that she hadn't taken in a single word he had said. And the expression in her eyes as she patiently waited for him to stop talking hinted that her anger now surpassed even his own. His voice trailed off under her angry stare.

'If you have quite finished instructing me?'

'I wasn't instructing, I was merely pointing out that I don't think you are cut out for this type of thing. You're nothing like this lot.' His gesture took in the other people in the room as he looked round almost contemptuously at his rich, shallow, pretentious friends. Chrissy followed his gaze. She saw the glamour: the beautiful women, with their expensive clothes, painted nails and glossy hair.

'Who says I'm not?' Her cheeks flamed with colour.

'I do. You're nothing like them.' You are far more beautiful and you have a mind of your own – not like these idiots, he added silently.

'So it's all right for one of Clarissa's rich friends to step in and sleep with your buddies, but not all right for me? What's wrong – am I not rich enough?' Chrissy was furious. She had not taken him for a snob.

'What?' Now Ross was puzzled. 'Who said anything about money?'

'I think you have said enough, don't you?'

They heard sing-song voices approaching from the next room.

'Clarissa, oh, Clarissa . . .'

She glanced at the door then back at Ross, an unfriendly distance between them now.

The door burst open and two laughing men staggered into the room.

'There you are, Clarissa. We thought you were avoiding us.' One of them waved a bottle of champagne and ground his hips suggestively, causing his friend to giggle and Ross to set his face in disapproval. In tight white breeches and matching red polo shirts, there was no doubt that these were Chrissy's polo players. Their tanned faces shone with drunken good-humour and she could see how hard and muscular their bodies were.

'Keeping her warm for us, Ross? That's OK. We'll take over now.' The speaker, the taller of the two, ran his hand familiarly over Chrissy's bottom, and pulled her towards him.

Ross gave him an icy look, then turned the look on Chrissy. 'Well, *Clarissa*?' he asked sarcastically, 'Have you made up your mind?'

Chrissy was still so angry that she had all but forgotten her earlier decision to cancel her date with the two men. All she could think about was Ross and his attitude. Who the hell was he to judge her, anyway? He had known her ten minutes but already he was criticising her lifestyle, offering unasked-for advice. She'd had enough of that over the last few years. She would show him!

'Yes, I have,' she smiled sweetly. 'Come on, boys, let's have some fun!'

The second man, who up till then had been silent, stepped forward, his eyes sweeping over her body and taking in every curve. 'Let's go,' he growled. 'I'm getting a hard-on just looking at you, and in these breeches I might get arrested.' His grin was so wolfish that for a second Chrissy hesitated; things were moving too fast. Nervously she licked her lips.

Ross deliberately misinterpreted the gesture. He gave her a look of such utter loathing that she knew she could not back down now. No way would she allow him to think he had any influence over her. Quickly, before she could change her mind, she linked arms with the polo players, and allowed them to hustle her out of the room.

Ross watched them leave, barely able to contain his anger, unsure how the argument had become so out of hand. They had been getting along so well. Women were all the same, he thought in disgust – they couldn't be trusted. It was a lesson he'd learnt long ago and would have done well to remember tonight. He felt someone come and stand by his elbow and turned his glare on Will Barnes.

'Was that Clarissa?' asked Will, wistfully. 'Isn't she just beautiful?'

Ross stared at him in fury. 'For fuck's sake! Not you, too?' He stormed out of the room without another word. Will blinked mildly at his friend's retreating back, then turned to look up the stairs to where Chrissy had disappeared.

The polo players, Luke and Scott, she learnt, seemed to know where they were going and swept her along with them to an empty bedroom. Chrissy was nervous but not frightened. The men had come straight from a photo session organised by their sponsor, which explained the polo shirts and breeches, but they were not as drunk as they had seemed at first; the champagne bottle was unopened.

Almost as soon as the door was closed, hands began roaming over her body. They talked to her, telling her what a great idea they thought this was, kissing her softly, their lips brushing her ears, her throat, her shoulders. It was delicious, but terribly distracting. Chrissy needed a few seconds to herself, to get her thoughts straight.

'Hang on, boys, just a moment. Is there a loo?' she asked, fending off some of their more intimate approaches. 'Won't be a moment.' She fled to the *en suite* bathroom and closed the door firmly behind her, catching sight of herself in the mirror. She was breathing heavily, her face and upper chest flushed a rosy pink. There was no doubt that what those two had been doing out there had been turning her on. So why was she in here now, staring in confusion at her own reflection?

She had come to this party with the intention of having sex with two strangers. Right. She had chosen this ultra-clingy, ultra-short dress, purely with that in mind. She had even come to the party completely naked under the dress, just for the anticipated pleasure of watching their reaction when they finally peeled it off her. So why was she now having doubts? What had changed?

That was easy. Ross Sinclair. It was true that she had spent the evening in a state of steadily increasing sexual excitement but for the latter part, at least, her arousal had been focused entirely on Ross and she knew he'd felt it too; she had known from the moment she set eyes on him how the evening would end.

But then everything had gone horribly wrong. After he remembered the polo players, he had made no attempt to hide his contempt of her and they had both lost their tempers. The fact that he had been telling her to do something she had already decided to do for herself only made it worse. Downstairs it had all seemed so clear-cut, but now she was confused. Was she up here with Luke and Scott because she wanted to be, or because she knew it would annoy Ross? The Treasure Hunt had barely begun and already she was getting herself into a mess.

Suddenly she reached a decision. The two men outside wanted her now purely for her body: no judgements, no emotional entanglements. And that was what she wanted too, she reminded herself. Wasn't that why she had agreed to join the Treasure Hunt in the first place? To hell with Ross Sinclair!

Slipping back into the bedroom, Chrissy found her two companions lying on the bed, waiting for her good-naturedly. They didn't seem to find it at all odd that she had left them alone for so long. Immediately they leapt to their feet, taking up where they had left off. One of them had found a radio, and they began to dance round the room, Chrissy sandwiched between them, their cocks pressing into her, back and front, hard and enticing.

The emerald green dress proved a great success, with both men taking it in turns to roll the stretchy material down. Her breasts tumbled free, her nipples already hard and aching for attention, and Luke and Scott both gasped in delight.

Under their inspection, Chrissy's breathing quickened. Feeling excited but self-conscious as she stood before them, she closed her eyes and was startled by a picture in her head of Ross Sinclair, his eyes smouldering with lust as he watched her undress. Boldly she pushed back her shoulders, causing her breasts to quiver as she thrust them towards him. The vision was so vivid for a second, that her eyes flew open in surprise when Luke spoke.

'My God, they're magnificent. Have you ever seen tits like that before, Scottie?'

'Never. Things of beauty. Veritable works of art.'

More slowly now, caressing her sensuously, their lips and hands slid over her skin. Chrissy moaned as two sets of lips fastened on her nipples while four hands continued to roll the dress down over her hips till it slipped to the floor. There were more gasps when they discovered that she wore no panties and the smooth, naked beauty of her sex.

'Lie on the bed.' Luke's voice was hoarse, his eyes fixed on her. The bulges in the fronts of their trousers were very obvious now, their cocks outlined impressively by the tight material. Obeying him, Chrissy moved to the bed and lay down, watching through excited eyes.

Quickly they undressed, hard muscles rippling as they pulled their shirts over their heads. The white breeches were next, and it was Chrissy's turn to gasp. Their erections bobbing before them, they climbed onto the bed and knelt on either side of her. Two cocks. She had never had two men before, never even considered the possibility – and the sight of them excited her beyond belief. What would Karen say if she could see her now?

'Now you relax,' Luke murmured, running his hands over her skin. 'Scott, the champagne.' Scott lifted the bottle and began to ease out the cork. 'We're going to drink this champagne off your luscious body. Just you lie still and we won't lose a drop,' he advised.

Chrissy, her eyes huge, watched Scott's fingers work busily on the cork. When it exploded she jumped, and jumped again when the cold liquid foamed out of the neck and onto her belly. Immediately two tongues began to lap it up, trying to prevent it from rolling off her tummy onto the bed-covers, and she squirmed beneath the ticklish onslaught. When the initial foam had died down, Luke rocked back on his heels and grinned at her.

'Now we can get down to the serious business. Scott?'

A little of the champagne was trickled into the dip in Chrissy's collarbone, then eagerly lapped up. She felt her toes and stomach clench in bliss as they worked their way down her writhing body; all thoughts of Ross, or anyone else, were driven from her mind. Now there was only sensation, searching, licking, pleasure-giving sensation, no part of her body escaping the delight of their probing tongues. As the fizzing liquid splashed onto her nipples, Chrissy convulsed, arching her back, and they had to lick faster in order to spill as little as possible, their mouths lingering for a long time on each creamy globe. Moving lower, they repeatedly filled the well of her navel, taking it in turns to swirl their tongues inside, missing not a drop.

From there they moved to her feet. Chrissy was disappointed that they had bypassed her aching sex until they started sucking and licking the champagne from each individual toe and she squirmed beneath this new delightful onslaught. She felt as drunk with pleasure as if her body was absorbing the champagne through her pores. Every nerve ending was tingling, sending urgent messages to her brain, desperate for release. They continued their slow, erotic progress along each leg and her writing increased as they drank from her knees, her thighs, drawing ever nearer to the centre of her excitement.

Her thighs had parted slightly of their own accord and now one of the men, she did not know which, tried to ease them further apart. Suddenly overwhelmed, Chrissy resisted, turning her head into the pillow, ashamed and embarrassed by how aroused she was, how exposed. She had never met either of these men before, and now here she was writhing wantonly before them, mewling soft sounds she had not known she was capable of making. She had forgotten that sex could be like this, how defenceless it could make you feel.

But he kept up a steady gentle pressure on her inner thighs, murmuring soft words of approval and encouragement, urging her to open her secret intimate places to them, soothing her, till she relaxed once again under his touch. Gradually she allowed him to push her thighs apart, but she whimpered softly as her sex came into view, knowing that her arousal must be blatantly obvious.

Pouring a trickle of champagne over her smooth, naked mound, they watched for a moment as it found its way down to her parted lips. When the fizzing liquid hit her most sensitive areas Chrissy jumped, then gasped as two tongues fought to lap it up. This action was repeated endlessly, the men jostling with each other to drink the champagne now mingling with Chrissy's own sweet juices, and she squirmed ecstatically under this erotic harassment. Closing her eyes again, it was Ross's mouth she felt upon her, Ross's tongue which probed so deeply, the pressure inside her increasing till it reached a peak, an explosion of pleasure that left her panting and she had to beg them to stop.

Grinning, they sat up and Scott held the bottle aloft.

'Still only half-finished. I know what I'm going to do with the rest.' Sliding up the bed, he sat astride Chrissy, his penis resting in the deep valley between her breasts and the swollen tip only inches from her lips. Dribbling a little champagne onto her cleavage, he began sliding his cock along the wet groove. She shivered at the vibrant strength of his manhood, so close to her mouth. Scott gathered her breasts in his hands and moulded them around his swollen organ, moaning as he engulfed himself in her softness.

When he could take no more of this he changed position, moving to the side of her head, his penis held in his hand, the tip nudging hopefully at Chrissy's lips. All her inhibitions were gone now; she wanted only to give these men as much pleasure as they had given her. Reaching for the champagne she drank some, holding the fizzing liquid in her mouth before sliding her lips down his shaft, bathing his erection in champagne.

Scott's head was thrown back as the cold liquid travelled over his cock; he groaned at the unspeakable bliss. Sighing in pleasure, Chrissy sucked as much of him into her mouth as possible, till he bumped the back of her throat. Tipping her head back slightly, revealing the graceful arch of her neck to his gaze, she swallowed the champagne in her mouth and with it felt Scott's penis slide in deep, then deeper, till her lips were kissing the very base of his shaft.

At that moment she felt Luke's penis part the lips of her sex and glide smoothly inside, the walls stretching snugly to accommodate him. And then she was lost in paradise once again. Nothing before had prepared her for this whole new realm of sensuous pleasure, this feeling of being filled at both ends, two men embedded deeply inside her.

Wildly out of control, she bucked her hips up to meet Luke, her mouth still loving Scott. Scott came first, his head drawn back in a silent scream, a tiny frantic pulse beating in his jaw. With his buttocks clenched and his balls drawn up tightly, his cock jerked and spasmed and she gulped eagerly, swallowing every drop of his creamy seed, just as her own orgasm streaked through her, every bit as powerful as the first.

Luke slid his penis from her slippery hold to shoot his white-hot seed over Chrissy's belly and breasts, groaning loudly as each jet spurted onto her over-heated skin.

Gasping for breath, he collapsed beside her, reaching once more for the champagne. 'And we've still got to do your back,' he murmured.

Chrissy left shortly afterwards. It had been very tempting to start again, to let them 'do her back' as Luke had suggested, but somehow she couldn't. She had already done more, been more sexually adventurous than she had ever been in her life before, and she needed a little time to adjust, to set her thoughts straight. And there was also a niggling sense of guilt. Neither Scott nor Luke need ever know that when she closed her eyes during their lovemaking, it had been Ross Sinclair's face Chrissy had seen, his cock she had imagined sliding into her.

They had been reluctant to let her go; Clarissa, it seemed, had promised them her company for the whole night. In the end they had waved her off with more good humour than she thought she strictly deserved, but only after they had made her promise a follow-up session later in the week to make up for what they were missing.

'We may have to spank your bottom for letting us down like this,' Luke warned.

'And tie you up,' added Scott. 'We're very disappointed, you know.' He said this straight-faced, but his eyes were laughing, and Chrissy had no idea if he was serious or not.

'OK,' she agreed, the idea suddenly appealing to her very much.

'Promise?'

'Maybe,' she laughed and fled the room.

Downstairs the party was over. Most people had already left. Chrissy was standing in the hall, undecided whether to walk home or phone for a taxi, when someone came up behind her.

'Hi.' It was Will, her partner from the previous night. She recognised him immediately.

'Oh, hi. I didn't know you were here. I didn't see you earlier.'

'I've been here a while. I said I'd see you around.' He smiled his gorgeous smile.

'That's right, you did.' She grinned back.

'Are you going now? I can call you a taxi if you like.'

'Thanks, I was wondering if I should. It's later that I thought.'

'No problem. I'll do it for you now.'

While they waited the few minutes for the taxi to arrive, they chatted. Although Chrissy cringed inwardly every time he called her Clarissa, she was amazed at how easy he was to talk to. Last night, he had been so tongue-tied, but tonight he seemed much more relaxed. Even though he must have known what she had been up to upstairs with Luke and Scott, he did not make her feel awkward or uncomfortable. How refreshing it was to talk to a man who wasn't judging or criticising.

All too soon, the taxi arrived and she had to go.

'See you around?'

'You can count on it,' he smiled.

Four

Portia de Havilland sat on the patio of her London home and poured another glass of Pimm's for her friend.

'I, for one, cannot abide it! Edinburgh in July? God forbid! No, I didn't really have any choice but to come back. It's just unfortunate that it's so damn hot,' she drawled in the bored tone that her friends knew only too well. Irritably, she fished an ice cube out of her drink and ran it over her elegant throat in an attempt to cool down.

Hilary looked at her admiringly. Portia had to be one of the most striking-looking women she had ever known. Her alabaster skin contrasted exquisitely with the glossy jet black of her hair and the deep scarlet of her painted lips. The dress she wore was also black, very short and tight, not really designed for the summer heat. Hilary had rarely seen Portia dress in anything but black. Both her toe- and finger-nails were painted a rich dark red, and Hilary had heard a rumour that Portia had recently had her nipples dyed the same alluring colour . . .

'At least you have the Treasure Hunt to liven things up for you this summer,' she suggested. 'Surely that will provide some entertainment? I hear that Clarissa has got off to a good start.'

Portia eyed her coldly, but did not bother to reply; the melting ice trickling into her cleavage provided no relief from the oppressive sticky heat.

'How are you getting on with the Hunt? Have you heard from Basil yet?' Hilary suppressed a shudder at the thought of the man appointed to be Portia's 'referee'. 'Honestly, Portia, Bas is such a creep. I don't know why you let Clarissa choose Ross,' she added slyly.

'Ross Sinclair?' Portia screwed up her face in distaste. 'Don't make me laugh! Ross has to be the most boring, self-righteous man I have ever met. He's so straight-laced these days that I would swear he was still a virgin if I didn't know better from personal experience.' She smirked, but her tone had taken on an edge at the sound of Ross's name, just as Hilary had known it would. Portia did not handle rejection well and even after all these years she still harboured a bitter resentment towards her ex-lover.

'No,' she continued, 'I think I'll do all right with Bas, thank you very much. He's so . . .' she struggled for the right word, 'so amenable. Anyway, you'll get to meet him soon, he's staying here. He's been out shopping for lunch. That should be him now.' She turned her head as she heard a car draw up, her glossy hair swinging over her face.

'Just watch, and tell me if you could ever imagine Ross Sinclair behaving like this.' There was a rather nasty gleam in her eye that Hilary recognised and she smiled, settling back in her chair appreciatively. Lunch with Portia was always unpredictable, and never boring.

A few moments later Basil Hardacre came round the side of the building. He nodded at Hilary but spoke directly to Portia, licking his thin lips nervously. 'Hello, Portia. I've finished the shopping.'

'You're late.'

'Late? I don't think so.' Bas's voice trembled slightly as he looked at his watch. 'I—'

'Are you calling me a liar?' Portia's eyes were hard as she turned them on the man standing before her. He was actually quite good looking in a dark, mild sort of way, but her look held only contempt.

'No, Portia, of course not. I must have been mistaken. I am late.'

'No. Maybe I'm the one who's mistaken. Mistaken in choosing you to be the one to help me. I don't think I'm going to be needing your services after all, Basil. Perhaps you should just go?' She arched an eyebrow.

'Oh no, Portia, don't make me go. Please. I know I'll be able to help you if you will give me the chance.' His tongue snaked out again to moisten his lips and, though he did not raise his eyes, Hilary was sure she could detect a glimmer of excitement in his voice.

'What will you do if I let you stay?'

'I'll do anything Portia, anything you ask. You know I will.'

'Anything?'

'Of c-c-course.' His voice trembled.

Portia appeared to consider. All right, you can stay. But I'm warning you, I won't put up with you questioning me. If you don't please me then you are out and I'll find someone else to help me, understood? Now make us some fresh drinks and then sit down. No! *Fresh* drinks, you idiot; we need more ice. You'll find it in the kitchen.' She rolled her eyes in exasperation at Hilary as Bas hurried eagerly indoors.

He returned a few minutes later and poured the drinks.

'Now, sit down,' she ordered.

Bas looked round in confusion for a few moments. There were only the two chairs on the patio, both occupied.

'On the ground then, idiot, if you can't find anywhere else. No not there, not in that suit. Perhaps you had better take it off.' She winked at Hilary.

'Off? What, here?' Bas looked around the patio dubiously. 'Couldn't I just go in and get—'

'Take it off, Bas, when I tell you. In fact, take everything off. I may as well take a look at what you are offering.'

'Everything? Here? In front of . . .? But, Portia—'

'Bas, if you are going to question everything I say, then we are not going to get along very well, are we?' said Portia with feigned patience. 'Now do it or get out.'

Bas seemed to struggle with his emotions for a few seconds before he began to remove his clothes in front of the women, as Portia had known he would. It was what he had come for, after all. She and Hilary watched as he removed his jacket then his shirt. Actually, his body was not too bad: thin, but fit and wiry. As his fingers moved to lower his trousers, Hilary's eyes quickened with interest. His penis was already hard and very erect, long and thin against the flat muscles of his stomach. Self-consciously Bas crossed his hands in front of himself, quivering slightly as his fingers brushed the hot skin of his own erection.

'Get your hands away!' snapped Portia. 'Did I say you could touch yourself?' Her black eyes shone now with excitement as she looked at the naked man in front of her. Bas obeyed immediately and though he hung his head in shame, his cock seemed to grow even longer at her tone.

'Well, that's a fine thing, Bas.' Portia's voice dripped sarcasm, which served only to excite him more; a low groan escaped his parted lips. 'I invite you here to my home and how do you repay me? You embarrass me in front of my friend. You're an insult. Get rid of it immediately.'

'What?' Bas was confused.

'Your erection. Get rid of it,' she hissed.

'But I can't . . . It won't – not with you watching me.'

'You have one minute, Bas,' said Portia, looking pointedly at her watch. 'If it's not gone by then, then you had better just get dressed and leave. I have no further use for you.'

Now Hilary sat forward eagerly in her seat. 'Perhaps if I just—' she started hopefully.

'Sit down,' snapped Portia to her friend. 'Don't be disgusting. This is his problem. One minute, Bas. What's it going to be?'

Already a tear of liquid had oozed from the tip of Bas's straining cock, and as he took his shaft in his hand he smoothed it over the purple tip with the ball of his thumb. He looked at the two women as his hand began to slide up and down his shaft. His stance was one of humiliation, his shoulders drooping as he stood with his trousers around his ankles, stroking himself, rubbing the smooth skin over the hardness within. His shame only added to his intense excitement. It only took a few seconds before his body stiffened and he groaned, shooting jet after jet of thick white semen into the air to land on the grass between him and the women.

Portia's eyes glinted as she stared at the white globules glistening in the sunshine. 'That's better. Perhaps we might get along after all, if you can do as you are told. Now go and wash up and make us some lunch. You won't be needing your clothes again. I'll find you something more suitable to wear while you stay here.' They both watched him disappear naked into the house.

'Well?' Portia asked, unable to keep the smirk out of her voice. 'Could you ever imagine Ross Sinclair doing that?'

The idea was so absurd that both women looked at each other and burst out laughing. 'No,' agreed Hilary, 'but I'll tell you

53

this, if you ever manage to persuade him to do it I'll pay money to watch!'

They were still laughing when Bas came back with the lunch and served it naked in the garden, biting his lip hard to try to prevent another erection. Portia nodded approvingly at his self-control. Although she seemed unmoved by his nakedness, she noted how Hilary's eyes followed his every movement. When Bas went back inside to make the coffee and Hilary leaned forward to whisper something in Portia's ear, she pretended to consider for a moment then nodded indulgently, like a good hostess. Her mood seemed to have been improved considerably.

When Bas returned Portia spoke sweetly to him. 'It seems that my friend is not as repulsed by your body as I am and she would like you to do her a little favour, Basil. A very special favour. I've told her you would be delighted; isn't that right?'

'Of course.' Basil turned questioningly to Hilary who merely looked back at Portia.

'Oh, don't be so bloody naive, Basil. Get on your knees and do her a "favour" when you are told.'

Hesitantly Basil dropped to his knees and approached Hilary. She was wearing a long flowing Laura Ashley skirt and she made no attempt to pull it up; she did not even look at him but merely parted her legs slightly. Bas understood. He pushed his head under her skirt, allowing the folds of soft material to settle over his naked back and shoulders. He was at once engulfed in a world of downy skin and musky feminine scents. The sunlight filtered through the gauzy fabric, bathing his vision in a rosy pink glow and allowing him to see clearly the swollen lips of Hilary's sex, glistening and ready, fringed by her wispy blonde curls. Through the skirt he could hear the women, their voices somewhat muffled, begin to chat about a party they might go to, as though oblivious to Bas's presence.

Reverently, cocooned from the outside, Bas breathed in deeply, scenting the rich aroma of Hilary's arousal before planting a tender kiss on the tip of her pubic bone. Hilary moaned slightly; she quickly turned the noise into a cough and, under the pretext of getting more comfortable, wriggled down the chair a little, increasing his access. She sipped her coffee and laughed at a joke Portia made while Bas's mouth slowly began to brush kisses over her inner thighs, before moving upwards to explore her folds with his lips and tongue. His movements were slow and expert as he probed and licked, sucked and nibbled.

Using his tongue he flicked up and down over her pleasure bud, the movement exposing the exquisitely sensitive tip. Hilary moaned. Beneath her skirt Bas allowed himself to grin, guessing that an audible reaction like that would have earned the disapproval of Portia. After a time he eased Hilary's legs further apart and pushed a finger inside her, then two, releasing a gush of moisture which he lapped up eagerly. She squirmed and, encouraged, he bobbed his head even lower, allowing his tongue to trace lightly over the highly sensitised skin of her perineum, exploring every intimate crevice of her body. Sensing the approach of her climax, Bas slid a third finger easily into her as his thumb began a lazy circling of her clitoris and his tongue continued its sensuous probing.

Hilary, forgetting the rules of the game, gasped loudly as the pleasurable sensations flowed through her body. Tightly, she clamped her legs around his head, pulling him towards her as the tension gathered within her. Throwing her head back, exposing her throat and face to the sun, she ground herself into his face, striving to meet his wet-mouthed kiss as she was tipped into a world of pulsing sensation. She moaned aloud as wave after wave of pleasure washed over her and was still panting when she finally released her hold on Bas and he emerged back into the sunlight, his face and chin glistening with her juices, a look of absurd pleasure on his face and another unwilled erection jutting from between his legs.

'Well, well, well.' Portia's hissing voice brought him back to reality with a snap. 'Hilary, I think it is time you left now, don't you? You must have lots to do for the party tonight.'

Hilary was well aware that Portia liked to play elaborate games of a sexual nature and that she played with a rigid set of rules. Unfortunately for the other participants, these rules could be changed at will – Portia's will. This unpredictability was what made her company so exciting, but it could also be a little unnerving. Recognising the gleam in Portia's eye, and glad to be able to escape her friend's wrath, Hilary got to her feet and made her excuses, her legs still somewhat shaky. She did not waste any sympathy on Bas, who was still kneeling on the patio – she was quite sure that he would enjoy any punishment Portia had in mind.

Neither Portia nor Bas got up to show her out.

Portia looked at Bas coldly, most pointedly at his erection which only seemed to grow with her disapproval. 'You seem to be in a rather defiant mood today, Basil. I think it's time you learned a lesson, don't you?' She stood up, her tall frame towering above him. 'And I think I'm just the one to teach you. Come here.'

Meekly, his body trembling with anticipation, Basil followed her into the house.

Later that evening, Portia stood on the platform waiting for her tube train to arrive. She always took the tube to her 'special' parties; it helped get her in the mood. Every inch of her skin prickled with anticipation as she waited; her nipples pressed provocatively against her sleeveless white silk top, their dyed cherry-red tips highly visible through the sheer silk and already aching to be touched. Restless and hot, she prowled the near-empty platform, her short, flirty skirt barely covering the naked skin of her bottom. Her face flushed with the promise of the pleasure to come, she impatiently eyed the dark tunnel through which her train would emerge. The time was carefully chosen, her intention to catch the tail-end of the rush hour. Not too quiet, not too overcrowded.

To the casual observer Portia appeared to be alone but she knew that Bas was on the platform somewhere behind her, carrying a suitcase with the clothes she would change into for the party. He knew better than to approach her until he was told.

Portia was excited. She was aware that all the men on the platform were surreptitiously watching her and wondered if they could sense how hot she was, how aroused. But she did not encourage them; they were not part of the game. She was almost trembling by the time a train rumbled into the station, and stamped her foot in frustration when she realised it was not suitable – too busy.

But the next train came in only a few minutes later, and that suited her fine: busy, but not overcrowded. Portia got on, knowing without looking that Bas would follow.

She saw her victim almost as soon as the doors opened: a stocky, good-looking man in a business suit standing against the opposite doors. Bas found himself a seat from where he could watch Portia. She allowed herself to be pushed by the crowd into a position just in front of her chosen prey, moving in close under the pretext of being jostled by the early evening throng. Portia did not once look directly at him, but made sure he had a clear, unobstructed view of her breasts through the semi-transparent silk before she took up her place with her back to him. As the doors closed, the crowding bodies caused her to press more closely into the man behind as she caught hold of the hanging strap for support.

She stared straight ahead, like all the other commuters, seemingly oblivious to her fellow passengers. But with every swaying motion of the tube-train she allowed herself to move gently backwards and forwards, her bottom rubbing against the crotch of the businessman behind her. She tossed her hair as though pushing it off her face, apparently unaware when it tantalisingly brushed over his nose and chin. He tried to back away slightly, but was brought up by the doors of the train, and Portia, grinning to herself, felt his startled response as she followed him back, pressing now against the hardening lump she could feel in his trousers. There would be no escape; she had never felt so hot.

Nothing happened for a moment as the stranger tried to gauge what was going on. Impatiently Portia waited to see what would happen. Some men were more reluctant than others and needed encouragement. The standing passengers lurched with the rocking movement of the train as it roared through the darkness and she felt his growing hardness jab into her behind. A second later she felt a tentative hand on her thigh and with a rush of exhilaration knew it would be all right.

She had to stifle a moan of excitement as the hand, encouraged at not being slapped away, slid further up her leg and over her buttock. She heard his sudden sharp intake of breath, quickly turned into a cough, as he discovered that she

57

wore no panties under the short skirt. He paused in his exploration and Portia had to urge him to continue by swaying back, as though thrown slightly off balance by the movement of the train. She continued to stare straight ahead, a bored expression on her face, as his hand slipped forward, cupping her warm sex before sliding two fingers along her already very moist channel. Portia clenched her muscles around him in encouragement, her whole body buzzing with excitement, ready for more than just a gentle touch. Now came the risky bit.

Still holding the hanging strap with one hand, she allowed the other to drop to her side. When she was sure the other passengers were paying her no attention, she allowed her hand to move behind her between their two bodies, till she could slide down his zip. He stiffened slightly as she eased her hand inside his trousers and massaged his cock, which was already very erect. Releasing him from the confines of his trousers, she dropped the hem of her short skirt lightly over his cock, pressing her buttocks against him encouragingly. The rest was up to him.

She bit her lip to keep from crying out as the cheeks of her bottom were gently eased apart and the stranger stroked his cock along her crease. Slowly, steadying her with his hands, he worked his stubby length inside her, stretching and filling her to the brim. For a moment his breathing was ragged as he savoured the sensation and Portia had to stifle a flash of irritation – surely he was not going to spoil things by drawing attention to them? But no. By holding very still for a few moments he was able to regain control and stare resolutely into space once again.

Resisting the urge to thrust backwards into him, Portia had to settle for surreptitiously using the movement of the train, swaying back against him and clenching and unclenching her muscles. This was what she loved. Her eyes were glassy and unfocused, all her attention on her hot sex and how well this stranger filled her; his pleasure, as always, was secondary to her own.

At the next station they both paused, their movements frozen until the train started moving once more. This time Portia worked her pelvic muscles furiously and she could feel his orgasm building inside him as they rocketed through the dark tunnel. As the train slowed for the next station she was ready.

Her timing was all now, the momentum gathering pace, and she milked his cock for all she was worth, even as the doors flew open.

Bas was watching closely, following the expressions fleeting across her face and he stood up, her suitcase clutched to him. The stranger, unable to hold back, gave a last frantic thrust and spent himself inside her just as she stepped forward and off the train, Bas close behind. Portia turned on the platform, her last vision as the train doors slid shut, of the startled stranger, his cock still out of his trousers, gushing forth the last of his milky fluid onto the floor of the train.

Portia blew him a triumphant kiss as the train pulled out of the station.

The other departing passengers, unaware, quickly left the platform. Portia and Bas followed a short way up the passage until she was sure all the other passengers were gone. She caught his arm and pulled him back.

'Now. Lick me. Quickly!'

Startled, Bas hesitated; but one look at Portia's feverish stare told him that he dare not disobey. Portia, her eyes glassy, pressed back against the cool tiled wall, tipping her hips towards him slightly. Sinking to his knees Bas lifted her short skirt enough to push his head underneath, breathing in her excited musk, mixed with the tangy scent of semen. She grabbed his head and pulled him towards her, squirming frantically on his tongue, her gasps loud and echoing along the empty platform as he sucked and licked her, eager to obey. Portia screamed as she came, oblivious to security cameras and the noise of approaching passengers – oblivious to everything but the massive orgasm which overtook her as Bas greedily sucked her clean. When she had recovered, Portia walked jauntily away without a glance, eager to get to her party, leaving him on his knees.

Admiringly, Bas scrambled to his feet, hurrying after her. He was going to enjoy his few weeks with Portia.

Five

It was almost ten when Chrissy was woken by a loud banging. At first she was groggy, unsure where she was as she stared blearily round Clarissa's bedroom. Then it all came flooding back and she sat up quickly in bed, wondering who on earth was at the door. The pounding continued as she grabbed a silk robe of Clarissa's and hurried down the stairs. There on the doorstep stood Ross, his hair gleaming raven black in the late morning sunshine, dressed in a white T-shirt and jeans. The jeans were old and frayed, the seams and button fly faded to near white. He looked way too sexy, Chrissy thought, conscious of her own sleepy and tousled appearance. Ross smiled guardedly, as if unsure of his welcome. He held up a brown paper bag with a baker's name emblazoned on the side.

'A peace offering. I've brought breakfast. Aren't you going to invite me in?'

Wordlessly she stepped aside and he made his way to the kitchen.

'I've had the devil of a time finding a baker open on a Sunday morning. You do like croissants, don't you?'

Chrissy nodded silently as he busied himself boiling the kettle and warming the croissants. Soon the rich aroma of freshly ground coffee filled the room. She found herself reluctantly impressed by his efficiency.

Ross handed her a mug of coffee and she closed her eyes as she sipped the steaming liquid, finally managing to pull herself together. She usually had no trouble with mornings, but it had been late before she had finally fallen into Clarissa's bed, exhausted and sated after her evening with Scott and Luke.

When she opened her eyes again, feeling the strong coffee coursing through her veins, she saw Ross watching her.

Remarkably she found herself blushing and wished she had stopped to put on more clothes. She felt very naked in her blue robe, even though it swept the floor.

'Rough night?' Something flashed in his eyes, something indefinable, that nonetheless brought goosebumps to her skin. 'No, don't answer that,' he said quickly. 'It's none of my business. I've come to start again, to offer the help I promised Clarissa.' His voice was husky, and he cleared his throat before pushing the plate of croissants towards Chrissy. 'Here, have some.'

'Thanks.'

'She talks! I thought for a moment that you were one of those zombies who can't speak before three o'clock in the afternoon.'

'I can speak. I'm just not as disgustingly cheerful as some people.' She helped herself hungrily to breakfast.

Ross watched her eat, astonished that someone with such a slim build could pack away so much food. 'I thought we should get to know each other a little better; I wondered if you would like to spend the day with me?'

'Doing what?' Chrissy was suspicious. This Ross seemed quite different to the one she had spoken to on the phone and met at the party. He was much more pleasant and cheerful, though certainly no less attractive. She found herself wondering what he would look like sitting at her breakfast table in just his faded jeans, without the T-shirt. Flushing, she looked away and busied herself pouring more coffee for both of them.

'I'm going to visit a friend who wants me to look at a horse he has bought. He doesn't know Clarissa very well and I thought you might like to come along. Don't worry – ' his voice took on a edge as he caught her expression – 'it's strictly a social visit. His wife has recently given birth to their third child – he is definitely not a candidate for your little game. I just thought we should get to know each other a bit better.'

'OK.' Chrissy shrugged, resenting his tone rather but finding the prospect of spending a day with him strangely appealing. 'Will you help me fill in my Treasure Hunt card before I get ready?'

Ross nodded and waited at the table while she fetched it, his

61

eyes following her as she moved out of the room; he was keenly aware that she was naked under her robe.

Since meeting Chrissy last night he had been unable to get her out of his mind. All through the fund-raising function he attended after the party, she had occupied his thoughts, though he had deliberately willed himself not to think of what she was doing at that moment. Later in bed, unable to sleep, he had tossed restlessly, the sheets twisted round his hard body, frustrated by visions of Chrissy and her impossibly provocative green dress.

The only reason Ross had allowed himself to be persuaded into helping with the Treasure Hunt was because of the money that had been promised to Down and Out. After all, he justified, both Clarissa and Portia would have slept with half a dozen men in a week just for fun. Someone may as well benefit financially. But already, since meeting Chrissy, he was regretting his decision.

He had come here today against his better judgement, hoping that if he saw her again, especially after she had spent a night with those two insufferable polo players, he would be able to think about her more objectively. He was wrong. The attraction and the hunger were still there, every bit as hot and aching as before.

Chrissy returned with her list, chewing on her pen and sat down opposite him. She seemed unaware that her robe had parted slightly at the front, revealing a tantalising glimpse of cleavage, which drew Ross's eye despite his attempts to resist. She ticked the boxes for 'sportsman' and '*ménage à trois*'.

'I'll need your help with the first two. Phil, for instance: who is he and where does he fit in?'

'Phil is a lawyer,' said Ross simply, not telling her that Phil's family were behind one of the largest law firms in the country. His voice sounded gruff, making her look up at him.

'And Will, what is he? Some kind of farmer?' She remembered him making a reference to horses.

Ross looked at her oddly. 'Richard William Frederick Barnes, eighteenth Earl of Mirton, owns estates in England and Scotland, as well as two Scottish islands, so yes, I suppose you could call him a farmer.'

62

'An earl? Gosh. I didn't know. Still, there are no earls on here, so he will have to go down as a farmer. He was a lovely man.'

Ross could hardly believe that she was so unimpressed by Will's title, but she ticked lawyer and farmer and carefully folded the list away.

'OK, give me five minutes to get ready.'

Up in Clarissa's bedroom Chrissy chose a sleeveless cotton dress which buttoned up the front. She would normally have worn her jeans, but it seemed a shame to let so many beautiful clothes go to waste. Anyway, she was playing the role of seductress, so she should at least wear a dress and not trousers. Impulsively she slipped the dress on without any bra or panties, feeling sexy and daring. No-one else need know, and she might as well be ready if the opportunity arose!

As she ran a brush through her thick hair she wondered at her chances of adding Ross to her list. He was a wildly attractive man, and she had seen the way he had looked at her over breakfast. What was it Clarissa had said about him? 'He has the biggest cock in Edinburgh, but he keeps it tucked well into his trousers.'

For a moment, with her hand on the doorknob Chrissy wondered what would happen if she stripped off her dress, lay down on the bed and called down to him. She shivered, anticipating the expression on his face as he came into the room, how his eyes would darken with lust at the naked invitation, how he would strip off his clothes – no, just his T-shirt at first, she corrected her fantasy – before joining her on the bed. Before she could get too carried away, Chrissy remembered the disapproval and anger she had seen on his face when she went off with Scott and Luke the previous evening. Maybe it would not be such a good idea.

Ross was waiting in the hall for her. The breath caught in his throat as she ran down the stairs towards him, her full breasts moving freely inside the soft fabric of her clothes. Daringly, knowing that she was not wearing panties, Chrissy had left the two lower buttons of her dress undone; it was perfectly decent, but allowed the skirt to swish and fold round her shapely legs as she walked.

Ross's voice was throaty as he held the door open for her. 'We'll use my car, if that's OK?'

'Fine.' She was almost out the door when the phone rang. Chrissy went back in to answer it, expecting it to be Clarissa, but it was Will.

'Hello,' he said, 'I hope I'm not bothering you, but I was wondering if you would like to come out for a drink tonight?'

Chrissy was surprised at how pleased she was to hear from him. She knew how much it must have cost him to call her – a man as shy as he was would not call up women very often and ask them out on a date. But she hesitated. Will was far too nice a person for her to continue lying to him. And if she saw him again it would certainly lead to complications.

Will seemed to sense her hesitation, because he hurried on, 'It's OK, I haven't forgotten what you said the other night – it's just a drink, nothing more.'

Still Chrissy was unsure. A quick glance at where Ross stood at the door, his face like thunder, helped her to make up her mind

'Thanks. That would be great. Nine o'clock all right? You'll pick me up here? OK. Bye.'

Before leaving she went into the kitchen and picked the last croissant off the plate, munching on it and smiling to herself as she passed Ross on the doorstep. Let him think what he liked. Maybe he should learn not to jump to conclusions about people!

Chrissy laughed when she saw Ross's car, a battered and rusty old Escort.

'I thought you would have a little red sports car,' she joked, 'one of those ones where your knees are up around your chin. Or at the very least, a convertible. This is even older than my car.'

'We can't all be rich,' said Ross, as he tugged with both hands at the passenger door to open it. 'Some of us have to work for a living, you know.'

Chrissy grinned back at him. Who was he trying to kid? His jeans might be faded, but she had already noted that they were Armani. The plain white T-shirt could easily have come from Marks and Spencer, if it had not been for the Paul Smith label sticking out at the back of his neck. Impulsively Chrissy reached up and tucked it in for him. The action brought them close, with his face only inches from hers. His blue eyes were inscrutable as he looked down at her; her breasts touched his chest, the nipples rising immediately to hard points which she was sure he could feel.

Ross was angry again and struggling to hide it. It was infuriating to have to stand there and listen to her make dates to have sex with other men – even worse when he recognised that that was exactly what he wanted to do to her himself. He wanted to make love to this woman more than he had ever wanted anything in his life. Something primitive moved inside him as her hazel eyes gazed curiously back at him and his own eyes took on a rather predatory glint.

Suddenly, without warning, he bent his head and his mouth found hers, his tongue flicking over her lower lip and capturing a tiny crumb of croissant. Startled at first, Chrissy closed her eyes, inviting his kiss. Though he only touched her with his mouth and then so lightly that she barely felt it, she was aware of a melting, liquid arousal flooding through her, could feel the matching heat flowing from him. Waiting, growing confused when he did not put his arms around her and kiss her properly, she opened her eyes and she searched his face, exhilarated by what she saw there, the raw intensity of his need for her.

But a second later his expression changed. It was though a shutter had come down, masking his emotions.

Silently Ross cursed. He really was going to have to keep a tighter grip on himself. He had to keep reminding himself what kind of woman he was dealing with here. Perhaps it was part of the game for her, to lure a man deeper and deeper with the unexpected innocence of her wide eyes. But the problem was his, not hers. Chrissy had never pretended to be anything other than what she was. He forced himself to smile.

'Sorry about that. You had a crumb on your lip. You shouldn't stand so close to men if you don't want to be kissed. You're just too sexy.'

He did not sound sorry at all and Chrissy matched his flippant tone when she spoke. 'Don't worry about it. Happens all the time. Men just can't resist me.'

He was still standing close and an erotic energy crackled between them as she broke contact and climbed into the car. This brought her eyes almost to a level with his crotch and she was relieved to see the tantalising bulge in his jeans before he slammed the door and moved round to the driver's seat. At least he wasn't as unmoved by her as he was pretending. She was totally confused by Ross Sinclair and the conflicting signals he was sending her.

'I feel like a teenager,' Ross muttered as they set off.

'Why?' she joked. 'Was that the last time you managed to get a girl in this grotty car?'

'Not quite. But it was the last time my jeans felt this tight.'

For a moment Chrissy said nothing, then she burst out laughing. Despite everything, she couldn't help liking Ross. Tentatively she offered, 'You know I'm on this Treasure Hunt. If you feel like it, we could always go back and . . .' She let the sentence tail off, hoping she had not revealed how much effort it had taken her to say the words. Despite what Ross obviously thought of her, he was the first man she had propositioned in years.

'No, thanks. I don't want to be a notch on anyone's bedpost. I'm not into one night stands. But it was nice of you to offer.' His tone was light as he concentrated on pulling out into the traffic but Chrissy felt as if she had been slapped. What was with this man? It was he who had made a pass at her, after all. But she did not let herself get annoyed. If she was honest, involvement with a man as complicated as Ross Sinclair was the last thing she needed.

They drove in silence for a while, the tension gradually dissipating. Eventually, as he turned the car towards Glasgow, they started chatting companionably, as if the kiss and Chrissy's offer had not happened. Chrissy told him about the changes she was making to her life and the university course she hoped to start in October. Ross talked about his work, his voice becoming impassioned when he talked of some of the people his charity had helped and his frustration at not being able to do more. If Chrissy was a little surprised at the strength of his feelings, she did not show it.

As he drove, Ross's eyes were repeatedly drawn to Chrissy's

long bare legs, exposed to his gaze by the buttons undone on her dress. In fact, now that she was sitting, the dress had ridden up and rather more leg was on show than Chrissy had anticipated, but she felt that any attempt by her to fasten the buttons now would only draw more attention. Maybe he hadn't noticed.

They had left the motorway some time before and, as they started up a bumpy farm road, the dress parted even higher. Ross felt his mouth go dry. My God, no woman had a right to have legs that long.

The narrow track did not do justice to the house when they arrived. Chrissy realised he had driven up the back way, but even from the back the house was spectacular – absolutely enormous. It must have at least forty rooms. She was still gazing in amazement when Ross parked his battered car next to a gleaming Bentley at the side of a stable block.

'Ross! Glad you could make it. How are you?'

'Fine. How are Penny and the kids? Especially the new one – are they here?' Ross shook hands with a tall middle-aged man who had emerged from one of the stables at the approach of their car.

'No. Unfortunately you've just missed them. They've gone to Penny's mother's. Aren't you going to introduce me?' He looked expectantly over Ross's shoulder at Chrissy.

'Of course. Greg Mitchell, this is . . .' Ross hesitated briefly and Chrissy knew he was uncomfortable lying to his friend about her identity.

'Clarissa Asquith.' She stepped forward and held out her hand.

'Clarissa? We've met before, but I never would have recognised you. How are you? How's your father?'

'He's fine,' cut in Ross. 'Now, where's this horse you're so proud of?'

Greg looked from one to the other, aware that something was going on, but then shrugged. 'In here. She's a beauty. Jim! Bring out Brittany, will you?' A gleaming filly was led out by a handsome stocky man in his forties. His eyes swept over Chrissy insolently as he led the filly past, but Ross and Greg only had eyes for the horse.

Chrissy knew nothing at all about horses, had rarely even

been near one, and was taken aback by the sheer size of this one. Somehow on television they did not look so big. Unconsciously, she took a step or two back and then jumped when she heard a loud snort and whinny from just behind her. Greg and Ross looked up from their discussion of the mare's legs to laugh at her nervousness.

'Pay no attention to Samson,' Greg grinned. 'He's got things on his mind.'

'Still up to his old tricks?' asked Ross.

'You bet. Plenty of life in the old devil yet. Jim! Saddle up Brittany and Jerry. What about you, Clarissa? Are you coming with us?'

'No thanks.' She was still nervously eyeing the box where she could hear a large horse stamping impatiently. 'I don't ride.'

Greg looked puzzled. 'But I thought—'

'You've hurt your back, haven't you? You're not allowed to ride,' Ross put in hurriedly, knowing that Clarissa was an accomplished horsewoman.

'Yes. That's right. I'm not allowed. I'll just stay here, if it's all the same to you. You go and enjoy yourselves. It's what we came for, after all. I'll be fine.'

'Well, if you're sure?'

Chrissy wandered round the yard, tentatively stroking the velvety noses of the horses who stared curiously at her from their loose boxes. She was not so nervous when they were contained by the stable doors. Ross, already mounted on Brittany, watched her while Greg changed into his riding boots. Chrissy found a kitten and she bent to tease it with a piece of straw, laughing as the furry little creature rolled and dived on the cobbles.

Ross's eyes drifted from her smiling face to the thrust of her firm breasts against the material as she bent down to tickle the kitten, her dress parting once again to reveal her long, long legs. He was too far away but he could almost imagine that he saw her hard nipples outlined by the fabric, then a flashing glimpse of shadow at the top of her legs as the folds of her dress fell back into place when she stood up. He was unaware of Greg's eyes upon him, looking from him to Chrissy, recognition dawning as he saw the intensity of Ross's expression.

Ross was imagining crossing the stable yard, pressing Chrissy down on the straw and sliding his hand up the smoothness of her thigh, when suddenly Brittany, bored with being ignored, gave a restless buck, almost unseating him.

'Now, now, Ross, keep your mind on one filly at a time,' Greg laughed, mounting his own horse.

'Piss off,' grinned Ross. 'Are you finally ready? See you later,' he called to Chrissy and the two horses clattered out of the yard.

Ross had not been the only one looking at Chrissy. Jim the stablehand had also been appreciating the way she fitted into her clothes but now he reluctantly moved away, disappearing round the corner of the stable block.

Alone, Chrissy found herself drifting to the half-door where the horse called Samson was stabled. He was still making a lot of noise, stamping and calling imperiously every few moments. Occasionally there was an answering whinny from a closed box further down the row, which only seemed to spur Samson on. Tentatively Chrissy peered over the half-door of the stable, ready to flee if the wild-sounding horse attacked her. The stable was divided into two large stalls and she breathed a sigh of relief when she saw that Samson was not roaming free like the other horses but was secured by a head collar.

He was huge, the biggest horse she had ever seen. His dappled grey coat was flecked with sweat and he tossed his black mane and tail restlessly, whinnying loudly. As he swung round Chrissy gasped to see his huge penis, bigger than she would ever have thought possible, curving along the length of his belly.

'You want to be careful.' Jim had crept back and was standing beside her. 'He's usually gentle as a lamb but there's a mare in season further down the row and he is a mite over-excited. In fact, if you'll excuse my language, he's as randy as hell. I wouldn't go in there, if I was you.'

Chrissy had absolutely no intention of going in. 'He's beautiful,' she said.

'Aye, he is that.' Jim's voice was full of pride as he looked at the horse.

'Why do you keep the mare so close if he's only going to be frustrated like that?' Chrissy motioned to the stallion's erection. 'It hardly seems fair.'

Jim was taken aback by the directness of her question. Most visitors to the yard were a touch more coy. 'He'll get his chance, miss, soon as his Lordship comes back.' He chuckled. 'I suspect he'd damn near kick the stable down if we kept him away from her much longer.'

The stallion pawed the ground and lifted his elegant head to sniff the air, his nostrils flaring, ignoring the two people. It was hot in the stableyard, the air heavy with the smell of sweat and hay, and the pervading pungent aroma of the stallion's arousal. Chrissy felt breathless, unable to take her eyes off the swollen massive length of the horse's penis, jumping and twitching with a life of its own. All morning, since sharing her breakfast table with Ross, she had been aware of a dull throbbing in her own sex organs, and felt a sympathy with the horse's frustration. But she was also very aware of Jim standing beside her and became self-conscious.

'I hope he doesn't have to wait too long,' she said, turning away from the stallion's box. 'Phew, it's hot, isn't it? I think I'll look for somewhere cool to sit while I wait for them to come back.' She ignored Jim's knowing smile as he nodded his head and turned to get on with his work. Even when he entered the barn Chrissy had the uncomfortable feeling that he was still watching her.

There was no shade to be found anywhere in the stable yard. She looked longingly at the house, but it was far too big and imposing for her just to let herself in to wait. Nor was she going to follow Jim into the barn. Although he was actually quite handsome in a swarthy kind of way and a 'groom' was on her Treasure Hunt card, Chrissy had no desire to complicate her life further at this moment. She could just picture Ross and Greg's faces if they came back to find her rolling in the hay with the hired help.

The only place she could find some shade was in the empty box next to Samson's. Sliding the bolt, Chrissy slipped inside, closing only the bottom half of the door behind her. There wasn't much of a breeze, but she thought she might as well take

70

advantage of what there was. It was still hot inside, but it was nice to get out of the direct sun. The box smelled of wood and horse and clean straw, smells Chrissy was unfamiliar with; she felt rather light-headed in the heat of the confined space. Shakily, she made her way to some bales of fresh smelling hay and settled herself down. She might as well be comfortable as she waited.

It was warm in the stable and very pleasant. Chrissy lay back, shaking her head to fan her hair over the straw, allowing what little breeze there was to play over the nape of her neck. Beads of perspiration were already forming in the deep valley between her breasts and she slipped the top button of her dress free, hoping in vain that the breeze would reach here too.

She had not had much sleep the previous night and as she lay in the warmth she began to grow drowsy. It was pleasant to lie there, allowing her mind to wander, her eyes to gently close. Idly, as she drifted to sleep, her thoughts turned to Ross. He really was an impossible man, but there was no denying how attractive he was.

For a second she allowed herself to imagine Ross standing over her in the stable, his shirt off, sweat glistening on his bronzed chest as he slowly unbuttoned his jeans, his remarkable eyes smoky with passion, unable to resist her. She smiled sleepily at the image. Maybe she should talk to him on the drive back, explain why she was taking part in the Treasure Hunt? Yes, that's what she would do. She would talk to him. Chrissy's eyes closed and her breathing deepened as she slept.

But even in her sleep she was hot. A piece of straw tickled her shoulder and she raised a hand to brush it away. The restless movement was enough to allow another two buttons on her dress to slip open and her heavy breasts tumbled free into the sunlight. Chrissy moaned, as the whisper of a breeze touched her nipples, causing them to rise and harden to rosy peaks. She squirmed slightly in the straw and the last few buttons on her dress slipped free. The soft breeze was now able to play all over her hot skin, drying the thin sheen of perspiration and in her sleep she sighed in relief, her lips parting slightly in a smile.

Ross had been the last thing she thought of as she drifted off and now he filled her dreams. A dark shadow passed over her

71

and she frowned slightly. She dreamt he had entered the stable and was standing over her, watching her, his blue eyes glittering with sexual intent. Instead of his jeans he now wore a crisp white shirt and jodhpurs and occasionally slapped a riding crop against the supple leather of his boots, but he made no move to touch her or to speak, and Chrissy whimpered in mounting frustration.

Jim's eyes were wide as he looked over the half-door. Whatever he had been expecting to find in the stable, it certainly hadn't been this! He could tell immediately that Chrissy was asleep, but still, as he drank in the sight before him, he was ready to duck back out of sight if she looked like waking up. She lay there semi-naked, her honey-gold hair, almost exactly the same colour of the straw, tumbling wantonly around her shoulders. Her breasts were there in all their naked glory for him to see but, frustratingly, her hand rested lightly on her mound, hiding her secrets in shadow. Jim licked his lips. God, she looked beautiful lying there!

Chrissy moved restively, as if her dreams were troubled. 'Ross?' The name was a soft whisper on her lips, but the movement caused her hand to slip away and Jim was treated to the sight of her smoothly shaven pubis. He gasped, then quickly stifled the sound. The last thing he wanted right now was to waken her. He had not even noticed until then that his hand was massaging his erection through the rough material of his trousers, but once he became aware of it, he knew he would have to release the swollen organ soon, before pleasure turned to pain. Feeling guilty for intruding on Chrissy's privacy, but completely unable to resist, he slipped the bolt on the stable door and silently crept inside.

Chrissy was having the most wonderful dream. Ross was still there with her, still watching her. And he wanted her. She could tell he wanted her though he did not move or speak. For the moment he was content to watch, to drink in her nakedness. No matter. They had all the time in the world. A delicious heat began to spread over her and she smiled happily. Lifting the heavy globes of her breasts in her hands she offered then to him and she knew, just *knew*, that he wanted to take them in his hands, his mouth. And she also knew just how good his lips and teeth would feel on her sensitive skin. It would be well worth waiting for. Moaning softly, she rolled her nipples between her fingers, lifting first one and then the other to flick the rising crests with her tongue.

Sensing the dream Ross's approval, she drew her legs up, allowing them to fall apart, showing him how ready she was for him. In her dream, Ross groaned and she was pleased with his reaction. Perhaps now he would lie down beside her, touch her as she longed to be touched? She sighed happily.

Standing just inside the stable door, Jim tucked his now limp cock into his trousers and zipped up as quietly as he could. Resisting touching Chrissy had been the hardest thing he had ever done in his life, but had certainly been the wisest. He could stand here all day just watching her, but it was time to go. His Lordship and his friend could be back any minute.

Jim had seen the way Ross looked at Chrissy – though they hadn't actually seemed to be a couple – and the last thing he needed was the wrath of a jealous man to deal with. Certainly not a man like Ross Sinclair, who looked as if he could be very dangerous indeed if crossed. But also Jim wanted to be away from here before Chrissy woke up. He was not normally a sensitive man, but he knew that she would be dreadfully embarrassed to know he had seen her like this, and she did not deserve that. Not after all the pleasure she had unknowingly given him – not to mention enough material to fuel his fantasies for months to come. Silently he closed the stable door behind him, looked surreptitiously round the yard to see if he was observed, and walked jauntily back to the barn.

Ross had cut his ride short. The mare was everything Greg had said she would be and more. She was a pleasure to ride and any other day he would have been happy to stay out for hours. But today he was on edge. He kept seeing the vision of Chrissy as she bent down in the stable yard to play with the kitten, her long legs exposed by the open dress. He would go back to her now, take her for a drink and talk her out of this stupid Treasure Hunt. Then, when she had agreed that it was a foolish way for a mature woman to behave, they would take some time to get to know each other and then . . . Well, then they would see.

He made his excuses to Greg, who was not fooled for a moment, and turned for home. Standing tall in his stirrups, while he was still some way away, Ross scoured the area for Chrissy, half-hoping she had got bored and set out to meet him. All he saw was Jim coming out of a loose box and crossing the yard, but the other man did not see him. There was no one in sight by the time he clattered into the empty stable yard.

Ross dismounted. He would have called out for Chrissy, but was reluctant to disturb the sleepy afternoon peacefulness of the horses. Where was Jim? He would know where she was. Heading purposefully for the barn, Ross strode past Samson's box, grinning to himself when he heard the big horse pawing restlessly. From what he had heard, Samson was in for a fine old time this afternoon, lucky devil. He was continuing to the barn when he heard an unfamiliar noise in the box next to Samson's, the one he had seen Jim emerge from. Curiosity made him go over and glance into what should have been an empty box.

Chrissy stirred in her sleep and half-opened her eyes. She came to slowly, groggily aware that a noise had disturbed her, but unable to place what it was or where she was. Still rubbing her eyes sleepily, she came up on to one elbow, opening both eyes fully when she was stabbed uncomfortably by a piece of straw.

A stable. She was in a stable. Ross. The Treasure Hunt. A wonderful dream. It all came flooding back to her at exactly the same moment that she realised she was lying in the straw, to all intents and purposes, naked! Appalled and confused, she looked around for an explanation and found herself staring directly at Ross, who was standing outside the stable door, his blue eyes wide with shock.

Six

Ross was standing by his car when Chrissy scrambled out of the stable a few moments later, her dress quickly pulled into place and refastened, surreptitiously picking pieces of straw from her hair, totally confused. She remembered the heat and feeling sleepy, and a wonderful, sensuous dream, though the details had already become a blur. But exactly how her dress had come undone, or why her nipples tingled so, or why her whole sex felt swollen with need and longing, she hadn't got a clue.

She could, however, see why Ross might be annoyed; though as usual he was grossly overreacting.

Greg rode into the yard.

'What? Not going already, are you? I thought you would both come up to the house for a drink. Penny and the kids will be back soon.'

'Sorry, Greg, I've just remembered something. We'll have to go. Some other time.' Ross's tone was cool, his face unreadable, but Greg could tell that something was wrong with his friend.

He looked from Ross to Chrissy, who, flushed with embarrassment, did not quite meet his eye. 'Ross?' he asked uncertainly.

'Everything's fine, Greg,' said Ross in a voice that betrayed that everything was not fine at all. 'But we have to go. I'll call you.' He climbed into the car and slammed the door, waiting for Chrissy to flash Greg an awkward smile and clamber into the passenger seat. His face white and drawn, Ross reversed out and drove off without a backward glance, leaving Greg standing bewildered in the stable yard.

He drove in silence for some time till they were back on the motorway, his knuckles white as he gripped the steering wheel. Chrissy felt it prudent to keep quiet.

'What the fuck do you think you are playing at?'

'What?' She was startled by the fury in his voice.

'Humiliating me in front of my friend like that. Look at you, for God's sake!'

The sun visor on the passenger side was down and Chrissy looked at herself in the mirror. She could see her eyes, bright but heavy-lidded, her face still flushed with sleep, stray pieces of straw caught in her hair.

'Can't you lay off sex for half an hour?'

'Lay off . . .? What are you talking about?'

'Oh, please! At least don't play me for a fool. I'm not totally stupid. You're like a bitch on heat, aren't you?'

'Ross, I haven't got a clue—'

'I presume groom is on your list? I should have checked it before leaving you alone, obviously. Maybe I am a fool after all!'

'Groom? You mean Jim? What has he got to do with—'

'For God's sake, don't make it worse by lying. I saw him, all right? I saw him leaving the box, still zipping himself up and I saw you, lying there, looking as if you'd just had the fuck of your life! And now you're trying to pretend that nothing happened? Give me a break!'

Chrissy was getting angry herself now. 'I haven't got a clue what you are talking about, Ross,' she said, her tone dangerously calm. 'I fell asleep on some straw, yes, I know it looked bad, but I can assure you that I have not had sex with Jim or anyone else.' The throbbing, unsatisfied ache between her legs was testament to that, but she was not going to tell him.

Ross cursed, not believing a word. 'Maybe I should be grateful,' he snarled. 'I was beginning to wonder if I'd got you wrong. Well, it's quite clear that I haven't. Now I know exactly what you're like!'

In the face of his fury, Chrissy had been relatively calm, but now resentment boiled inside her. Who the hell was he to judge her? And even if he had been right, even if she had had sex with Jim, what business was it of his? But strangely, despite her anger, Chrissy felt a perverse pleasure. The old Chrissy, the one who had lived with Marc for so long, would have fallen over herself to explain to Ross, to try and placate him and apologise. This Chrissy did not need to.

'Treasure Hunt, Ross. That's what my game is! You promised to help, remember? I thought that's what you were doing, leaving me alone,' she lied, 'I thought you were helping.'

He swore again. 'Helping? Yes, I'll help you. Not that you seem to need much help.' He spun the wheel recklessly, pulling the car off the motorway onto a slip road, causing several cars behind to beep furiously. 'Here we are. Motorway service station. That's on your list, isn't it? Happy to oblige. I'm sure you won't have any trouble picking someone up, looking like that. Now get out!' His tone was scathing and his eyes glittered dangerously.

For a moment Chrissy could not believe he was serious, but then, angry beyond words, she jumped out of the car. As soon as he heard the door slam shut Ross drove off; he had not looked at her once since finding her in the stable.

Chrissy was outraged. Who the hell did he think he was? He had known her for less than twenty-four hours and here he was carrying on like some jealous husband. And she had thought that Marc had been unreasonable! The idea that Marc – or indeed any man – finding her in the same situation would have jumped to exactly the same conclusion, crossed her mind, but she pushed the thought aside. She did not want to have rational thoughts at the moment. She wanted to fuel her anger. Well, that was it. She was finished with Ross Sinclair – before she'd even started with him. She stamped through the car park to the service station, too angry to think what she was going to do next.

There were two rows of lorries parked close to her, about twenty in all, and Chrissy's steps slowed as she drew near them. So Ross was going to teach her a lesson by leaving her here? She did not think so.

There was no-one in the cabs of the first few lorries and she had almost decided to abandon her plan when she realised that she was being watched by a man sitting on the steps by the open door of a large tanker.

She wondered if he had been watching since Ross drove off, but it did not really matter. He was young, younger than Chrissy, wearing a soft chambray shirt; his long blond hair hung to his muscular shoulders. Slowing her steps, she walked towards him, swaying her hips slightly as she did so.

This was what the Treasure Hunt was really about.

'Hi.' She stopped before him, not too sure how to proceed.

'Hi.'

'All on your own?'

'Not any more.' He smiled, a wide grin that would have melted any woman's heart, and Chrissy felt the blood singing in her veins. He was absolutely perfect.

She smiled and reached out to stroke his hair, her gesture an open invitation which he accepted immediately.

'Shall we go into the cab?' he asked her, looking rather doubtfully around the deserted car park.

'No need. It'll be too hot.' There was another lorry parked beside them and now Chrissy angled the open door of the tanker so that they were hidden on three sides. They were still on open view to anyone who approached from the rear but she couldn't have cared less. Chrissy's knees felt weak now that she had made up her mind, but she did not hesitate. She placed one hand on his flat belly, feeling his skin hot beneath the fine cloth. Tugging the material free of his trousers, she slid her hand down inside. The man did not speak now, unable to believe his luck, content to let Chrissy take charge.

When his zip was down he lifted his hips slightly so that she could lower his trousers just enough to could see his penis nestling among his blond curls; he wore no underwear. Quickly, before she changed her mind, Chrissy dropped her head into his lap, breathing in his warm, musky maleness. She nuzzled right into his pubic hair, causing him to groan, before taking his still soft cock between her lips. He was obviously a little more nervous about this unexpected encounter than he liked to let on.

She loved to do this. To hold a soft penis in her warm mouth, not moving her head at all, feeling it come alive and growing inside her until it pushed her lips apart and she could barely contain it. This was exactly what happened. The stranger's cock began to grow and swell inside the warm, wet cavern of her mouth. A persistent pulse throbbed at the base till he had grown so big Chrissy had to wrap her fingers around his shaft to keep him from slipping from her hot lips.

The sounds of the car park were muted as Chrissy

concentrated on sucking his vibrant length far into her mouth. She was aware on some level of his deep gasping groans, the pressure building at the base of his shaft, as she continued to caress him with her mouth, her lips and her teeth.

As her movements became more excited, his desperate cock sprang from her lips and she caught it in both hands, licking down his shaft then rubbing his slick penis over her face and cheeks before welcoming him back between her lips. Chrissy knew he would not be able to hold out long; but she did not want him to. A few moments later he slipped from her lips again, and she held the throbbing base of his shaft with her fingers as he spent himself, each jet of semen splashing on her face and throat, the sight drawing forth a long ecstatic groan from his lips.

Only when she had milked him of every last drop of his creamy seed did she release him. Her eyes were hot and feverish as she straightened up before him and bunched her skirt around her waist, revealing the moist naked flesh at the top of her thighs to his startled gaze. Her sex was still swollen and ready for her fingers as she slid them desperately through her own damp furrow to ease the ache of her throbbing clitoris. With one hand she held her skirt aloft while the other flashed across her sex, bringing her swiftly to a shuddering climax, there in the car park with the stranger's semen still on her skin.

When the shuddering finally stopped and she could trust herself to speak, she opened her eyes and looked at the driver. She dropped her bunched dress and smoothed it back in place, smiling.

'Thanks,' she said.

'Any time. Thank you.' He handed her a tissue. 'What's your name?'

She shook her head. 'Doesn't matter.' Grinning, Chrissy turned and made her way across the car park. She did not look back.

Ross had driven only a few miles before the rage left him and he was overcome with shame for his action in abandoning Chrissy. The truth was that he was jealous. He had wanted Chrissy from the moment he saw her at last night's party. He had continued to want her even when she went off with those two clowns, Luke and Scott. He could not understand how he had allowed a woman like that, a woman with the morals of an alley cat, to sneak past his defences. But he could not put her out of his mind; he had not slept, the previous night, for thinking about her. He had made an excuse to be with her today because, quite simply, he could not keep away.

So when he saw her lying in the straw after Jim . . . His hands tightened on the wheel again and he breathed deeply till he had regained control. It was not Chrissy's fault. She could have no idea of the depth of his feelings for her. He had to go back.

He had to drive a few more miles before he could leave the motorway and circle back to the service station. He was surprised to find Chrissy standing exactly where he had left her about ten minutes before, and was racked with guilt at her faith in him returning.

Chrissy was even more surprised. She had just been crossing to the café when she had seen Ross's battered blue car return. She resented the way her heart leapt when he pulled up beside her. The door opened but she was wary of getting in.

Ross was staring straight ahead, his hands slowly loosening their grip on the wheel. 'I'm sorry, Chrissy. I behaved like a shit.' He looked at her now, his expression so bleak that Chrissy took pity on him.

She climbed into the car. 'How many men have I slept with, Ross?' she asked softly.

'What?'

'How many men have I slept with in my life? I'm asking you.'

'I . . . How could I—'

'Do I sleep with men on a first date?'

'I don't know.'

'Exactly.' Her voice was cold. 'You don't know. You don't know anything about me, but still you are prepared to pass judgement on me and my behaviour. You don't want to sleep with me but you don't want me to sleep with anyone else, either. Don't you think that that's an odd way to behave with someone you have only just met, someone you don't know at all?'

Ross turned to look at her, an emotion she could not recognise burning in his eyes. 'You're right,' he grated, annoyed that she had not accepted his apology and forgiven him, knowing that this expectation was unreasonable. 'I don't know anything about you. And I am sorry. I'll take you home.'

As they drove off, they passed Chrissy's stranger, still sitting on the steps of his tanker, a bemused expression on his face as he watched them. Wondering what he had made of the whole episode, Chrissy hid a smile.

They had left the M9 and were on a minor road, several miles from Edinburgh, when the car began to choke and splutter and lose power. Even as it cruised to a halt and Ross pulled into the side of the road, Chrissy, although she was no longer angry, was reluctant to be the first one to break the stony silence. Ross once again held the steering wheel in a white knuckled grip.

'What's wrong?' she asked eventually, once it had become clear he was not going to volunteer any information.

'We're out of petrol.'

'We're what?' She turned to him incredulously. 'Out of petrol? I don't believe this!'

'It's all right,' he snapped and she realised he was embarrassed. 'There's some in the boot.' He climbed out of the car and slammed the door, walking round to the back. Chrissy stayed in her seat and stared straight ahead. She heard him rummaging around, then rummaging a little more frantically, then a muttered oath. Next moment he came round to her side and yanked the door open.

'I seem to have forgotten the petrol can.' He could not quite meet her eye. 'It was in the boot, but I took it out yesterday to pack some sacks of cement, and I must have forgotten to put it back.'

'Sacks of cement?'

He said nothing.

'So what do we do now. Walk?'

'Yes, but it's not as bad as it looks. My house is just over those fields,' he pointed. 'I can go and get the can and be back in half an hour, three-quarters at most.'

Chrissy climbed out of the car. 'God, I don't believe this.'

Her mouth twitched slightly, but she suspected that he would not appreciate her grinning too widely at his embarrassment. 'Which way?'

'What? You don't have to come. You can wait with the car.'

'In this heat? Forget it. I'm coming.'

'It's through those fields, over some fences,' he warned.

'I'll manage,' she said wryly.

With that she set off determinedly. It was unfortunate that she had forgotten she wasn't wearing any panties and as she swung her leg over the first gate, Ross probably got a flash of more than she bargained for, but at least that silenced any more of his protests. He tried to help her over the next fence, but she shrugged his hand away and clambered over, glad she was wearing a pair of flat white pumps.

It was the pumps that proved her undoing, however. The fields were dry as a result of the hot weather, but the only possible place they could climb the final fence was just behind a water trough, where the ground had been churned to mud by the feet of what looked to Chrissy like a whole stampede of cattle. She eyed it dubiously.

'I warned you.' Ross was standing beside her.

Chrissy shot him a look and marched over to the fence. She almost made it, too, but at the last moment, one of her pumps sank into the quagmire. The shoe slipped off her foot and Chrissy let out a yelp as the mud oozed over her ankle. She gave a little hop in a futile attempt to regain the shoe, lost her balance and fell her full length into the squelching mud, screwing her eyes against the slimy feel of it against her body and the mouldy, vaguely animal smell that clogged her nostrils.

Struggling to sit up, she slipped again and would have floundered there indefinitely if Ross, without regard for his own clothes, hadn't scooped her up in his powerful arms, carried her to the fence, climbed over with her and placed her safely on the grass. Wordlessly he returned and retrieved her shoe which he handed to her solemnly, his shoulders shaking with silent mirth. Ungraciously, Chrissy snatched it from him and placed it back on her foot, her face screwing up in disgust when she discovered it was still full of mud.

'Is that your house?' she demanded, pointing at the only

cottage on the deserted road, ignoring the handkerchief he offered her.

Ross nodded, his jaws clamped firmly together, barely containing the laughter that was bubbling inside him as her eyes flashed furiously from her mud-spattered face.

With as much dignity as she could muster, Chrissy stomped ahead of him towards the cottage. As she got closer and had a better look at it, she was surprised by what she saw. The house was small and fairly run-down, with piles of bricks and a cement mixer in the front garden, but even from the outside she could see how cosy and homely it would be when the work was finished. Like his car, the cottage was not at all what she would have expected of Ross.

They both had to bend to get in the door, but Chrissy was transfixed by the kitchen. A beautifully restored range occupied one entire wall and the long scrubbed oak table matched the bare floorboards perfectly. A wooden rack was suspended above the range, and Chrissy allowed herself to imagine it hanging with wild herbs and gleaming copper pans. She suspected Ross didn't possess either.

'It's lovely,' she said in surprise, forgetting the mud drying on her clothes for a moment.

'Most of it's a dump.' Ross grinned, unable to keep the pride out of his voice. 'But it's going to be great when it's finished; there are only one or two rooms that are habitable. One of them's the bathroom,' he added tactfully, a wide grin finally splitting his face.

Chrissy wasn't mad any more, she was tired. It had been an unusual day, fraught with emotion and she was exhausted.

'I've got a bathroom at home. I'll wait and use that.'

'OK,' Ross agreed, 'I'll go and get the car. Will you be all right?'

Chrissy nodded. 'I'll put the kettle on. I think we could both do with some coffee.' She managed a thin smile. She must look a sight.

For a moment Ross looked as if he was about to say something, then nodded, and left her sitting in the quiet, somehow restful kitchen. Wearily Chrissy got to her feet and put the kettle on. Coffee was not what she needed at the moment. The feeling of being carried in Ross's strong arms, feeling the hard power of his muscular chest and the strong, steady beat of his heart next to her, had unsettled her once again. Had he held her to him longer than was strictly necessary? Probably not. What was it about the man that affected her this way?

As she drank the hot coffee, Chrissy caught sight of the mud on her hand. She had been stupid to turn down his offer of a bath. Exactly what point had she been trying to make? Reaching a decision, she finished the coffee, then set off in search of the bathroom. Ross would be at least another twenty minutes; she had plenty of time.

The bathroom was another of the rooms Ross had finished restoring, like the kitchen; Chrissy approved of his priorities. She ran water into the deep, claw-footed Victorian bath and found a bottle of expensive herbal bath oil on the windowsill. Instinct told her that no man would buy such an extravagant product for himself, but she was gratified to find a thick layer of dust on the blue glass. At least the woman who'd bought it had not been here to use it for some time.

The lock on the bathroom door did not work. What was more alarming for Chrissy was that the door would not even shut properly. Whatever she did, it just would not catch. Exasperated, she finally left it, fully intending to be out of the bath before Ross got back.

But after stripping off her clothes and sliding into the luxuriant, fragrant bubbles, Chrissy forgot about the door and the time. The bath was slightly too hot and her skin immediately flushed pink, but it felt so good. She lay back, eyes closed, allowing the warm water to wash over her, realising only then how tense she actually was. She stretched out her long legs, easing her tired muscles. The movement sent small eddies of scented water swirling around her and she parted her knees, allowing the water to ebb and flow between her legs, the gentle waves splashing against her sex. Dropping her hands below the surface, she lightly stroked the skin of her inner thighs, so soft in the warm water. One hand brushed her mons, still smoothly depilated, and she felt the erotic thrill of the velvety skin against her palm. She was tempted to slide her fingers deeper, to stretch her lips wide, allowing the warm water access to her innermost secrets. But she shouldn't; there wasn't time.

Her heavy breasts, buoyed by the water, floated gently on the surface, the sensitive skin tickled by the bubbles and her nipples swollen by the heat of the water. Abandoning for the moment the soft flesh at the top of her thighs, Chrissy turned her attention to these firm globes. Soaping them gently she quickly brought each nipple to a firm peak, the rosy crests bursting through the surface of the water. Her legs continued to scissor gently, keeping the water flowing over her body, the sensations too delicious to stop. But she concentrated on her breasts now, as, her eyes still closed, she brought one soapy orb up to her mouth, her tongue flicking out to lick the bubbles off the rosy tip.

There was a sharp gasp from the doorway. Chrissy's eyes flew open and she sat up quickly, causing the bathwater to lap over the edge of the bath and soak the floor. Ross was standing in the open doorway, his chest bare, his T-shirt in his hand and his blue eyes wide as he stared at her. There was less water in the bath now, and Chrissy crossed her arms over her breasts protectively.

'I'm sorry,' said Ross, his face flushing with embarrassment, but unable to tear his gaze away. 'I called your name; I thought you'd gone, somehow. I was going to take a shower.'

'That's OK.' Chrissy couldn't take her eyes off the sight of his naked chest, broader and harder than she had imagined, roped with muscle, spread with tightly curled black hair. They stared at each other.

Chrissy reached a decision. She licked her lips, then very slowly lowered her arms. Squaring her shoulders slightly, she pushed her breasts forward, the action and the invitation in her hazel eyes obvious. She held her breath. If he rejected her now, again, she would die. Did he have any idea how attracted she was to him?

Ross stared for a very long time. Then he stepped forward, towering over the bath, his eyes burning with a fierce passion.

The air thickened around them. A visible tremor passed through Ross, and he closed his eyes for a second, taking a deep breath. Then he handed her a snowy white towel.

'The car's fine now. I'll wait for you downstairs,' he said thickly and left.

85

Chrissy stared at his retreating back. Her vision was blurred with tears of humiliation as she jumped out of the bath and pulled her dress on without drying herself, oblivious to the dried mud on her clothes. Twice in one day Ross Sinclair had seen her naked body; twice she had blatantly offered herself to him; and each time he had turned her down. He hadn't even found it too difficult. Well, it wasn't the first time a man she cared for had rejected her. Maybe this time she would learn her lesson, she thought bitterly.

In the car neither of them spoke; Chrissy because she was so totally and completely mortified and Ross because he could not trust himself to. He knew that Chrissy was embarrassed and he was sorry, but it was better this way. It was better that she had no idea how difficult it had been for him to walk out of that bathroom. The visions he had of her glorious body covered in suds in his bath, and of her lying in the stable, her clothes spread around her, were ones he would carry with him for the rest of his life. And the memory of how she had clung to him as he carried her over the fence, how right it had felt to hold her in his arms . . . No. It was much better this way, he reminded himself, changing gear savagely.

He dropped her off at Clarissa's house. Somehow, 'thank you for a lovely day' did not seem appropriate, so they parted like strangers and Chrissy let herself into the house with a sense of relief. Ross was a very strange man indeed. His rejection of her had been total and complete; so why was it that the mere thought of him still made her body throb with longing?

Her date with Will that evening was a surprising success. For a while Chrissy had been tempted to call him and cancel it, but the alternative was to sit alone at home and brood about her day. That idea held no appeal at all. Of course, there still was the problem of having to confess that she had lied to him – that she wasn't Clarissa. Well, the rest of her day had been appalling. Having Will despise her, too, would just about round it off nicely!

But it wasn't like that at all. Will picked her up at nine, just as he had said he would, looking every bit as handsome as she remembered and much more at ease in casual trousers and a polo shirt. They walked only as far as the pub at the end of the road and sat in the beer garden, making the most of Edinburgh's long summer evening. When he came back with their drinks, Chrissy decided to get the confession over with straightaway.

'I'm not Clarissa Asquith,' she blurted.

Will looked at her, his beer glass poised half-way to his mouth.

'I mean it. I'm not Clarissa. I lied to you. I'm sorry,' she continued quickly. 'It was Clarissa's idea, but I agreed to it. It was stupid and I'm sorry. I didn't mean for anyone to get hurt.'

Will said nothing at first, but took a long drink of his beer. 'Well, who are you then?'

There was nothing in his tone to say how angry he was. 'Christine Fielding,' she said, 'Chrissy.'

Will held out his right hand. 'William Barnes,' he said solemnly, shaking hands.

'Aren't you angry? I would be furious.'

Will grinned. 'What's to be angry about? I don't know Clarissa.'

'But aren't you shocked?'

'Shocked? No. But maybe a bit surprised. Things like this don't usually happen to me. I lead an extremely boring, mundane life, normally.'

That was all he said. Chrissy fiddled nervously with her hair. Will was entitled to an explanation, but now that the time had come, she found she didn't know how to begin. She liked Will and didn't want him to think too badly of her – but however carefully she chose her words, it was going to sound awful. 'I wanted lots and lots of uncomplicated sex so Clarissa and I set out to deceive everybody.'

No, it was not going to make her look good. On the other hand, she reminded herself, Will had been an eager partner in the Treasure Hunt after all – he could hardly judge her too harshly. In the end, she settled for the bare facts, rushing quickly through her meeting with Phil and Clarissa, not dwelling too much on the intimate details. Will listened attentively, neither criticising nor judging, and Chrissy was surprised to find herself beginning to relax.

This was a new experience for her, having a conversation

with a man who did not immediately jump in with his opinion of how she should behave or what she should do next, and she discovered she was enjoying herself. She even recounted the tale of how she had slipped in the mud and had to be rescued by Ross and laughed along with Will as she told it. At the end he had only one question.

'Has it been as much fun as you hoped it would be?'

Chrissy gave the answer careful consideration. 'I've met some nice people.' She flashed him a quick smile. 'I've had some great sex, but no, I don't think it has been quite as much fun as I expected.' Largely thanks to Ross Sinclair, she added silently.

'Ross is a great guy,' said Will, causing her to jump. It was as if he had read her mind. 'I've known him a long time.'

'He and I don't quite see eye to eye on a number of issues. Like he thinks I'm a slut, for instance.'

'No, he doesn't.' Will smiled. 'He's a better judge of character than that. He's had a lot of bad luck with relationships over the years, it's made him a bit . . . careful.' Chrissy would have dearly loved to continue talking about Ross, but knew that it was pointless. Despite what Will said, she knew exactly what Ross's opinion of her was.

They had another few drinks. Will was so easy to talk to that Chrissy found herself telling him about Marc and what she now considered the wasted years they had spent together. He was silent when she had finished and she felt guilty, convinced that she had bored him to tears, but then she realised that he was angry – angry on her behalf about the way she had been treated. She was deeply touched. It was wonderful to spend time in the company of a man who was interested in you as a person. And, if she was honest, very soothing indeed to spend time with a man who gazed at you with such open admiration and demanded so little in return.

When the bar closed, they walked companionably back to Clarissa's house.

'You know something,' Will said suddenly, 'I'm glad you're not Clarissa. Since all this started I've heard some unusual things about her. I think I much prefer Chrissy Fielding.'

Although it was nice to receive a compliment, Chrissy could

not let this go without comment. She stopped walking and waited till he turned to face her. 'Listen, Will, don't try to fool yourself that I'm something I'm not. I went into this with my eyes open. Really, Ross is right – I'm no better than Clarissa.'

'Oh yes, you are,' said Will, confidently. 'You're quite different, I'm sure.'

When they reached Chrissy's doorstep she turned to him again. 'Please don't take this the wrong way; I've had a wonderful evening, but I'm not going to invite you in, Will.'

His dark eyes missed nothing as he looked at her. 'Probably very wise,' he said, his grin surprisingly wolfish. He bent his head and kissed her very lightly on the lips, a kiss that sent a warm glow spreading throughout her body.

For a second she was tempted to change her mind. Maybe sharing her bed with this warm, kind, very sexy man was exactly what she needed. But the second passed. She had already slept with Will, knew exactly how good his hard body would make her feel. It was maybe that which made it feel odd: the time scale and the order of things. She had the feeling that if she and Will took the time to get to know each other, that if they made a more natural progression towards bed, then it would be even better. She couldn't think how to put this into words, but Will seemed to understand.

'Goodnight,' he said softly, 'I'll be seeing you again, I hope.' And he walked off into the night.

Seven

Over the next few days Chrissy did little to further her chances of winning the Treasure Hunt. She was busy, visiting the university to collect a reading list for her course, then trawling round the many bookshops of Edinburgh trying to pick up bargains, something she normally enjoyed very much. But she was restless; things were unresolved.

The whole concept of the Treasure Hunt, in theory, should have been both liberating and exciting, and she still held firmly to the belief in her right to participate. But somehow a lot of the fun had gone out of it for her.

Unfortunately, nothing in life was simple. Already she had feelings for both Ross and for Will, when she had, most definitely, not intended to get involved with anyone. She was not as emotionally detached as she had planned to be. Chrissy did not like the idea that she cared so much what Ross and Will thought of her. It was unsettling that the good opinion of a man should be so important to her, especially after what she had been through in her last relationship. Hadn't she learnt anything? It was a damn good thing she had enrolled in this Women's Studies course. She knew in principle that she should be able to live quite happily without any man's approval, but she seemed to be badly in need of some positive reinforcement.

Coming home on Tuesday afternoon, she found two messages on Clarissa's answer-machine: one from Karen in the Orkneys, the other from Ross. Karen's message asked eagerly for an update and left a number for Chrissy to ring her back. Ross's message was short and brusque, inviting her out for a meal that evening, despite the fact they had not spoken since Sunday. There was no warmth in his tone and Chrissy made a face at the answer-machine. What on earth could he possibly want with her now, and why did her heart still leap at the sound of his voice, no matter how unfriendly it was?

She was disappointed when she couldn't get hold of Karen. It would have been nice to get her opinion of Ross and of Will. Also, Chrissy had to admit, she sneakily enjoyed shocking her friend and looked forward to telling her the juicier details of her recent escapades – details she had, of course, kept back from Will.

Next she returned Ross's call. He was not home either but she left a short message on his machine, formally accepting his invitation.

The rest of the day was filled with tidying up and checking the situations vacant for any part-time jobs she could do to support herself at university. Life was not going to be easy as a mature student but Chrissy was very much looking forward to it. She relished a challenge.

Ross was waiting impatiently in the foyer of the restaurant. He caught sight of himself in the mirror above the small bar and took a minute to fasten the button of his jacket and straighten his grey silk tie. He felt tired and dishevelled, the result of two sleepless nights. In fact, he didn't honestly think he had slept since Saturday. Also he had had a difficult day at work, constantly distracted by thoughts of Chrissy and what he hoped to say to her tonight. Unfortunately, when he thought about her he was eaten up by a raging jealousy, making him snap at everyone, and adding guilt and remorse to his already overstretched emotions. He knew he was in a foul temper but could not shake it.

When Chrissy arrived, five minutes early, looking so good it made his heart pound desperately, he acknowledged her without a smile. 'You came, then. I wasn't sure you would.'

'Why wouldn't I?' She smiled. It was so good to see him again, though her heart sank when she recognised that he was not in the best of moods.

Ross shrugged but did not reply. As he helped her out of her jacket, his fingers brushed against the warm, bare skin of her shoulders and he pulled back quickly as though burned. Chrissy looked at him curiously. A beaming waiter led them to a table near the window of the empty restaurant, but Ross needed privacy for what he had to say and moved to a secluded table at the back. Chrissy and the waiter followed. Smiling and chatting and fussing with her chair, the waiter managed to glance down the front of her dress, angling his head slightly to better see her cleavage. Looking up he saw Ross scowling at him and scurried away.

While Chrissy examined the menu, Ross studied her unobtrusively. Her shift dress was simple and elegant but short enough to show off her long legs. Her hair was worn simply around her shoulders and shone like burnished gold in the soft lights. With her eyes lowered reading the menu, her lashes appeared so long and curling they seemed to brush her cheeks. Ross stared at her, unblinking and unsmiling. How could she sit there like that? Didn't she know the effect she was having on him? He could feel desire churning through him, every nerve ending firing as he watched her breasts rise and fall with each breath.

As though feeling his scrutiny, Chrissy looked up. Her hazel eyes were frank and curious and she seemed faintly puzzled by his behaviour. 'Have a good day at work?'

'Yes.' He answered curtly.

'The food smells good. I do love Italian.'

'Yes.'

'Ross, why are we here if you are not going to talk? I can think of pleasanter ways of spending an evening than watching you sit there glowering.'

Her directness startled him.

'I am going talk to you.' It came out more harshly than he had intended and he was glad of the waiter arriving to take their order. The man hurried away again quickly. He had been a waiter too long not to recognise the tension in the air.

Ross cleared his throat and started again. 'Chrissy, I need to talk to you.' I'm obsessed by you, I love you, I can't get you out of my mind, he wanted to say, but couldn't. Instead, he said, 'Can I be frank with you? I would like you to give up this Treasure Hunt. It's childish and unworthy of a woman of your intelligence.'

Oh God, I sound like a pompous ass, he thought, but hurried

on, encouraged by her silence. 'It was a stupid idea from the beginning, but no more than I would expect from Clarissa and Portia. It ceased to be a joke when they involved you in it. No, hear me out.' He held up a hand as Chrissy was about to interrupt. 'Playing with people's emotions is second nature to those two. Portia especially doesn't care who she corrupts with her stupid games. I think you should get out. I'll speak to Clarissa, if you like.' He was warming to his theme, relieved that he was finally able to tell her how he felt. He did not notice Chrissy's stunned expression, nor the anger that replaced it.

'So that's your opinion of me, Ross? A poor little innocent, easily led astray by the promise of glamour and wealth, however temporary? Hasn't it occurred to you yet that I know exactly what I'm doing and that I might like it? Thank you for your concern, but I can take charge of my own life.' She met his gaze, her eyes glittering dangerously.

Ross's lip curled slightly. 'So you're prepared to live without commitment or respect? A different man in your bed every night, then on to the next one? That's what you want from life?'

'How dare you! You have no idea what I want from life.' She was white with anger.

For a moment Ross glowered. This had all gone wrong. But he tried again. 'Chrissy, please. Hear me out.' He reached across and took her hand but she snatched it away.

'Don't touch me!'

Something inside Ross snapped. Don't touch her? Why the hell not? She invited every other man in the world to touch her, didn't she? Then ticked him off on her list and moved on to the next one. Well, maybe that was it, then.

'OK,' he snarled. 'As long as you think you know what you are doing. Have you brought your list with you?'

'Now you're just being childish.'

'Have you got your list?'

Wordlessly, Chrissy bent down for her handbag. Ross stared openly down the front of her dress. So that was the view the waiter had enjoyed. Who could blame him? Catching the direction of his gaze, seeing desire struggle with the rage in his eyes, Chrissy shivered. Even now, when she was seriously beginning to wonder about Ross Sinclair's mental stability, Chrissy had to admit that he was a devastatingly attractive man. His thick unruly hair flopped over his eyes and he pushed it back in irritation as both of them glared at each other. The waiter, too far away to eavesdrop but sensing the growing tension, fled to the kitchen to check on their order.

Ross picked up the Treasure Hunt card and let his eyes roam down it, managing not to flinch when he saw the extra ticks.

'OK, here's one.' His finger stabbed the card at 'sex in a public place'. 'We can probably manage that now.'

'What are you talking about?' hissed Chrissy. The man really was insufferable.

'This!' Theatrically Ross dropped his napkin to the floor. Then he sank down and pushed his way under the long, red-chequered tablecloth until he was completely hidden from view. Startled, Chrissy was about to lift the hem and ask him what the hell he was playing at but, just then, the door to the kitchen swung open and the waiter reappeared, bearing their food. He looked confused to see Chrissy on her own, but she smiled tensely.

'My friend will be back in a moment,' she assured him, sipping from her wine glass, then almost choked when she felt a hand on her knee gently easing her legs apart. Furiously, she pressed them together. What on earth did Ross think he was doing? With a concerned backward glance, the waiter fled again to the safety of his kitchen.

At first Ross persisted, increasing the pressure, as though he would force her, but then he seemed to change his mind and his tactics. Ever so gently his fingertips began to trace little circles along her outer thighs, each circle inching higher, pushing up the edge of her dress. Chrissy gasped, folding the tabecloth over her lap, making sure she was covered. She heard what sounded like a soft moan, then a whisper from under the table.

'You'd better co-operate. You wouldn't want the waiter joining us, would you?'

'Ross!'

'Shh. Open your legs. Open them!' The whisper was slightly louder and terrified of drawing attention, Chrissy did as he asked. She forced herself to relax and moved her legs apart. Blushingly aware that she was wearing no underwear to impede

94

him, she felt his cool hands push her legs wide. There was no sound or movement from him for a long moment and Chrissy shivered as she imagined the view he must be enjoying of her naked sex, the swollen labia protruding temptingly. Desire clenched her stomach as she anticipated his touch.

Ross took his time. His fingers continued to caress the delicate skin on her inner thigh, but moved no higher. Each touch of his fingers sent ripples of pleasure shooting through her body. Her mouth and throat were dry as she gave up all pretence of eating her meal, merely pushing her food around the plate as her breathing grew ever more shallow.

In spite of herself, in spite of the fact that she was still angry with him, she was longing for the moment Ross would emerge and they could go back to Clarissa's house to quench together the fire he was lighting within her.

'Ross,' she breathed his name. She was unprepared for what happened next as she felt his warm breath inches from her sex. He couldn't! He wouldn't! Not here, in a restaurant with the waiter no more than fifteen feet away, sticking his head round the kitchen door, watching her? But he did. She felt the very tip of his tongue flick the tender point of her clitoris and jumped again, the pleasure so intense it was almost painful. Thankfully the waiter, though obviously confused by Ross's continued absence, returned to the kitchen, and she was able to relax slightly.

Swallowing hard, Chrissy closed her eyes, dropping her hand to her lap to make sure the tablecloth was still covering her.

She could barely breathe as Ross replaced his tongue with a finger, bringing up the silky moisture from the lip of her vagina, smoothing it over her delicate folds with a tenderness that made her ache. This slow, sensitive loving was not at all what she would have expected after the rage she had seen in Ross's eyes, but for the moment she forgot the complexities of his moods, just allowed his touch to bathe her in an erotic, sensual glow.

Without even being conscious of doing so, Chrissy opened her legs wider, inviting more intimacy. Ross obliged, spreading her fleshy pink lips with his fingers before embracing her sex with his mouth, kissing and sucking, lapping then nibbling, teasing and stimulating her bud till she felt she would explode.

Her hand trembled so much that her cutlery dropped to the table. Biting her lip to keep from groaning, she was only dimly aware of the restaurant door opening and another couple entering, being greeted by the waiter.

Her orgasm was intense, electrifying, all the more so because it had to be secret. She was still shuddering involuntarily and struggling to control her breathing when Ross emerged from under the table, wiping his lips delicately with his napkin. He stood beside the table and Chrissy looked up at him, her eyes dazed.

The waiter, having seated his new customers hurried over. Ross's eyes were like blue ice as he looked down at Chrissy, but it was the waiter he addressed as he dropped some money on the table.

'I'm sorry, I can't stay. But I understand, if you're lucky, the lady may prove an excellent tipper.'

Chrissy stared after his retreating back in shock. He couldn't just walk out, not after that! But he had. She smiled reassuringly at the waiter and slowly picked up her fork, pretending to eat while she gathered her thoughts, her legs way too shaky to permit her to go after him. He would come back – surely he would come back? But the memory of the cold fire she had seen in his eyes stayed with her. With the aftermath of a delicious orgasm still tingling through her, she was unable to think straight, trying to work out how the evening had grown so out of control.

Ross's behaviour had always been erratic where she was concerned. He seemed to pick a fight with her deliberately every time he saw her. What exactly had he been trying to say this evening? Did he really want her to give up this Hunt because it was bad for her soul, or was there something else? Chrissy had seen hurt as well as anger in Ross's eyes several times now when he talked about her involvement in the Treasure Hunt. Sadly it occurred to her that the longer she and Ross spent in each other's company, the less they seemed able to communicate.

'Chrissy? I thought it was you. Was that Ross I just saw?'

'Will?' She looked up, flustered. What was he doing here? How much had he seen? A look at his cheerful, sexy smile reassured her a little. Surely he must have come in too late to have seen anything. 'What are you doing here?' she asked quickly, trying to mask her confusion. 'I didn't see you come in.'

'I've just arrived,' Will said easily, indicating a large group of people seating themselves noisily at tables. 'I've come with some friends.' When they realised they were being watched, the friends called out a cheerful greeting to Chrissy, who managed to smile back.

'It's my estate manager's birthday. We're having a party,' Will explained. 'Would you like to join us?'

'No thanks; it's sweet of you to ask, but I'm not really in the mood for strangers.'

He looked at her, understanding in his brown eyes. 'Have you and Ross been fighting again?' he asked sympathetically. 'If you won't join us, why don't I join you?'

She smiled at him, the idea appealing very much. A nice relaxed evening with Will would be very soothing after another abrasive encounter with Ross. And she definitely needed something to take her mind off Ross. 'I couldn't let you do that. Your friends would think me terribly rude.'

'No, they won't. I'll have a word with them.' Will did not bother to explain that his friends were stunned that he had actually accepted their invitation out that night, when he had never accepted in the past. They would be absolutely speechless if he left them to join a beautiful woman!

He was wrong about that. They were anything but speechless, and he had to put up with a great deal of ribald teasing before he was allowed to rejoin Chrissy. Blushing furiously, he sat down opposite her. Chrissy was amused. It was nice to see that there were apparently no class barriers between Will and his staff, despite his title. They seemed to treat each other with genuine affection.

'Sorry about that. Would you like something else to eat? That looks a bit cold.' He indicated Chrissy's pasta which was congealing on her plate.'

'No thanks, I'll just have a glass of wine, if you don't mind, but you order – you must be starving.'

The waiter, when he was called over, glared disapprovingly

at Chrissy. He had absolutely no idea what was going on, but he was beginning to suspect that she was not the sort of woman he wished to encourage in his restaurant. He looked pityingly at the pleasant-looking man who was now sitting with her, wishing he could somehow warn him, then hurried off muttering darkly in Italian.

'I think his opinion of me is even lower than Ross's,' said Chrissy, after he had left. 'Tell me something, Will; does Ross have any kind of emotional problems? I mean, he doesn't seem to have much control over his temper.'

'Ross?' Will was astounded. 'Ross is the most controlled man I've ever known.'

Chrissy digested this piece of information. Was it significant that Ross seemed to lose control over his emotions only where she was involved? A warm feeling began to spread over her, but Will was still talking.

'Ross is a friend, so maybe I shouldn't say anything, but I hate to see you two at loggerheads. He hasn't really got any emotional problems as such, but . . . Have you met Portia yet? Portia de Havilland? No? Best to try and keep it that way, if you can. Now Portia really does have problems. To be honest, I don't like her very much,' he confided, gratefully accepting his meal from the waiter and replenishing Chrissy's glass.

Chrissy stifled a smile. Portia must indeed be the bitch everyone said she was for someone as mild and easy-going as Will to admit to disliking her.

'She and Ross were a couple once. For quite a long time, actually. Ross was absolutely besotted. He wouldn't hear a bad word against her, though some of us tried to warn him that when he wasn't around, Portia was maybe not quite as committed to the relationship as he was. But Ross wouldn't listen, he loved her too much to believe any of the rumours.' Will became uncomfortable and began to concentrate on his food. It looked as if he wasn't going to say any more, but Chrissy couldn't leave it like that.

'So then they split up?' she prompted.

Will looked sorry he had started this story. He nodded. 'Ross played rugby. He was very good, better than I ever was. Portia sometimes came along on a Saturday to watch us play –

goodness knows why because she didn't have a clue about the rules of the game. One time Ross injured his knee and had to miss a few games. We always went out for a drink afterwards and he would come along to meet us after the game.' Now Will seemed to lose his appetite and pushed the food around on his plate, not quite meeting Chrissy's eye.

'One afternoon when he arrived, Portia was in the changing room. It wasn't the first time she had been there without Ross knowing. Her excuse was that she had been late, and was not aware that Ross hadn't been playing, but I don't think she offered any excuse for what happened next. When Ross saw her she was naked and . . . enjoying herself with several of his team-mates. Ross went berserk. He almost killed the men who were . . . were with Portia at the time, and almost killed me too before I managed to drag him out. Portia actually seemed surprised that he was so mad. She told him that he should be flattered to see his girlfriend "desired" by so many men. Ross didn't quite see it that way. I don't think he has spoken two words to her since.'

'Well,' said Chrissy, feeling a sharp sympathy for Ross, 'it's no wonder he's so big on commitment now, though it's a shame that one awful experience has so soured him against all women.'

'It wasn't just one.' Will spoke with a finality that told her the subject was closed, that he already felt he had said too much. 'Would you like some coffee?'

They said no more about Ross. Nor was the Treasure Hunt mentioned. Now that he was no longer shy with her, Will proved a witty and easy companion. Chrissy liked the way he made her feel, relaxed and good about herself. They smiled and laughed easily with each other and she was aware of his friends staring at them curiously. It was such a total contrast to the stressful start of the evening and Chrissy felt her earlier tension dissolve, aided by the wine and the warm glow of Will's admiration. When Will offered to see her home, reaching across the table to stroke the inside of her wrist lightly with his fingers, an unasked question burning in his brown eyes, Chrissy had no hesitation in accepting. Before they left she went over with him to be introduced to his friends and to apologise for monopolising his company all evening. They were charmed by her friendliness and not at all put out when she and Will left together shortly after.

Clarissa's house was within easy walking distance, probably why Ross had chosen the restaurant in the first place. Chrissy slipped her arm through Will's as they walked; it seemed such a natural thing to do and she liked the way his hard, fit body felt against her. She felt close to him and content, and found that she was sorry when they reached home, sorry the walk was so short. At the front door she turned to face him, not letting go of his arm.

'Would you like to come in?' Would he be able to tell that she was offering more than coffee?

Will looked down at her, a smile spreading across his face, lighting a slow fire in his eyes. Stepping closer his mouth nuzzled her ear, his voice warm and dark. 'That would be nice.'

His lips barely brushed her, but Chrissy's legs turned to water, her nipples and thighs tightening as though he had touched them. She swayed slightly and Will caught her and pulled her firmly against him, crushing her breasts against his hard, muscled chest. Rubbing his cheek on the top of her head, he breathed in the clean scent of her hair. 'Are you sure?' he asked.

'Very sure, let's go in.' She couldn't control her breathing or her pulse rate as she fumbled her key into the door, aware of Will standing very close behind her. She did not know at which point in the evening she had decided that she wanted Will Barnes, wanted to feel his hard weight lying on top of her, to have him inside her once again, only knew that she wanted him desperately, tonight. But once inside the door she felt she should slow things down. 'Shall I make some coffee?' Her voice did not sound quite as firm as she would have liked.

Will, it seemed, had other ideas. Without a word he drew her back into his arms, then bent his head and captured her mouth in a kiss that was both tender and passionate. Chrissy, taken by surprise, was frozen in place, her nerve endings going wild as he deepened the kiss, his tongue delving into her mouth. She hesitated only a second before her hands came up, circling his back, reaching up to his neck to pull him even closer, her tongue moving against his in an age-old rhythm. She could feel the enticing imprint of his hardness against her flesh and her legs almost gave way, her body flooding with warmth. The kiss stripped away all pretence, leaving them gasping, clinging to each other when they finally broke apart. Will began to softly mouth her throat, his hand coming up to roughly massage her nipple through the fabric of her dress.

'I . . . I thought you were meant to be shy?' Chrissy gasped, arching her back, glad of the strong arm that supported her as uncontrollable shivers vibrated through her body, emanating from everywhere his roaming lips and hands touched.

'I seem to be cured.' Will's hands slid over her buttocks, pulling up her dress, till he could caress the firm satiny flesh, groaning when he discovered she was naked under her clothes.

It took all Chrissy's strength and willpower to press her hands against his chest and push him away slightly. 'Go in there,' she said breathlessly, 'I'll bring the coffee. I won't be a minute.'

Will recognised her stalling tactics for what they were, and grinned. 'OK, but don't be too long.' His cock, which had been semi-hard all evening, was now pushing painfully against his trousers. Maybe a breather was a good idea.

Chrissy almost ran down the passage to the kitchen. She needed to get away for a few moments before they ended up writhing naked on the tiled floor of the hallway, their limbs entwined around each other. The image was one which made her heart race faster, causing her whole body to tingle in sweet anticipation. Will had been more than satisfying the other night, but who would have thought him capable of such heart churning passion? That kiss . . . If anything, Chrissy liked this new Will even better than the old one.

'Come on, come on,' she muttered impatiently to the kettle, already regretting the panic that had made her rush away from him in the first place.

'Here you are.' The voice came from just behind her and Chrissy jumped as she felt warm hands on her bottom, callused fingers stroking the peachy skin. 'I got bored waiting for you.'

She straightened up and would have turned into his arms, but Will held her firmly round the waist, gently biting the back of her neck while he began to explore her body more intimately. Chrissy moaned, leaning back slightly against his hand, the sensations too delicious for her to want him ever to stop. When his fingers slid inside the damp warmth of her sex, her control slipped completely and she pushed herself backwards, sinking deeper onto his probing, teasing fingers. She almost wept when his caress stopped, then realised it was his own male frustration that had caused him to leave her unsatisfied.

'I need to see you,' he grated roughly, pulling down the zip of her dress, 'I need to touch you all over.'

Chrissy, eager to comply, shrugged her shoulders and the dress dropped easily to the floor. She heard the rustle of Will's shirt as he pulled it over his head, then her naked body was once again engulfed in his powerful hold.

'You are so beautiful,' he murmured, gripping the lobe of her ear between his teeth, and cupping the weight of her breasts in his large hands, 'so beautiful. I'm going to take you now, here in the kitchen.' His voice was no more than a whisper.

Chrissy shivered at his words, unable to trust herself to speak, and wriggled restlessly against the hardness of his crotch, the material of his trousers rasping over her buttocks. She heard the sound of his zipper coming down, then the delicious sensation of his cock-head moving, sliding, coating itself in her slick juices, ready for entry.

'Now,' Will continued to murmur, 'now. Oh, yes.' With a strangled groan he buried his rock-hard penis smoothly inside her, willing himself to hold still for a second till he felt her body soften against his invasion, moulding to him, gripping him like liquid velvet.

Chrissy braced herself for the thrust she longed for, leaning her elbows on the kitchen worktop, her eyes half closed, her lips moist and parted with desire, unknowing and uncaring that they could be seen by anyone looking in the kitchen window. Holding her hips firmly in his grasp, Will withdrew slowly, savouring both the mind-blowing sensation and the vision of his glistening cock as he watched it emerge from her slippery hold. With a wild, deep cry he plunged inside her, again and again, and Chrissy rocked back to meet him, striving to deepen the penetration. She gasped and cried out with each heavy surge of his hips against her buttocks, driven wild by the feel of his cock stretching and filling her. Her heavy breasts swung in time to his rhythmic pounding, only adding to the delicious sensations coursing through her body.

But Will wanted more. Sweet though the vision of her arched back and the curve of her bottom were, he needed to hold all of her in his arms, to feel her yielding softness cradled against him. Withdrawing completely, he spun her round to face him, stifling her whimpers of protest with his lips on hers as his hands ran feverishly all over her body. Cupping his hands low on her buttocks, he lifted her easily, pausing only to allow her legs to wrap tightly around his waist before lowering her onto his rigid, straining cock, sheathing himself once more in her heat. In this position he could bury his head in her breasts, mouthing the hard nipples till Chrissy thought she could stand no more and ran her fingers frantically through his hair, kissing his head, his neck, any part of him she could reach, wriggling ecstatically in his strong hold, her body firmly anchored to him by the hardness of his cock.

When his hands began moving against her splayed buttocks, softly stroking the tender flesh, she almost lost control, bucking wildly on him, thrusting her breast even deeper into his mouth.

She sobbed his name, begging for release, with a pleasure that bordered on torment, the sound bringing a response deep inside him. With the blood singing in his veins, Will took a firmer grip on her then strode out of the kitchen. Not knowing where the bedroom was and his need so urgent now that he did not take time to ask, he carried her easily to the living room where he dropped her down onto the sofa.

For a second Chrissy was dazed by his hurried dash, then bereft of the warmth of his body, but he had only left her for as long as it took him to pull off his trousers and kneel on the sofa, nudging her legs apart with his knee, his cock rising powerfully along his belly. As she lay in this position with her legs spread, Chrissy's sex was held wide open, the pink lips pouting with need and desire. Will took just a second to admire the beauty of the vision before him. He rubbed a knuckle appreciatively over the smoothness of her hairless mound and would have lingered longer, had not a low moan from Chrissy, embarrassed but wildly turned on by this very personal scrutiny, sent his temperature soaring even higher. He lowered himself onto her, covering her with his hard masculine body and Chrissy arched

103

deliriously as he thrust into her, filling her again with his long thick cock, knowing this time he would not stop till he had given them the release for which their bodies screamed.

Chrissy surrendered completely to the rhythm of his pounding, her body surging upwards to meet every thrust. Higher and higher he took her, until there was nothing left for her but release. A shuddering pleasure engulfed her, rippling through her body in ever-widening waves, till she could no longer hear her own sobbing gasps and was barely aware of Will's deep cry as his body heaved convulsively against her one last time before he joined her on the verge of ecstatic oblivion.

Drifting back on a warm sensual fog, aware of the heavy weight of him lying on her, Chrissy couldn't keep from smiling. When her stroking hand on his damp hair finally made Will look up, he was grinning too.

Chrissy opened her mouth, but Will pressed a finger to her lips.

'Sh, don't say anything,' he murmured. 'there's nothing you need to say. I'm not looking for any promises, remember? I'll never put you under any pressure, Chrissy, believe that.'

Tears sprang to her eyes at the generosity of his words. Will was giving her the freedom to make her own choices, her own mistakes. Will Barnes was a man in a million, and she snuggled deeper into his shoulder, glad that she did not have to speak.

Eight

After Ross left Chrissy in the restaurant, he strode through the early evening streets, too angry to go home. Eventually, finding himself outside a pub that he recognised, he went in and elbowed through the crowd to the bar. The other customers, though annoyed at being pushed aside, took one look at the fury in his eyes and gave him a wide berth. He ordered a large whisky, with the firm intention of drinking himself into oblivion or at least to have enough to guarantee him some sleep tonight and deaden his emotions.

His groin still ached with longing for Chrissy and he imagined that he could still taste her musky sweetness on his breath. He shook his head bitterly, as if to clear it of any other stupid thoughts. Why had he even tried to speak to her tonight? Why hadn't he just trusted his instincts and had nothing more to do with her?

Cursing, Ross downed the drink and immediately ordered another, which the barman brought reluctantly. Everything about the darkly glowering newcomer spelled trouble. The angry glint in his blue eyes singled him out as a man to be avoided – a man whose turbulent emotions and anger were only barely being held in check. He looked dangerous, and the barman was already looking forward to the moment when Ross left.

Ross stared broodingly at the glass which had been put in front of him. Alcohol was not the real answer to his problem, but he had to admit that at the moment it did make him feel better. He raised the glass of golden liquid to his lips, but his arm was nudged violently and the glass fell from his hand, shattering on the bar. The room went silent and the barman stepped forward apprehensively. Ross spun round, his hands already clenched into tight fists.

'What the—' He found himself looking down into a pair of soft, grey eyes framed by a halo of blonde curls.

'Oh, I'm sorry. Did I knock your arm? I'm terribly sorry, it's just so crowded in here.' The grey eyes, which belonged to an elfin young girl, were wide and anxious.

Ross was immediately ashamed that she looked so afraid of him. 'It's OK,' he mumbled. 'An accident.' He turned away but the girl, encouraged by the fact that he seemed a little calmer, was unable to let it go.

'Are you sure? I'm not normally so clumsy. Can I buy you another?'

'Really,' said Ross, his mouth still set in a hard line, 'it's OK. I'd probably had enough anyway.' The girl, he noticed, was wearing an extremely short skirt and looked far too young to be in a pub at all. Just then her companion appeared beside them.

'Oh, Sophie, what have you done now? Honestly, I can't leave you alone for two minutes.' She smiled affectionately at her friend, then seemed to notice Ross for the first time.

'Ross? Ross Sinclair? It is you, isn't it? How are you? It's Tara – Tara Caversham. Don't say you don't remember me!'

Tara Caversham? Ross looked at the tall good-looking woman with no sense of recognition. Then something about her frank, brown-eyed stare jogged his memory a little. 'School?' he hazarded and then remembered. 'A school trip. A skiing holiday. Four of us got sent home early for "behaving in an improper manner, likely to bring the school into disrepute".'

'That's right.' Tara's eyes twinkled and she turned to her friend. 'I'd be very insulted if he hadn't remembered me after what we did that night.'

'And what was that?'

'Tell you later. It'll make Ross blush. You've already met Sophie, haven't you? Look, we just live around the corner. Why don't you come back with us and have a drink? We can talk about old times.'

'No thanks,' said Ross quickly. 'Some other time. I'm not the best of company tonight. I'd spoil your evening.'

'Says who?' Tara was amazed. 'You were always great company. Come on, it'll do you good.'

'He might be right,' Sophie warned, smiling. 'I honestly

thought he was going to thump me when I spilled his drink.'

'I'm sorry about that.' Ross shuffled in embarrassment. 'I was in a bit of a foul temper, but that was no excuse to take it out on you.'

'Well, you're not in a foul temper now, are you? Obviously we're good for you. Come on – it'll do you good to talk to someone, I suspect.' Tara was eyeing Ross's dishevelled appearance shrewdly.

'Well . . .' Ross knew that he really did not want any more to drink, so there was no reason to stay in the bar. And he did not relish going home alone to brood about Chrissy. He allowed himself to be persuaded out of the pub by Tara and Sophie.

The flat the two women shared was warm and cosy and Ross was soon settled in an armchair with a cup of hot coffee in his hand. Sensibly, Tara had not offered him an alcoholic drink. She sat on the settee and Sophie settled beside her, drawing her knees up to snuggle beside her friend. There was something so domestic and comfortable about the way they looked together that Ross was jolted by another memory of Tara. At first he couldn't remember, then it came to him. Tara's family had more or less disowned her when she had come out and admitted she was gay. It had been a shock to Ross and their other friends too, he remembered, especially after their short but highly enjoyable skiing trip. Tara had spent less and less time at home and eventually they had all lost touch. Ross realised that Sophie and Tara were watching him, waiting for a reaction.

He cleared his throat. 'So how long have you two been together then?'

Tara smiled in relief. 'I wasn't sure if you remembered or not.' She put her arm around Sophie and pulled her close. 'Three years.' The women shared a look of such tenderness that Ross felt a stab of jealousy. Then he realised what Tara had said.

'Three years?' He could not keep the surprise out of his voice.

Sophie read his mind. 'I'm twenty-one,' she said defensively. 'Look!' With her hand she indicated the birthday cards which were all around the room. 'Twenty-one yesterday, as a matter of fact.'

'Sorry,' Ross grinned, realising this was a sore point with the young woman. 'I didn't know or I would have brought you a present.' He said this lightly, but noticed a sudden tension in the room at his words.

'It's funny you should say that.' Tara leaned forward and looked at him carefully. 'Maybe there is something you could give Sophie for her birthday.'

'What do you mean?' He looked from Tara to Sophie, who was blushing furiously and refused to meet his eye. 'What kind of present?'

'It really was lucky meeting you tonight. I thought I was going to have to disappoint Sophie on her birthday. Promise you'll hear me out?'

Ross shrugged, curious. 'Sure.'

Tara took a moment before she began to speak. 'As I said, Sophie and I have been together for three years now.' Unconsciously her hand dropped onto her friend's knee and began to trace tiny circles. Despite himself, Ross's eyes were drawn to Sophie's smooth thighs while he listened. 'We've been very, very happy together and recently Sophie has been talking about us making a formal commitment to each other.' They smiled fondly before she continued. 'I love her very much and would like nothing better. But as you have already noticed, Ross, she is very young. Yes, I know, love.' Her hand moved higher to pat Sophie reassuringly on the lap, neither of the women noticing that the hem of Sophie's dress had also ridden up. Ross noticed.

'You see, the thing is, I've had a lot more time than Sophie to experience life.' The younger woman no longer seemed to be listening to her partner. Her eyes were closed, and her entire being seemed to be focused on her lap and the tiny circles Tara was tracing there. Ross could see that her nipples had hardened and were pushing through the material of her dress.

'I've had lots of partners, both male and female – enough to know that Sophie is everything I will ever need.' Sophie moaned and her thighs parted slightly under Tara's caress. Ross was mesmerised, his attention focused on Sophie's soft skin and his own growing erection, so he was quite unprepared for Tara's next words. 'Sophie has never experienced sex with a man and I told her I would find her one for her birthday. Then, if she still wants to make a commitment to us, then that's fine. Ross, will you have sex with Sophie as my birthday gift to her?'

'What?'

'Don't be so shocked; you know you want to.' Tara made a wry reference to Ross's erection, visible through his trousers. Embarrassed, Ross pulled his jacket round him. Both women were now leaning forward, awaiting his answer.

'Are you in a relationship at the moment? Sorry, I should have asked you before propositioning you.'

'No, but—'

'Please, Ross. It means so much to both of us. It was horrible having to disappoint Sophie yesterday on her birthday, but you have to realise that I love her too much to let her sleep with just any man. Hopefully, this will be the only time she does it in her entire life, so I wanted it to be really special. When I saw you in the pub tonight, I knew it must be fate. It'll just be sex. We don't want anything else from you, honestly. There's no catch.'

Just sex. Ross had given up casual sex some time ago – even before Portia – unable to reconcile what he wanted from his own relationships with the free-and-easy attitude of most of his acquaintances. Still, this meant that he had not had sex for some time. The recent advent of Chrissy in his life, and more especially his encounter with her in the restaurant this evening, had left him aching with sexual frustration and his cock was rock-hard again as he looked at the two women.

Sophie's soft grey eyes, still glowing from her recent arousal, now turned on him. 'Please, Ross. I really do want to do this. Tara is right; I'm very curious to know what it's like with a man. She's told me, of course, but that's not really the same, is it?'

Ross took a deep breath. 'OK. If you are sure it's what you both want.'

'Great!' Tara, her eyes bright with excitement, immediately took charge and moved them all into the bedroom. It became clear to Ross that whatever she had planned for the rest of the evening, she fully intended to take part herself. 'You don't mind, do you? It would be hell for me, sitting out there and wondering what was going on. I want this to be so special for Sophie.'

'Sure.' Ross, now that he was in the bedroom, realised that he was the most nervous of the three. 'Where do you want me?'

'Just lie on the bed, please, and relax. You're Sophie's present and she is going to unwrap you.'

Ross felt a thrill of pleasure at the words and hurried to do as he was told. The women undressed quickly and unselfconsciously, and approached the bed where he lay, propped on the pillows. Tara was magnificent. Her golden skin glowed like butterscotch in the light of the bedside lamps and her generous breasts bounced with every movement. She perched herself on the edge of the bed, out of Ross's reach, but he caught a tantalising glimpse of glistening pink at the apex of her thighs when she drew one leg under her, causing her labia to part slightly.

He was distracted from this delight by Sophie, also naked, climbing onto the bed beside him. Her body was slender, as he had known it would be, her skin so white that it appeared almost translucent. A sparse covering of soft golden hair was all that protected her sex from his gaze. She looked fragile and delicate, though her small girlish breasts were tipped with the largest nipples he had ever seen. Ross ached to touch her but understood that for the moment this was against the rules. There was a deep insistent throbbing in his groin.

Sophie, kneeling beside him, seemed unsure of what to do next. She turned to Tara who nodded encouragingly. 'Go on. He's your present. Unwrap him.'

Sophie laid a tentative hand on Ross's chest. He had already removed his jacket, so her small hand rested on his shirt. Ross could feel the heat of her fingers and see a steady pulse beating at the base of her throat as she leaned towards him. When her fingers started to undo the buttons on his shirt, he had to resist the urge to help her, to rip the shirt off and pull her naked body down against him. He groaned.

Sophie paused at this, then smiled, pleased at his reaction. My God, Ross thought, looking up at her, she has no idea what effect she is having on me. He glanced at Tara who was watching them both avidly, her eyes aflame, one hand cupping her own breast and tugging gently at the nipple.

Sophie, meanwhile, had finished with his buttons and spread his shirt wide so that she could look at him. Curiously she rubbed one of his nipples with her thumb. Ross hissed with pleasure and Sophie looked startled.

'Oh! I'd no idea that a man's nipples would be sensitive.' She tweaked the other nipple and giggled at his reaction before lowering her head and flicking him with her tongue. Ross groaned again, gritting his teeth with the pleasure of her touch. Sophie moved her hands over the coarse hairs on his chest, then impulsively leaned over him and brushed her own erect nipples over the roughness. The delicious friction drew a moan from her own lips and she pulled away quickly, sneaking a guilty glance at Tara. But Tara's eyes were heavy with love and lust.

'Go on,' she urged, 'you know how I love to see your pleasure.'

Warming to her task, Sophie now began to explore every inch of Ross's skin that she had access to. Her tongue and lips and hands caressed him as she nibbled and tasted, gauging his reaction to her touch. Ross was lost in a world of pleasure, the contact of her soft skin against him heightening his senses till he thought he would explode.

For all her inexperience with men, some instinct seemed to warn Sophie that her victim was nearing the end of his tether. Anyway, she had been feeling the urgent heat of his erection against her leg for some time now and she was eager to take her exploration further. Her hands were shaking as they settled on the fastening of Ross's trousers, and it was with difficulty that she lowered the zip around the straining bulge. Before she could fully part the fabric, Ross's cock, too long restrained, sprang free, standing up straight and proud from his pubic hair.

Sophie gasped and rocked back on her heels. 'Oh! It's huge! I never thought—'

Tara had crept across the bed till she was now kneeling on the other side of Ross. The two women looked at each other across his erection.

'It is big, isn't it?' Tara licked her lip hungrily. 'I'd forgotten what a big boy you were, Ross. You're in for a real treat tonight, Sophie. A lot of women go through their whole life and never encounter a cock like this. We'll just have to make sure that you are good and wet enough to take it.' Her wicked grin took in both Ross and Sophie.

Sophie was mesmerised. 'I've never seen a real cock before. I just can't believe it. Can I touch it?'

'Please.' Ross thought he would die if one of them did not

touch him soon. The sight of two naked women crouching over him, discussing his erection in tones of awe, was enough to send any man over the edge. He closed his eyes and gritted his teeth as he felt Sophie's fingers reach out to stroke him; she giggled as his cock twitched out of her grasp, then closed her fingers more firmly around him.

She squealed like a child with a new toy. 'I can feel it! I can feel it throbbing. It feels wonderful, as if it has a life of its own! Touch it, Tara.' Her hands moved up and down the shaft, inadvertently sliding the loose skin over the shiny purple glans. Ross gasped audibly, his entire body tensing with pleasure under the naivety of her touch, and Tara took pity on him.

'I think you'd better leave him for a moment, love. Men tend to get very excited very quickly when beautiful women touch their cock. Isn't that right, Ross?'

Ross nodded, his breathing ragged, not trusting himself to speak.

Tara smiled at him. 'I think we had better make a slight alteration to our plans,' she said to Sophie. 'I do so want your first time to be memorable for all the right reasons. Poor Ross is really very excited and I think we should try to relieve some of his tension first, so he can take his time later.'

She kept her expression carefully casual, looking down at the bed. 'Would you mind if I asked him to fuck me first? I know it wasn't really part of the plan, but it would be quite nice to feel a man inside me again.' She glanced up quickly to check Sophie's reaction.

Sophie's eyes sparkled with excitement as she scrambled round the bed to take her lover in her arms. 'Would you? Would you do that for me? I'd love to see you.' Sophie kissed her hard, hungrily; their tongues explored each other, thrusting, expressing their love for each other. Ross, lying beneath them, could have felt excluded, if only the sight of them entwined in each others arms had not been so totally erotic that it sent his cock twitching and jumping once again. He groaned loudly and Sophie broke off the kiss.

'Don't worry, Ross, we haven't forgotten you. I can't wait to see you make love to my lover; but first I have to prepare her for you.' Gently she lay Tara down on the bed. Ross raised himself onto his elbow so he could see, as Sophie spread Tara's legs to reveal her sex, already swollen and aroused, to their gaze.

With her fingers Sophie spread Tara's labia even more before pushing two fingers inside her deep, moist opening. A moment later she slid them out, glistening with the honeyed dew of Tara's body. She held them up for Ross to see and for a second his nostrils were assailed by the sharp piquant scent of female arousal, before Sophie put them in her mouth, sucking them eagerly between her pink lips.

Ross was breathing hard now, from the sheer excitement of the erotic stimuli assaulting his senses. He watched Sophie's head drop between Tara's legs – the blonde curls in stark contrast to Tara's jet-black pubic hair – and kiss her vulva with the same passion she had used on her lips only moments before. He heard Tara moan, saw her arch her back in pleasure. And then his own lips sought and found the cherry tip of her nipple which he brought to a bursting peak with his tongue. This was the first time he had actually touched either of the women and he felt his excitement rising once again as he reached for the other nipple. But Sophie had beaten him to it and for a few moments they each sucked contentedly, while Tara moaned and writhed beneath them, lost in a spiral of pleasure.

Eventually, knowing her lover's every nuance, every whimper, Sophie recognised that Tara was close to coming. She sat up. Ross, taking his cue from her, stopped too.

'I think you're ready for him now. Turn over. I want to see this.'

Before doing so Tara reached for the packet of condoms she had left in a drawer beside the bed and handed them to Ross. He nodded and quickly rolled one into place while Tara scrambled onto her hands and knees, the sight of her upraised bottom drawing gasps from both Ross and Sophie. Sophie spread the soft cheeks, opening Tara as Ross took up his position behind her.

'You look so damned exciting, I don't think I'm going to be able to last,' he warned her, his voice sounding harsh and throaty.

'Put it inside me, Ross. I want to feel a man inside me tonight. I want to feel what Sophie will feel.'

Ross ran his hands over her buttocks before taking his cock in his hand and inserting just the tip inside her welcoming passage. Sophie's face was only inches away from his cock, and Ross was aware that her hand had disappeared between her own legs; then a wave of sheer pleasure jolted through him, starting at the tip of his cock and quickly spreading to every nerve in his body. He penetrated Tara slowly at first, then suddenly pushed all the way in.

She cried aloud, 'Oh yes, yes, that feels so good!'

Her words sent shivers racing down Ross's spine, and he pushed even more deeply into her. Tara gave little cries and thrust vigorously back against him as the rhythm accelerated. Neither of them held out long and they came noisily together, Tara's convulsing internal muscles wringing every last drop of pleasure from him as they collapsed on the bed.

Ross was allowed to rest for a few moments, but Sophie fell on top of Tara's sweat-slicked body and kissed her hard, possesively. 'Was it good?' she whispered. 'It was so exciting to watch you come.' She slid down to rest her head between Tara's legs, breathing in the unfamiliar mingled scents of man and woman, before beginning a delicate lapping at her partner's swollen sex lips. Her tongue was tender and loving, sliding over every fold of flesh, pushing gently inside, wanting to share her lover's recent experience. Only after she had brought Tara to another whimpering orgasm, did Sophie turn her attention to Ross.

He had been watching them and his penis was already semi-erect when he felt her warm breath approaching; her tongue flicked out to lick his glans quickly and repeatedly, as though she were daring herself to do so. Closing her eyes, she sucked Ross into her mouth as far as she could, remembering how he had slid into her lover's pussy and how deep he had gone. Ross entwined his fingers in her curly hair and held her, even in his growing passion, remembering to be gentle. After a long, delicious moment, Sophie let him slip from her mouth and enclosed his hot slippery shaft with her hand, working the velvety-soft skin up and down his length, varying the speed and gauging his reaction.

'Is this good, Ross; am I doing it right?'

'Yes,' he gasped. 'It's . . . wonderful.'

'I want you to come, Ross. I want to see you come.'

Ross was on fire, the sweat trickling down his body doing nothing to cool his passion. His entire being was focused on his penis and the hand that held it. And then another hand slipped between his legs, softly exploring his scrotum with infinite tenderness. He moaned loudly. Tara had joined Sophie, adding her hand to the one already on his cock and together the two women brought him to orgasm, his semen shooting forth in huge spurting jets to land on his belly.

'OK, you have a little rest now,' purred Tara, 'while I prepare Sophie. We'll have to get her nice and relaxed.'

She held her arms out to Sophie who slipped into them. They seemed so comfortable with each other, so relaxed, that Ross felt another pang of jealousy. It was obvious that they loved each other deeply. Tara had been right. With him it was 'just sex' but what they were experiencing with each other – that was love.

Sophie lay on her back, her eyes closed. Tara was propped at her side, sometimes kissing her lips, sometimes nibbling at her lover's breast, drawing forth soft cries of pleasure. Her hand was buried between Sophie's legs, her fingers knowing from long experience when and where to rub, how fast or how gently, how to tease and when to rest to bring Sophie to a quivering peak without allowing her to fall over the edge into orgasm. With a sigh, Sophie allowed her legs to fall apart, and Ross could see how pink and swollen she was, as Tara's fingers kept up their delicious friction. Sophie bucked her hips and a long low moan escaped from her lips. Tara removed her hand only reluctantly but could not resist one more long lingering kiss with Sophie before turning heavy-lidded eyes on Ross.

'You will be gentle with her?' she asked, unable to hide her anxiety now that the time had come.

Ross nodded, his mouth too dry to speak, his penis already hard again. Slowly, he moved to cover Sophie with his body, supporting his weight on his elbows. She felt tiny and fragile beneath him.

Sophie could feel his massive cock pressing hard into her belly and had opened her eyes to watch him apprehensively, awaiting his first thrust. But Ross took his time. He grinned down at her, in full control of his masculine strength now, stroking her hair gently till he felt her relax beneath him. Only then did he begin to place soft fluttering kisses over her face, covering every inch, allowing her to get used to the unaccustomed roughness of his skin, before kissing her on the lips for the first time. She tasted soft and sweet, and he played his tongue across her teeth till her mouth opened and she welcomed him in, to explore her. His lips traced a path down the line of her neck, and she arched her neck towards him, so he could suck and nibble the sensitive skin of her throat.

Without warning, Ross's head moved lower and closed over a hard nipple. His mouth was bigger than Tara's and he could suck the whole of her small breast into his mouth, a new experience that caused Sophie to cry out in pleasure. Ross too, savoured the sensation, her moulding softness filling his mouth, the tip of her nipple pressing exquisitely on the roof of his mouth. He did not neglect her other breast, and teased it to a hard peak with his lips.

Ross continued to trail his tongue downwards, licking across her flat stomach, lingering a while over the sweet indent of her navel. The light covering of hair on her mons was no defence against his tongue as he gently parted her labia to taste her musky sweetness for the first time. Her juices were flowing freely, like nectar from the most exotic of flowers, coating his lips and chin; he fastened his mouth over her, drinking every drop.

Laying his hand flat on her belly, Ross could feel her quivering and hear her moan softly; he deliberately slowed his pace, savouring the experience. Sophie's hips were writhing. She pushed herself towards him, but he held her firmly with his strong hands, staying in control. He had to struggle against the urge to suck the tiny bud of her clitoris between his teeth and nibble on it, knowing that this would bring her to instant orgasm, wanting to prolong the pleasure for both of them.

Only when he was fully sated on her nectar did he move up once more to cover her with his powerful body. Sophie's knees were drawn up as Ross settled between her parted legs. He paused with the tip of his cock nudging against her entrance, waiting for her to open herself to him. Sophie moaned and spread her legs even further.

With a sigh, Ross inched forwards. It was like sliding into velvet. He met no resistance and continued in one slow sensual movement until he was buried to the base of his shaft in her tight, virginal passage, content to rest there for a few moments, allowing her to get used to him. But he felt Sophie tighten and tremble in his arms and he pulled back slightly, frightened he had hurt her, till he realised that she was in the throes of a gentle orgasm. Ross felt exhilarated and held her tightly in his arms till the trembling stopped, sharing her orgasm as her convulsing internal muscles rippled along his cock. Sophie opened her eyes and gazed at him in wonder, her face only inches from his own.

'Nice?' he murmured.

'Heaven,' she breathed.

When he began to move he did so only slowly, kissing and nibbling her throat once again, coaxing small cries of pleasure from her parted lips. His rhythm was gentle, but the tension built steadily nonetheless. A fine film of sweat formed between them, allowing their skin to slide smoothly, the friction causing a delicious heat to spread through them, adding to their pleasure. Sophie clung to him, instinctively adjusting her hips so that the base of his shaft ground against the swollen bud of her clitoris.

Ross, in control and still wary of hurting her, allowed her to set the pace, matching his strokes to her own thrusting, watching the pleasure flit across her face as he savoured the tightness of her hold on him.

But gradually Sophie's movements grew more frantic. She clamped her legs around his waist and tried to pull him even deeper inside her.

'Harder,' she gasped, 'as hard as you did it to Tara. Please!'

This was almost more than Ross could bear. With every stroke he increased his pace, but Sophie only seemed to love it more, urging him with her hips. On and on he drove into her, till he lost track of everything else, aware only of Sophie's heat beneath him and the powerful, pulsating pleasure spreading from his cock to every nerve-ending in his body. A part of his mind allowed him to hold out till he felt Sophie's orgasm streak through her and she screamed her pleasure, arching away from him. Then Ross came too, an cry of release bursting from his lips as he shuddered above her, his third orgasm of the evening sapping his strength; he collapsed gasping onto the bed.

Sophie, her youth giving her more energy, immediately wriggled from under him and into Tara's waiting arms. 'Thank you, Tara, thank you. It was the best birthday present ever,' she wept, kissing her lover hard. Then, not forgetting Ross, she kissed him too. 'And you, Ross. Don't try and tell me that all men are like you because I won't believe you. That was so special. I think I could love you if I didn't love Tara so much!' She kissed him again.

'Thanks,' said Ross, weakly. 'It was special for me, too.'

Tara came to him and there were tears in her eyes as she kissed him. 'She's right. You're one in a million. Thank you for making it so good for her.'

'Any time,' murmured Ross, but they all knew this was not true.

He lay on the bed and the two women nestled at his side, their heads resting on his shoulder and one leg thrown over each of his. But they reached across his chest and linked fingers – needing contact, sharing a closeness that Ross could never be a part of. He was happy for them, but the glowing strength of their love for each other made him feel very alone.

Unbidden, thoughts of Chrissy came into his head. 'Just sex, no commitment,' Tara had said to him. That was what Chrissy had been doing, these past few days. Maybe, Ross thought, just before he drifted off to sleep, just maybe, he should ask her why she was doing it, why she was so keen to take part in the Treasure Hunt, instead of being so quick to condemn her for it.

Nine

Portia de Havilland lay naked on top of a white fur bedspread, in her London home. She was on her front, enjoying the sensation of the soft fur tickling her belly; she knew without checking that her nipples were hard and erect. In fact, every breath she drew sent soft ripples of pleasure coursing through her from the sensuous contact with the fur. She stretched and tried to relax, but knew she would not. The news she had heard at last night's party was preying on her mind.

Clarissa, it appeared, was taking the Treasure Hunt very seriously indeed. Bitch. Clarissa was not exactly renowned for seeing things through to the end – just Portia's luck that this particular game had captured her interest. It was not in Portia's nature to lose and she did not intend to do so this time.

She heard a faint noise and rolled over onto her back, expecting to see Bas, but the room was empty. Then a movement caught her eye, and she saw the startled face of the window cleaner staring in at her naked body. Stupid man. He was going to fall if he was not careful.

Portia looked at him coolly, for a long moment, then, slowly, she opened her legs wide, allowing him an unhindered view of her sex, watching his expression. His eyes widened even further, if that was possible, and she imagined she could hear his ladder rattling against her windowsill, he was shaking so much. She stretched languorously and arched her back.

Above her on the ceiling was a large mirror. As she stretched, she looked up at it, examining a version of the view the window cleaner was enjoying. That she looked spectacular against the white fur, she had no doubt. Her flawless porcelain skin was almost as white as the fur and her glossy black hair spread over her pillow like a halo. Her pubic hair, also black, was bushy and

119

luxuriant – she never, never trimmed it and was proud of the way it curled over her thighs and lower belly. Each deep red nipple – the red colour tattooed on – was pierced by a small silver ring which held the nipples permanently erect, and created exquisite sensations when they came into contact with anything, even her clothes. The nipple rings were linked by a fine silver chain, suspended between her breasts. Her lipstick and nails were a deep crimson against the white background.

She glanced back at the window. The man seemed to have got over his initial shock. In fact he had climbed a few rungs higher on his ladder to improve his view. Well, maybe she should give him something worth looking at. Portia stretched over to the bedside table and picked up the gleaming black rubber dildo she always kept there. Not looking at the window, she slowly licked from the base of the dildo, up the side, before wrapping her red lips around the bulbous tip and easing it into her mouth. Forgetting her audience, she closed her eyes and sucked it deeply, her lips and cheeks stretched wide by its monstrous size. She sucked contentedly for a while, then slowly eased it from her mouth. It was slippery with saliva and, cradling it with both hands, she trailed it down between her breasts and over her flat tummy, the shiny rubber coming to rest on her thick pubic tangle.

With her eyes half-closed, Portia spread her legs wide and parted the hair with both hands, entwining her fingers in the luxurious growth and tugging gently, teasing her outer lips apart. Taking the dildo in her hand she stroked it over the stretched skin till it glistened with her body's own sweet lubricant.

Still watching her reflection, she held herself open with one hand and slid the dildo inside, not roughly, but quickly, savouring the feeling of the sudden invasion of her most private of places. Her inner lips gripped tightly around the monster as she pushed it hard and fast, the rhythm she preferred, and her other hand flew to twist and tug at her nipple, sending bolts of pleasure arrowing through her body.

Reluctant to tear her eyes away from the vision in the mirror, Portia nonetheless sneaked a look at her audience and for a second felt herself tense with annoyance. The awful little man, although he was still watching her avidly, had removed his cock from his trousers and was rubbing it vigorously. How dare he!

Then Portia realised that she could not care less. If he fell off his ladder, that was his problem. She could not stop now, she was so near her crisis; the first tingling tremors of orgasm were rippling outwards from her womb. Her attention went back to the mirror above and she quickly forgot about him. Digging her heels into the bed she raised her hips and was able to push the dildo even deeper, her other hand now skimming across the slippery bud of her clitoris. Gasping her pleasure, she bore down on the black cock, her thighs clamping shut to hold it inside as she came, writhing on the white fur.

She lay for a few minutes gathering her breath. As her muscles relaxed, the dildo slipped out and she stood up, facing the window. The window cleaner was still rubbing himself, a rather puny cock Portia now noticed as she walked towards him. Her breasts seemed to tremble as she moved, the silver chain which linked them shimmering. He came just as she reached the window, but if he made a sound she did not hear it through the double glazing. But she saw the white globules of his come spattering the glass as she reached up with both hands and pulled the curtains shut.

'And if he doesn't clean that up he's fired,' she muttered to herself, turning away.

She called to Bas. It was time she came up with a plan to beat Clarissa. Portia needed to make a phone call.

Unlike Bas, Portia was not ill at ease in the seedy dressing room of the working men's club in south London. She had been to clubs like this many times in the past – every time she fancied a bit of rough, as her friends put it. Bas laid her costume out on the dressing table, jumping nervously as the door was thrown open and a large man in his late forties marched in.

'I'm Brian Rhodes, Master of Ceremonies and bouncer. Everything all right, love?' He had a strong Yorkshire accent, stood at least six foot three and was a huge, physical presence.

'Perfect,' purred Portia. 'Is there a good crowd?'

'About fifty. Tuesday's never a busy night, but there's nothing like a stripper to pull them in. You'd better not disappoint them – they'll not be shy about telling you they don't like the show.'

Portia was completely indifferent to whether they liked the show or not. She started to undress, revealing that she wore nothing under her jacket or her short skirt.

'Nowt to complain about there, love.' Brian eyed her figure appreciatively when she was naked.

'I would like a drink,' Portia said, ignoring his familiarity.

'A babycham?'

'A double malt whisky.'

A look passed between them. 'I'll send it through. What about you, lad?' He shook his head sadly when Bas asked for a glass of dry white wine.

'Wait. I intend to hold a raffle,' Portia told him. She snapped her fingers at Bas, who sprang forward, several books of raffle tickets in his hand.

'We don't allow the acts to do anything like that, love.'

Portia smiled knowingly. 'You will this time, when you know what the prize is. Perhaps you would like to buy one yourself?'

'What prize?' Brian asked suspiciously.

'The first ticket out of the hat has half an hour to do exactly what he wants to me. On stage. Anything at all.'

'How much are they?

'Just a pound. The profits go to charity.' In fact, she had given the money no thought at all.

Brian tore ten tickets out of the proffered book and gave Bas a ten pound note. 'You'd better come with me, lad. I reckon you'll be able to sell those, no problem.'

When they had gone, Portia turned to the costume that Bas had laid out for her. It consisted of many different layers, all of them in black leather. First she stepped into a tiny thong and a strapless platform bra. The thong did nothing to hide her luxuriant public hair but separated the cheeks of her bottom beautifully and caused a delicious friction between her legs as she walked. On top of this went her favourite leather basque, pinching in her tiny waist and pushing her breasts up high. Black fishnet stockings were attached to the suspenders on the basque, and she slipped her feet into a pair of excruciatingly high stilettos. On top of this ensemble went a nurse's uniform. Cheap, tacky and utterly tasteless – but just the sort of thing men expected in a place like this.

Before she left the dressing room, Portia added her long black leather gloves, smoothing each finger into place and rolling them up past her elbows. They did not go with the nurse's outfit at all, but there was no way she was actually going to touch any of these people. Except possibly for the large Yorkshireman. She smiled without warmth.

Stepping out the door, she signalled to Brian that she was ready.

The lights dimmed suddenly, loud music started to pump out of the sound system and bright spotlights illuminated the stage. Portia strode out onto the stage, to an appreciative roar from the crowd.

Her hair was black and glistening, her face heavily made up, her eyes outlined with kohl and her lips scarlet. She looked brutally and efficiently attractive, like no nurse any of them had ever seen before. She stalked the length of the stage a few times, lifting the hem of her uniform's skirt to show her stocking tops, but this was little more than a token gesture. Dancing was not really her style.

Without further preamble she turned her back and began to undo the buttons of her dress, taking her time and throwing coy looks over her shoulder at her audience; they were hooting and cheering. She slipped one shoulder down, then pulled the hem up again, giving them another tantalising glimpse of creamy buttock, the firm curve of her behind. Then she quickly allowed the dress to rustle to the floor and turned to face the cheering men, more comfortable with her outfit now. The effect was electrifying and she knew it. The room fell to an instant hush as she gently pushed her full breasts towards them, pouting suggestively. One of her nipples slipped from its cup and she toyed with it for a moment before slipping it back out of view.

Moving gently to the music, she allowed them to study her glorious body thoroughly; her long legs with smooth thighs and her pubic mound barely covered by its scrap of soft leather. Turning, she exposed her firm, taut bottom, the skin glowing whitely in the lights of the club, the thong hiding little from their appreciative eyes.

She paused to survey her audience then, with an imperious finger, signalled to a slender young man from the front row.

Nervously, he clambered onto the stage and stood in front of Portia's magnificent body.

'You're not going to touch until you've been invited, are you?' The meek young man shook his head silently. Rewarding his acquiescence, Portia lifted his hands and placed them on her leather-clad breasts. 'What do you for a living?'

'I'm a librarian.' At the back of the stage Bas pulled out Portia's Hunt card and checked it quickly. He looked up and shook his head.

'Have you ever been with a woman, little boy?'

'Of course I have,' he squeaked, turning bright red.

Portia turned to Bas. 'Put him down as a virgin.' The crowd roared with laughter. 'Did you buy a raffle ticket?'

'Yes. Ten.'

'And what would you like to do to me if you win?'

He said nothing, his blush deepening.

'That bad,' she sneered, to more guffaws from the other men. 'Well, just in case you don't win, this is your big chance. I want you to remove my stockings.' He stood, looking confused, but Portia encouraged him. 'Come on; how difficult can it be? Surely you've done it before? Do the back first.'

She stood with legs apart, gloved hands on her waist. Obediently, he went behind her and studied the fastening of her suspender. It actually was very simple, but he took his time, his fingers trembling as he crouched with his face inches from Portia's smooth white backside. The front fastenings took even longer, distracted as he was by the musky scent emanating from her thick pubic hair, but eventually these too were undone. Portia perched her bottom on a bar stool and lifted one leg so he could unroll each stocking. His hands lingered over the smooth curves of her calves, but his eyes fixed on the top of her thighs, to the dark secrets he hoped to glimpse as she held her leg up for him.

He stepped back as he dropped the second stocking. Portia slipped her feet back inside the stilettos; the floor after all looked none too clean. 'Thank you. You did that very well. Now take out your cock.'

'What?'

'Your cock. I want to see it.' Still sitting on her stool, she eased her legs apart, treating him to a view the rest of the crowd could not quite see.

Mesmerised, he undid his trousers and released his straining penis, holding himself protectively in his hand.

'Very good. Now, I want to see you come.'

Beyond arguing now, the young man began to move his hand up and down the length of his cock. Within seconds he came to a gasping climax, his semen dripping onto the floor.

'Well done,' Portia approved. 'You go back to your seat now and keep your fingers crossed for the raffle.'

One of the crowd clambered onto the stage now and, leering drunkenly, made a grab for Portia's breasts. Brian appeared from the side, but before he could reach them, Portia smiled sweetly at the drunk, slipped her hand to the bulge in his groin, and squeezed mercilessly. He dropped to the stage, clutching himself and Brian scooped him up and removed him, to loud approving cheers.

Imperiously, she summoned another man from the back of the hall. He was young and very attractive, wearing expensive clothes and a flashy gold watch. He was cocksure and arrogant, reeking of expensive aftershave.

'What do you work as?'

'I'm a personal trainer,' He grinned over his shoulder at his friends, but watched her warily, legs braced ready for an insult or a caress.

'OK, Mr Personal Trainer, take your clothes off.'

'What? Now?'

'I'll make it worth your while,' she cooed, slipping a gloved finger into her mouth and sucking on it.

'Come on, Gary, show her what you're made of!' Hoots and calls accompanied their words and, encouraged, Gary quickly removed his clothes. His erection jutted out straight in front of him, long and thin, in contrast to his thick stocky body.

'Mm, lovely,' Portia licked her lips. 'I do hope you bought a raffle ticket. Now. I want you to undress me. No,' she cautioned, as he reached eagerly for her, 'with your teeth.' She turned around and presented the back of the basque to him. It was laced together and tied tightly.

Gary looked around at his friends for support and, good-naturedly, they egged him on. Hesitantly, he took the lace in his mouth and slowly began the task of freeing Portia from the basque. His friends laughed and yelled encouragement at first, but fell silent as he settled to his task. Portia could tell he was no longer paying any attention to anyone else in the room. She could hear his breathing grow laboured as he became more involved in what he was doing. The first few times his lips touched her skin he jumped, but gradually he grew to savour the contact, touching her skin more than was entirely necessary with his mouth, occasionally nipping her back with his teeth as he grew bolder. Every now and then his erection jabbed into her buttock.

He took a long time, but eventually he stepped back, flushed and sweating, the long black lace held triumphantly in his teeth.

Portia turned to face her audience, holding the leather basque in place with her hands. She faced her willing victim. 'Would you like me to drop it?'

He nodded eagerly.

She flung the basque aside to stand in front of them wearing only her thong and the platform bra, her nipples peeping brightly over the top. The room went silent.

'Do you like what you see?'

He licked his thin lips and nodded.

'Would you like your reward? Now? With all your friends watching?'

He thought for a moment, then nodded again.

'Do you think he deserves a reward?' she demanded of the crowd. They yelled their assent.

'Remember,' she warned, 'don't touch.' Turning her back on him, she wiggled her buttocks against his erection. He gasped, but obeyed her instructions not to touch her with his hands, thoroughly enjoying the contact he was allowed. Portia rubbed him along her crease for a few moments, feeling his cock grow even longer. She aimed his cock between the top of her thighs, feeling him brace himself, convinced he was being allowed inside her at last.

Instead she slid his cock along her moist furrow, allowing it to drag deliciously on her quivering clitoris as it continued to slide through, denied the entry that it desperately sought. Portia looked down to see the shiny swollen head of his cock appear between her legs, peeping out through her own pubic hair. The room was silent as she began to rock her hips, increasing the tempo so that her breasts swung to and fro and her hair flew in front of her face.

The rigid shaft, now gripped tightly between her thighs, teased and massaged the whole centre of her pleasure. Her engorged little bud pulsed maddeningly but before she could achieve the orgasm she craved, Gary, unable to contain himself, suddenly gave a loud grunt and spurted his copious white seed onto the floor in front of them both. Contemptuously, Portia released his shrinking cock from the iron grip of her thighs. 'I hope you last a lot longer than that with your wife,' she told him.

'No, but I do!' yelled an anonymous voice from the darkness, to much laughter. Gary gathered up his clothes and left the stage to good-natured jeers from his friends.

Frustrated, Portia surveyed her audience, her eyes finally lighting on Brian, who was lounging on the bar and watching her closely.

Slipping off her thong and her bra, she stood naked, apart from her shoes and gloves, her legs wide apart. With one finger she beckoned him closer. 'What about you, big boy? Do you think you can satisfy me?' she scoffed.

'I'll give it a bash,' he answered mildly, not intimidated.

Portia looked at him narrowly, wondering if she had made a wise choice. 'OK. You'll do.' She sat back on the stool, holding her legs apart with her hands. 'Mouth only,' she instructed him; 'anything else is for the winner of the raffle.'

He nodded and crouched down in front of her, breathing in the rich aroma of her musk. 'Spread your lips further for me.'

Portia's eyes narrowed at being ordered about, but she did as he instructed, holding herself open for him.

The room was silent now as everyone watched his mouth seek and find her soft hot opening. With one sure upward sweep of his tongue he separated her folds, sending a jolt of pleasure shooting through her so intense it felt like pain. Her whole body jumped, almost losing her precarious balance on the bar stool.

Pleased with this reaction and satisfied he had asserted

himself, Brian settled to his task. His tongue continued its long sweeping strokes, occasionally breaking the rhythm to flick relentlessly over the swollen bud of her clitoris. Each time he did this, Portia gasped and felt her muscles clench, an orgasm almost within reach. But he always drew away slightly before she could achieve the release she craved. Desperately she wanted to take his head in her hands and press him closer, into her sex, but something about the way he moved so confidently between her legs prevented her from doing this. She hated to display any sign of weakness.

So it was that the Yorkshireman set his own pace, bringing her repeatedly to the brink, yet each time deliberately stopping before she could explode with excruciating pleasure. Her skin glowing with perspiration, Portia lifted her hands to tug and pull at her red nipples, ignoring the straining muscles in her thighs as she held herself open for him, oblivious of the audience now leaning forward avidly in their seats, conscious only of the ever-widening circles of pleasure emanating from her sex and his swirling, masterful tongue.

At last she could stand no more. Grabbing his head in her hands, she ground herself against him, shaking in violent rapture, her screams echoing round the silent club. When the last few violent spasms had passed, Brian gently prised her fingers from his curly hair.

'That was lovely, but what do you say we have that raffle? I think everyone is in the mood for it now.' Straightening his tie, he waved to Bas to bring over the waste-paper bin filled with raffle tickets.

Portia, recovering rapidly, sat on the stool, still naked, and crossed her legs elegantly as Bas hurried over. Brian held the waste-paper bin out to her. Flicking her hair back Portia smiled at the tense audience and pulled out a ticket stub.

'Which of you lucky men has number fifty-three?' There was a lot of rustling as tickets were checked but nobody spoke out. Portia uncrossed her legs. 'Come on. We're not shy, are we?'

Brian put down the bin. 'Hang on a minute,' he muttered, and pulled out his own tickets, holding one up triumphantly. There were good natured shouts of 'fix' round the room but also an element of relief. Most of the men, if they were honest, were frightened to death of Portia. Brian was well-liked and respected in the club, so no-one was disappointed enough to question the outcome seriously.

Portia eyed Brian suspiciously, but he smiled back innocently. She put her hands on her hips, her breasts bouncing. 'OK, I'm yours. For half an hour.'

There was a small pause while the crowd filled their glasses and reseated themselves ready for the performance. Brian fetched Portia another large whisky and bought himself a pint of bitter which he barely sipped.

When everyone was once again settled, Brian asked her to lean over a high bar stool so that her tummy rested on the worn velvet, then lifted her up so that her feet were off the floor and she had to hold the crossbar of the stool to keep from falling off. She looked and felt extraordinarily vulnerable.

'You did say owt, didn't you, love?'

'No, you fool! I said "anything".' Her voice was muffled by the position she was was in, but the anger in her voice was apparent to all of them.

'My, but you've got a beautiful arse!' Brian slapped her backside playfully, his large hand landing with a resounding smack.

Slowly and deliberately he poured the foam of his pint over her bottom, the creamy liquid oozing over her cheeks and into her crease. Portia gasped at how cold it was, but said nothing. Brian began to massage it into her with a thoroughness that made her gasp, especially when the pad of his thumb worked deftly inside the puckered hole of her anus, twisting around inside its tight walls for a second before slipping out so quickly she was unsure if the audience had even seen. Bent over the stool, the blood rushing to her head, Portia moaned at this unruly invasion, her pleasure intense.

Nonchalantly Brian unbuckled his belt and allowed his trousers to drop to the floor of the stage, so he could step out of them. In reply to the catcalls, he turned and wiggled his bottom at the throng before removing the rest of his clothes and folding them onto a chair. While he was undressing Portia tried to sit up, but Brian kept one huge hand on the small of her back, holding her gently but firmly in position. She twisted her head, trying to see what she could of his naked body. Brian was heavily built with broad shoulders and hair so thick on his chest it looked like fur. Surprisingly he looked more muscular without his clothes, his body firmly toned and without flab. His penis was jutting from his curly pubic hair, thick and eager and amply proportioned.

Naked, he stood behind her again. She had a beautiful bottom, firm and round and, placing his hands under her, he raised her buttocks till she was positioned just as he wanted her. Portia had to cling tightly to the legs of the stool to keep her balance. Without taking his eyes off this vision, Brian reached to where he had left his jacket and took a condom from his pocket, pulling it over his massively hard penis. The latex-covered organ rested on the crack between her buttocks and he happily ran it over her crease a few times, reaching his hand between her legs to collect her slippery moisture and rub it on himself. The strange position he had put her in, combined with the feeling of his fingers probing her tender opening to gather her juices, was making Portia feel quite light-headed. She was desperate to feel him inside her.

It wasn't long before he complied with her wishes. Egged on by the excited crowd, he sank his cock into her wet and willing passage, her flesh gripping him tightly as he did so. He really was huge, filling her as she had seldom been filled before.

At first he moved slowly and carefully in and out. The sensation was delicious as he penetrated her again and again. Gradually, he grew more excited. His breath became rasping and his tempo quickened; he held her in place with his hands on her hips, his fingers biting deep into the well-toned muscles of her buttocks.

Dizzy, her most sensitive flesh being pounded by an animal-sized cock, Portia came again and again. This time Brian seemed in no hurry, capable of carrying on forever. Suddenly she felt his thumb probing the tight sphincter of her anus once again. He circled it slowly, urging her to open and let him in, sinking his whole thumb inside when she did so, moving it around her smooth, tight walls.

'Oh God, I'm coming! I'm coming again,' she cried.

'That's it! Let it go. Let it go,' urged Brian, pumping his hips hard into her, his heavy balls banging against her over-stimulated sex. As he felt her body convulse once more, Brian came with a gargantuan yell and a violent jerk of his hips, the tip of his cock touching the mouth of her womb, intensifying her orgasm to excruciating heights.

Portia tried to rise to her feet and Brian offered her a helping hand, his powerful arms supporting her till she could walk unsteadily back to the changing room. Once there she sent Bas for another double scotch, well-pleased with her evening. She was sure she had done enough to give Clarissa a run for her money in the Treasure Hunt and she herself had had the best fuck she had had in a long time.

The door opened and Brian came in. 'Any time you fancy a return booking, the lads said they'd be delighted to have you back. Here's your cash.' He smiled broadly, and passed her a buff envelope.

'Wait,' said Portia. 'For our survey, what do you do for a living?'

Bas sat, his pen poised above her Treasure Hunt card.

'Can't see that it matters, love, but I'm a policeman.' And he lumbered out of the room.

Twenty minutes later, dressed only in her skirt and jacket, Portia was standing on the kerb waiting for Bas to bring the car around. But when he pulled the black BMW up beside her, she changed her mind and sent him home. She would take a cab. After all, mini-cab driver was on her list. A deep voice behind her startled her.

'It's dangerous for a woman like you to be out on these streets on her own.' It was Brian.

'A woman like me?'

'A beautiful woman, with expensive clothes.' His breath was warm on her neck, he was standing so close. Portia could feel the soft hairs at her nape begin to tingle.

'I can look after myself.'

'I'm sure you can.'

'I need a mini-cab.'

'I'll drive you home.' His voice was strong and assertive, already convinced she would not say no.

'Are you a cab driver, too?'

'I can be anything you want me to be, love. Come on.' He wrapped his strong arm around her waist and led her to his car. Portia, smiling widely at the prospect of battle, offered no immediate resistance.

Ten

On the phone next day at eleven o'clock. Portia was no longer smiling. 'Yes, I suppose I will have to be in Edinburgh by Saturday. It's so tedious, but I may as well see this Hunt thing through to the end.' She listened for a moment to the voice on the other end. 'No, dear. Clarissa's been there all along – bonking her brains out, apparently.' She listened again, rolling her eyes in exasperation.

'Stephanie, darling, you're not listening. You could not possibly have seen Clarissa in the Caribbean on Tuesday – she hasn't left Edinburgh. Yes, of course I would expect you to recognise your own cousin when you saw her, but it's just impossible!' She was interrupted again, and this time listened for a long time. There was a calculating, unpleasant smile on her face as she put the phone down slowly.

'Basil! Basil! Come here at once. We are going to Edinburgh.'

Will had not asked to stay with Chrissy on Tuesday night, for which she had been grateful. Their love-making had been incredible – even better than the first time, but once again her mind was in turmoil and she needed time to herself. The fact that Will had understood this without being told only complicated the issue. He seemed determined not to put any pressure on her and, although he hadn't said anything, Chrissy suspected that he was falling in love with her. Never before had she met such a wonderful man, a man so in tune, and considerate of another person's feelings. Not to mention good-looking, rich and a fantastic lover to boot. She should have been delighted. Should have been – but wasn't.

After Will left, she had gone to bed, replete and exhausted, falling asleep instantly. But her sleep had been restless, her dreams disturbed by a faceless man with chilling blue eyes who watched over her with icy disapproval. In the dream Chrissy had tried desperately to talk to him, to ask what she had done to make him hate her so, but he could not or would not hear her. She had wanted to please him, wanted to melt the ice she saw in his eyes, but he had remained tantalisingly out of reach, ignoring her pleas, brutally cold and distant.

Eventually she had awoken, the sheets twisted round her damp body, the dream already fading.

Chrissy was confused and cross. She had spent a wonderful few hours making tender love with Will, but still it had been Ross who'd invaded her dreams, as indeed he had every night since she'd met him. In the previous night's dream Ross had hated her, but that was not always the case. Sometimes she awoke with the memory of a caress, a warm glow suffusing her body, the dream so real she could almost feel the softness of his kiss on her lips.

Things were just too complicated. She was developing strong feelings for both men: Will, who had been nothing but nice to her, and Ross, who had often been horrible. Why couldn't she fall for the nice guy for a change? Chrissy doubted very much if Portia was making the same mess of her Treasure Hunt.

The day was fresh and sunny and she decided to go for a run. She hadn't kept up her exercise regime since moving to Edinburgh and she missed it. A good run would loosen her up, clear her mind, and allow her to get her thoughts straight. Maybe she could get back into the spirit of things and have sex with the first man she met in the park, she mused. That would get her back on track.

Clarissa's bottomless wardrobe did contain clothes obviously designed for fitness, but like so many of her things they looked as if they had never been used: bought on a whim and then forgotten. The more Chrissy perceived of Clarissa's lifestyle, the more curious she became. What exactly did Clarissa do, she wondered, when she wasn't shopping?

A few moments' rummaging produced a pair of blue satin running shorts, edged in white and cut very high around the legs, and a cropped yellow top that left her midriff bare and stretched tightly over her breasts. Luckily she had brought her own running shoes with her; they weren't quite as grand as some of Clarissa's but definitely more functional.

She was just finishing tying the shoes when there was a sudden loud knock at the front door. Chrissy hoped fervently that it was neither Ross nor Will. She did not particularly feel up to facing either of then. It was this thought that made her nip into the sitting room and sneak a look out of the window before going to the door. Standing on her doorstep, lounging lazily against the railing, was a tall, sandy-haired teenager. She did not recognise the boy, but certainly recognised the type: the macho swagger of male youth combined with the arrogant self-assurance so often seen in the children of the rich. The thought came to her, unbidden, that Ross would have been just such a teenager; though probably not Will.

The young man's composure dissappeared when Chrissy opened the door in her shiny blue shorts and crop top. He gawped awkwardly, somewhere in the region of her breasts and bare tummy.

'Yes?' She tried not to smile at his expression.

'What? Oh, I'm sorry. Ms Asquith? I'm Dominic Somers. My grandmother sent me with this.' He held out a small flat package wrapped in brown paper.

'What is it?' Chrissy reached out curiously, aware of how her breasts jiggled when she moved her arm, and aware of his eyes following their movement. He was actually quite good-looking, close up, and a little older than she had first thought. His T-shirt bore a political slogan and his sandy hair was cut in a short spiky style. But a smattering of freckles across his nose gave him a boyish charm that the gold ring through one of his nostrils could not entirely cancel out. He might have been aiming to look like a rebel, but she suspected that he was just another polite, well brought-up boy underneath. She smiled at herself, feeling old.

'Jewellery, I think,' he answered her question, still addressing her breasts. In a grown man Chrissy would have found this habit irritating but in the youth it was quite endearing. It did not help that she could feel her nipples rise and harden from the cool air of the doorstep. Dominic gulped before continuing, finally managing to drag his green eyes to her face. 'I'm not sure, but it's something she borrowed from you? She doesn't trust the post and she was too ill to return it herself so she asked me to bring it.'

Thank God for that, thought Chrissy. His grandmother, whoever she was, would have been sure to recognise her as an imposter.

'Thanks very much. It was good of you to bring it.'

She waited for him to say something else, or leave, but he seemed hypnotised by her breasts, his only lapse of concentration when his eyes briefly strayed to her legs. Chrissy ought to have been annoyed on principle but found his awkward admiration rather sweet.

'Would you like to come in?'

Using considerable strength of will to keep his eyes on her face and away from the magnets of her protruding nipples, Dominic tried for a casual tone. 'Yes. That is, if you're not too busy.'

'No, I was just going for a run, but that can wait. Would you like a drink? Coffee? Or there's coke in the fridge.'

'Do you have any beer?' he asked, squaring his shoulders.

'Beer?' she tried to keep the smile out of her voice. 'It's nine o'clock in the morning. Isn't it a little early?'

'Oh, right.' He grinned sheepishly 'I'm making a complete prat of myself, aren't I? Coke would be great.'

Chrissy grinned and led the way to the kitchen. She turned from the fridge to find him staring at her satin-covered bottom. His legs and lower half were tucked well under the table, out of sight, and she suspected she knew why. Oh, the trials and tribulations of youth!

Dominic pressed the cold can against his forehead. 'It's hot.'

He did indeed look hot. Chrissy smiled, knowing exactly where his thoughts were and beginning to have a few ideas of her own. What had she just been thinking about after all, but getting back on track with the Treasure Hunt?

'Are you a student?' she asked, seating herself beside him.

'Yes. Well that is, I start in October.' Which made him at least eighteen.

'Oh? I'd have thought you'd have been off somewhere this

summer – on a kibbutz or trekking across America or whatever it is students do these days.'

Dominic was visibly more at ease now. 'I should be,' he said, his expression glum. 'All my friends are. But Gran was taken ill and I felt I should stay. It was the responsible thing to do.' He looked at Chrissy for approval, confirming her opinion of him as a nice, likeable lad.

'That was kind of you. Is she OK?'

He shrugged. 'Just one of her turns, you know? She'll be fine.'

'Actually, Dominic, I don't know your grandmother. I'm not Clarissa Asquith. I'm a friend of hers. My name's Chrissy.'

Dominic didn't bother to ask why she hadn't put him straight earlier. It didn't matter to him one way or another – except that he was relieved that he hadn't got a hard-on from looking at one his grandmother's chums. That would just have been too gross.

'So, have all your friends gone, then?'

'Yeah. It's a pain. Seriously boring.' He was regaining his self-assurance, beginning to relax. 'In fact, this is the worst summer of my life,' he added theatrically.

'Can't be that bad,' laughed Chrissy. He had very nice eyes. 'What about your girlfriend?'

'Girlfriend? Gran doesn't approve of girlfriends. She thinks they distract me from my studies.'

Chrissy looked at this lanky youth with his nose ring and green eyes and felt that his grandmother was probably a very wise woman.

'What's worse,' confided Dominic, warming to his theme, and relaxing even more now that he knew she had no connection with his grandmother, 'is that when they come back they'll do nothing but brag about all the . . . stuff they've got up to.'

'Stuff?'

'You know. Sex and stuff. Everyone knows that girls in Europe are gasp—er . . . more mature and physical than British girls.' He was blushing to the roots of his spiky hair. His intention had been to shock her, but he had only managed to embarrass himself.

Chrissy laughed again. 'Well, can't you just bluff, pretend you've done "stuff" too?'

'Won't work,' he assured her dolefully. 'That's what we've always done in the past, but if they've actually done it then they'll be sure to know I'm lying. They'll see right through me. It'll be months before I know any girls at Uni well enough to get very far. I'll be so self-conscious being the only virgin on campus that I'll probably do something really stupid. Word will get round and I'll never live it down. I can see it all. No. I'm obviously doomed never to have sex; I'll be the eternal virgin. I think I'm just going to kill myself now and save myself the embarrassment.'

'Well, we can't have that,' Chrissy laughed again. 'How would it be if I gave you a few pointers?'

He was silent for a moment, suspecting she was making fun of him. Gorgeous women did not come on to boys like him every day. 'What kind of pointers?' he asked cagily.

'Anything you like.' She smiled again. It was obvious he found her attractive – correction, found women in general very attractive – but she wasn't going to push him into anything.

'Are you trying to seduce me?' he asked suspiciously, 'Because if you are then I'm all for it!'

Chrissy leaned closer and touched his hand. Dominic jumped then cursed as he knocked over his can of coke. When the cold liquid trickled onto his lap he leapt to his feet, hot and embarrassed by her words and his clumsiness.

'Hey, don't worry.' Chrissy was there, dabbing at his jeans with a tea-towel. She could feel the hard heat of his erection through the wet denim, and felt an anticipatory flush begin to creep over her own skin. She rocked back on her heels and looked up at him, hazel eyes glittering. 'You can't go till we get these dried, anyway, can you?'

'I . . . I don't suppose so.' Disbelief wrestled with hope as Chrissy knelt down and pressed her hand lightly on the hard bulge she could feel through his damp jeans.

'About those pointers?' She massaged his erection through the denim.

Dominic closed his eyes, enjoying what her hand was doing to him, but still not believing it. He took a deep breath, then blurted, 'Can I see your breasts?' as if testing her.

'I think we can do better than that.' Slowly, with infinite

care, Chrissy began to undo the buttons on his jeans, looking up into his face as she slipped each stud through its buttonhole. There was no mistaking his desire for her. Desire for sex, Chrissy corrected herself. The erection she revealed was long and slender, like its owner, and Chrissy longed to take it in her mouth, to see if it fulfilled its promise of youthful firmness.

'You have a beautiful penis, Dominic,' she told him. He grinned at her, a mixture of boyish pride and relief that it was normal. With a sudden burst of confidence he pulled his T-shirt over his head, revealing a smooth, hairless chest. His body was thin but not soft, and Chrissy could already see the promise of the man's body he would soon achieve. She tugged at the waistband of his jeans, eager now to see him naked. The jeans were wet from the coke and proved difficult, so Dominic had to help her ease them down. By the time he had struggled out of his Doc Marten boots and wriggled out of the wet jeans, they were both laughing and more relaxed.

Chrissy was still kneeling in front of him. 'Do you know what I want to do now?'

He shook his head, but licked his lips excitedly. 'I want to taste your cock. What do you think your friends would think of that?'

He tried to hide his shock at her use of the word 'cock'. 'I don't think they'd believe me.'

'As long as you believe me.' Chrissy gently reached out and cradled his testicles in one hand while wrapping the fingers of the other over the base of his shaft. As she had expected she could feel the vibrant throbbing of his arousal, the blood pumping through her grasp to swell his erection even further. Experimentally, she moved her hand up and down his shaft a few times, thrilling at the power she could feel flowing through him.

Suddenly Dominic gave a groan and a hot jet of semen splashed onto Chrissy's T-shirt.

'Shit, shit shit,' he moaned, close to tears with embarrassment.

Chrissy jumped to her feet to reassure him, but he would not meet her eye. 'Dominic?' She took his face in both hands and forced him to look at her. 'Dominic, it's all right. It's not over.'

Eventually her words seemed to get through and he raised his eyes to look into hers. 'I'm sorry. I knew I would do something stupid and . . . God, I'm so embarrassed.'

Chrissy pressed her lips to his, cutting off his words. 'Have you any idea how exciting it was for me to watch you come? To know that you were so turned on just by my touch?' Chrissy was breathing hard and began to run her fingers through his short hair, kissing him again, harder this time, her passion rising. As her tongue slipped between his lips, she met his initial resistance, coaxing her way further in, till he greedily countered her thrusting tongue with his own. By the time they broke away, each gasping audibly, Chrissy could feel him already growing hard again, his cock rising up to press into her belly.

'Would you like to take my top off?' she whispered, her lips brushing his ear. 'It can go in the machine with your jeans.'

'Could I?' Dominic's green eyes glittered like jewels but he took his time as he eased the stretchy fabric over her head, revealing her breasts to his gaze for the first time. Chrissy had to lift her arms high to help him off with it, and each breast bounced with the movement. Dominic's eyes followed them with awe.

'Do you like my breasts, Dominic? Why don't you touch them? It feels so nice to have a man's hands on them.' Holding his eye she cupped her breasts in her hands and offered them to him, inviting his caress. Dominic's hand shook, but he reached out and tentatively stroked down one smooth slope, rolling the nipple gently between his fingers. Chrissy hissed, a thrill of excitement running through her.

'Did I hurt you?' He pulled his hand away as if she had slapped him and she hurried to reassure him once again.

'No. It was wonderful.' She took his hand and placed it on her breast again. This time he needed no second bidding. He massaged her gently, then with more assurance as Chrissy moaned and leaned into his touch. Finally he bent his head and kissed each rosy tip, and Chrissy cried out as his teeth raked over the sensitive skin. She felt an answering pull deep within her womb, felt her own sex swell. She longed to have him inside her, but she was enjoying her role as teacher too much to hurry things.

'Come here.' She led the way through to the living room; his erection bobbed alluringly in front of him. Chrissy lay on the settee and pulled him down on top of her. Dominic was fascinated by her breasts and buried his face in them, responding willingly to Chrissy's gentle guidance, and soon learned how to drive her wild with pleasure with his mouth and his hands. She moaned and writhed, her fingers entwined in his short hair, and yearned for him to touch her between the legs, to relieve the pressure that was building there. But he was too inexperienced, waiting for more guidance.

'Why don't you take my shorts off?' she whispered in his ear.

Dominic froze for a moment at her words, then slowly sat up, perching on the edge of the settee and looking down at her. Chrissy was breathing hard, her chest heaving up and down, and the movement of her breasts held his attention for a moment. Then his gaze settled on the skimpy satin shorts, his eyes lingering on the darker patch at the crotch, dampened by her arousal.

Chrissy held her breath and waited, desperate for his touch. Eventually, as if in a dream, Dominic hooked his fingers under the waistband of her shorts and slowly rolled them down. At the first touch of his fingers Chrissy felt her stomach muscles tighten in anticipation and eagerly raised her hips up to help him all she could. But Dominic was not to be hurried. He continued to roll the shorts down slowly over her mound. If he was surprised by the lack of pubic hair he did not show it, only continued the infinitely slow movement until he slipped the shorts over her ankles and dropped them on the floor. Chrissy lay naked before him.

'Can I see your—' his voice was hoarse and his face flushed as he could not quite bring himself to say the word.

Understanding, Chrissy allowed one foot to fall on the floor, In this position her labia parted slightly, her inner lips, excited and swollen, opening like the petals of a flower to his gaze. Chrissy could feel the warm sweet honey lubricating her body and wondered if Dominic would recognise the extent of her arousal. Well, she was the teacher. It was up to her to tell him.

'I want you, Dominic. I want you to make love to me. See how I need you?' She touched her own fingers to the entrance of her body, drawing up the heavy moisture which bathed the lips of her sex in glistening dew.

Dominic seemed to snap out of his trance. He moved swiftly to cover her with his body, supporting himself with his arms while his cock nudged instinctively for her opening.

'Wait!' Chrissy stopped him. If she was being his teacher she had better make sure he learned all his lessons. 'Have you got a condom?' she asked.

For a moment he looked at her in confusion. Then his eyes cleared. 'Yes,' he told her proudly. 'There are some in my wallet. I've had them since I was fifteen.'

'Great,' Chrissy laughed. 'But perhaps we'd better use one of mine.' She leapt to her feet and returned with a condom which she quickly rolled into place. 'OK, where were we?'

But now Dominic did not seem to be in quite so much of a hurry. Chrissy spread her legs as far as the cramped settee would allow. It was impossible to move much, so she closed her eyes and waited, inviting his touch, but careful not to demand too much before he was ready. Her body tensed when she finally felt his fingers delicately touch her sex, moving across the stretched membranes to explore and separate each sensitive fold.

'Yes, Dominic, that feels so good.' She murmured encouragement, covering his hand with her own, guiding him to the pulsing core of her excitement. He was an eager pupil and soon learned the rhythm and pressure that Chrissy liked most, bringing her repeatedly to the brink of orgasm, but not allowing her the release she now sought. After the third such time Chrissy looked at him suspiciously through lowered eyelids, but he seemed entirely innocent in the pleasure he was drawing from her willing body. It was so wonderful finding such an enthusiastic pupil, that she forced herself to relax. It was not often one came across a man who so genuinely wanted to learn how to please a woman. But eventually her over-sensitised flesh could take no more.

'Please, Dominic, I need to feel you inside me now,' she whispered urgently. He grinned at her, absurdly pleased with himself, and for a second he looked as if he might resist a bit longer. Enough, thought Chrissy, reaching for his cock and expertly rubbing it to full hardness. His resistance disappeared as she had known it would and he clambered to lie on top of her. Chrissy took his face in her hands and kissed him deeply. This time when his cock sought her entrance, she tilted her hips up to meet him, still kissing him hard as he glided smoothly inside her. Chrissy scissored her legs around his waist, pulling him even closer as his hips began to buck in an instinctive, primitive rhythm. She ground her swollen clitoris against him, striving for orgasm. When it came, she broke off their kiss to cry out, and as she arched away from him Chrissy saw the momentary elation in Dominic's green eyes before he pushed harder into her convulsing body, grunting his triumph and release as he ejaculated deep inside her.

'That was absolutely fantastic,' he crowed, still on a high.

'Mmmm.' Chrissy at this point would have liked to snuggle up to him and rest but Dominic, with the enthusiasm of youth, intended no such thing. As his penis slipped out of her he removed the condom and wriggled down her body for a closer look at her sex.

'You are just so beautiful,' he murmured, glancing up into her eyes. 'I've seen pictures, you know, but I never expected a real woman to be so ... so delicious!' He rubbed her naked mons with the palm of his hand. 'What happened to your pubic hair? Did you shave it off?'

Chrissy nodded, not trusting herself to speak. Did he have any idea what his restless hand was doing to her? She felt a familiar stirring and tingling spread across her skin.

'For a man?'

'For myself,' she stated and began to moan as his head dipped lower to touch some tentative kisses over her belly and inner thighs.

'Your skin is so soft,' he murmured, as if to himself. 'Why did no-one ever tell me women were so soft, or that they smelled so wonderful?' He breathed in the hot musky scent of Chrissy's aroused sex, moving his face ever nearer to her as he did so. 'I wonder if they taste good, too?'

His mouth was so close to her hot flesh that she could feel his breath as he exhaled. When his tongue came out to taste her, Chrissy jumped as though electrified, so intense was the sensation. Dominic only seemed half-aware of her reaction as he closed his eyes in bliss for a few seconds, before beginning a series of long slow sensuous licks over the entire area of Chrissy's throbbing pussy. With his tongue he teased the sensitive tip of her clitoris from its protective hood, and sucked it softly between his teeth for a few seconds before releasing it. Ripples of pleasure chased through Chrissy's body and she tangled her fingers in his hair again, urging him closer.

Dominic pressed his mouth against the open lips of her sex, kissing her as he had on her mouth, pushing his tongue to swirl inside and explore her opening, eagerly drinking the honey that flowed there. Chrissy moaned and writhed on the end of his probing tongue and he slipped his hands under her buttocks to lift her towards him, feasting on her pleasure, wanting to taste more and more of her.

Her excitement built to a point where she was almost delirious, as she wrapped her thighs tightly around his head. Dominic crushed his face into her, grinding his nose against the quivering bud of her clitoris. At last she gave a cry and shook in violent rapture as wave after wave of orgasm crashed through her. Gasping air deep into her lungs, Chrissy felt as though her entire body was melting, liquefying, as her straining muscles relaxed and she slumped once again onto the settee. Dominic grinned wickedly at her. 'This is great,' he enthused. 'I could keep this up all day!'

In a panic, Chrissy scrambled out of his grasp. 'Oh no you don't,' she warned. 'Even women need some time to recover.' She patted the settee and invited him to sit beside her. 'That was glorious,' she told him. 'If you continue to learn so quickly, there won't be a woman in Edinburgh who is able to resist you.'

'Yeah? Well, I have a great teacher. Come here.'

'Oh, no,' Chrissy squirmed away from him and slipped onto the floor between his knees. 'Now it's time for your reward for being such a willing pupil.' His cock was still rigid and pointing straight at the ceiling. It seemed to tremble when she brushed her fingers along its length, tracing the thick vein on the underside. The loose skin covering the satiny tip was so soft and silky that she spent a few moments sliding it back and forth, making Dominic gasp aloud. Chrissy was in no hurry. With her other hand she reached between his legs to gently cup

144

his scrotum, feeling the weight and heat of his balls, as she explored him with infinite sensitivity.

The room was quiet, save for Dominic's ragged breathing. Chrissy continued to indulge herself, playing with his erection, sweeping her long hair back and forth across his belly, driving him to distraction and prolonging the pleasure for both of them. Eventually, holding his eye with her own, Chrissy took his shaft in her hand and lowered her mouth over the tip, eagerly sucking him in till he bumped the back of her throat. He seemed to grow and swell even more in the warmth and moisture of her mouth, but she held him firmly, one hand working the base of his shaft, as her lips and tongue swirled around his glans, drinking the dewy moisture she found there, coaxing more from the tiny slit with the tip of her tongue.

Dominic was breathing heavily now, his hands entangled in Chrissy's hair as he gazed at her in wonder. His skin felt hot and damp beneath her fingers and she could sense from the growing tension in his body that he was very close to coming. Chrissy began to suck him in earnest, her head moving up and down as she flicked her tongue firmly over the bulbous head. Her hand returned to massage his balls and she could feel the seed gathering there, ready for its sudden race along his shaft. She sucked even harder, drawing him in more deeply. Dominic cried out, his body rigid, his cock slipping from between her lips, pumping jet after jet of semen in the air as she continued to work him expertly with her hand. Chrissy lay her cheek on his flat stomach as they both rested.

'I want to move in with you and be your sex slave. To hell with university,' said Dominic, stroking her hair.

'Tough!' Chrissy slapped him on the thigh. 'This is a one-off lesson.' She jumped to her feet, pulling him up with her. 'Still, it should give you a few things to tell your friends when they come back bragging of their exploits.'

Dominic surprised her. 'Oh no,' he murmured. 'I won't be telling them anything. This is just for me to remember – the best day of my life.'

'Well, it's not quite over yet. Why don't we go and have a shower? Then we can do some revision. I want to be sure you have learnt your lessons well.'

'Great!' Laughing, he grabbed her hand and they ran towards the stairs, his youthfully enthusiastic cock leading the way.

In the queue at the delicatessen, Ross glanced impatiently at his watch, awaiting his sandwich and coffee. As usual he was in a hurry. It was always the same at work – either he was rushed off his feet, or he sat about idly with nothing to do, waiting for the phone to ring. Today was one of the busy days. Handing his money to the assistant, he took the bag containing his lunch and turned towards the door.

'Hi, Ross. I thought it was you. Hang on, we can have lunch together.'

'Will? Sorry, I'd love to, but I don't have time.'

'Come on, what's the rush? Everyone's entitled to a break. Ten minutes won't kill you.'

Ross looked at his watch, shrugged and grinned at his friend. 'OK. Ten minutes. I'll grab a table.'

He was seated, already snatching bites of his sandwich by the time Will sat down.

'I just missed you the other night. At Orlando's. With Chrissy.'

Ross choked on his sandwich, wondering exactly what Will had seen. Then he choked again, when he realised what Will had said. 'Chrissy? What do you mean Chrissy? Who told you? Who else knows?'

Will thumped him on the back till he was sure that Ross had stopped coughing. 'You OK? She did. Chrissy did. Said she hated to lie to me.'

Ross let this sink in for a second, working out the implications. 'So you've seen her again?' he asked carefully.

'Sure. A couple of times. Isn't she a great girl?'

'What do you mean, a couple of times? For God's sake, Will, what do you think you are playing at? A woman like that will chew you up and spit you out.'

'No, she won't,' smiled Will. 'You've got her all wrong, Ross. She's much nicer than that. You just don't know her as well as I do.'

Ross bit back the comment that he knew her type very well, thank you. He was appalled to hear that his shy, gentle friend had been taken in by Chrissy's act. Appalled and more than a little jealous, if he was reading the dreamy look in Will's eye correctly. What the hell was Chrissy up to now?

Will was still talking. 'You've misjudged her from the beginning, Ross. She just has some things to work out of her system, that's all. She just needs some time.'

Ross couldn't believe what he was hearing. 'Some things to get out of her system? That's a novel way of putting it. I for one would not be prepared to sit at home while the woman I loved screwed around, just to get things out of her system,' he snarled, crushing the polystyrene cup his coffee had come in.

Will was watching him closely, had been since the start of the conversation. He was neither stupid nor as naive as Ross always believed him to be. Now he saw beyond the anger to the pain in Ross's eyes. Even worse, he remembered the animated light in Chrissy's beautiful eyes whenever Ross's name was mentioned, even when she was complaining about his unreasonable behaviour. Now he saw the same light, tinged with hurt, in Ross's eyes. It occurred to Will that Ross was in love with Chrissy; and even worse, she with him. He wondered if either of them had admitted the truth to themselves yet.

He sighed deeply. Well, he might have the reputation for being Mr Nice Guy, but he certainly wasn't going to make things too easy for Ross; let him work it out for himself. Suddenly he remembered the reason he wanted to speak to him. 'Ross. Portia's back.'

Ross, having finished his lunch, was already on his feet. 'Shit,' he said and sat back down with a bump.

Eleven

All afternoon Ross wondered about phoning Chrissy to warn her of Portia's return, but didn't. Hell, maybe Will had already phoned her. An emotion that wasn't – couldn't be – jealousy twisted through him at the thought. He and Chrissy had not spoken since he'd walked out on her in Orlando's. Guilt and embarrassment shot through him, sharp and painful, every time he thought of his behaviour that night. He'd behaved like such a jerk. More than anything he wanted to call and apologise, but what could he say, what excuse could he give? Chances were she wouldn't even speak to him, give him enough time to tell her how sorry he was.

Christ, he really had made a mess of this.

No matter what he did, no matter what he told himself, he could not get Chrissy out of his mind. Even now that he knew Will was involved with her too, he could not stop thinking about her. Every night he woke, hard and aching from wanting her. However he tried to fight it, however he pushed the memory away, he could not forget the sight of her, the feel of her, the taste of her. She was like an illness, a fever he could not shake. He wanted her more than he ever had done. Only now, after the way he had behaved, she would surely have nothing to do with him.

He should phone and warn her that Portia was back though; but he was frightened to. Frightened of what she would say, of how much hurt a few well-deserved words could bring him. Ross despised himself for his cowardice, but still could not make himself pick up the phone. He would wait. Give her a little more time to calm down, then she might be more likely to listen to his apology, even if she didn't accept it. He didn't allow himself even to think of Will and how his friend's love for Chrissy would complicate the issue.

But events the next day forced his hand.

The day had started early for Ross. Despite fierce competition from developers, Down and Out had managed to acquire a dilapidated tenement in one of the ancient streets behind Edinburgh Castle. It was largely thanks to Ross's fierce campaigning that the building was not to be turned into yet more luxury flats. Instead it was to be carefully restored to provide comfortable and quality short-term accommodation for the many people who slept rough in the all but derelict property and others like it. It was planned to be a half-way house to independence: a home of their own.

Ross had argued that throwing these people back on the streets would only worsen a problem that Edinburgh liked to keep well-hidden from the tourists. And, thanks to his fierce determination, he had won. Ruthlessly using his impressive connections, he had gained the support of the media, the church, the people of Edinburgh and eventually, largely because they had no choice, the City Council.

The task before them had been daunting. The building was really not much more than a shell, but Ross was determined that it would be finished and fully occupied by the time Edinburgh's cruel winter set in. Today he had gone to the site to do a spot check on how the work was progressing. He liked to go early before any one else arrived. It wasn't that he didn't trust the contractors – he had appointed most of them himself – it was just that this job was so important, meant so much to him, that he had to ensure that it was done properly. So he often looked around on his own.

And today he was glad he had. One of the flats, more than likely the one he would have been shown if he had announced his arrival, was progressing nicely and contained the bathroom, kitchen and central heating system that Down and Out had paid for. Only one of the flats though. In the others he checked, many contained fittings of inferior standard. For instance, fires and boilers of lower specification had been installed in some of the flats. In others some equipment was missing altogether; showers were missing from bathrooms and fridges were in the kitchen where fridge-freezers should have stood.

As Ross wandered round, he could feel the anger beginning

to boil inside him. But by the time the first of the workmen arrived it had been replaced by a chilling rage that was reflected in the stiffness of his shoulders, the hard set of his jaw and the cold glitter in his pale eyes. Though he was dressed casually, in jeans and T-shirt little different from their own, the workmen recognised the authority and anger in his eyes and did not question his right to be there.

They started work, but watched with wary interest as Ross tore a strip off the foreman, the contractor, and finally the architect who was hurriedly brought from his office to try and placate him. Ross paced in fury, making a visible and not very successful effort to control his temper as he listened to their excuses, exclamations of surprise and horror, and attempts to pass the buck. Finally he cut them short, barking a promise to involve his lawyers and the media first thing on Monday morning if the work was not put right over the weekend, storming out before they could tell him it was impossible.

He was glad to get out of the place before he hit someone. How he despised dishonesty and petty corruption! Especially when someone was stealing from a charity – from the poor – to line their own, already well-filled pockets.

Ross walked back to his own office, his hands stuffed deep in the pockets of his jeans and his body tight with tension. He did not want to take his foul humour back to work with him. God knows he had been ratty enough with his colleagues these past few days. The walk took half an hour, and did manage to calm him a little, so he was able to smile an almost cheery greeting to his assistant.

'Ross,' she called out as he headed for the closed door of his office, 'there's someone waiting for you. She's been there a while.'

She? Chrissy? Still moving quickly, he pushed open the door, but two strides into the room he stopped dead. 'What the hell are you doing here?' A day that started out badly had suddenly turned much worse.

'Ross,' purred Portia, sitting at his desk and ignoring the sharpness of his greeting, 'It's so lovely to see you. Where have you been? Darling, I've been waiting ages!' She pouted slightly, the expression emphasising her deeply crimson lips and heavily made-up eyes. She was a strikingly good-looking woman, probably one of the most beautiful women he had ever seen, but Ross was unmoved by her. He stayed where he was near the door, keeping it open.

'What do you want, Portia? I'm afraid you've come at a very bad time. I'm rather busy.'

He had noticed the odd way Portia was dressed and had even known the significance of it, though he hoped he had kept this recognition out of his eyes. The black shiny silk trench coat, unbuttoned but cinched in tightly at the waist with a belt, was totally incongruous considering the beautiful July sunshine outside. The soft material clung to her body, its shiny surface catching the light, reflecting every curve and seeming to shimmer with movement.

Ross's mouth went dry, but he consciously did not allow himself to lick his lips. He was not going to let Portia know that he remembered when she had last worn the coat. It had been on their very first date. They had been on their way to a party at someone's country house and stopped off at a pub for a drink. Portia had leaned towards Ross as he stood at the bar and whispered that she was naked under the coat, her tongue lightly brushing his ear.

Ross had managed to choke out his order to the waiting barman, had even managed to finish his drink, before he had marched her outside and had taken her right there in the car park, first against the wall of the pub, then again in the back seat of his car, both of them so turned-on they hadn't cared if anyone saw them. They had never made it to the party that night. Despite his attempts at indifference, Ross could tell that Portia knew exactly what he was thinking.

She gave a knowing little smile. 'Yes, Ross, I wore it just for you,' she said softly, tugging gently at her belt as she spoke, allowing it to fall open, revealing that she was, once more, naked underneath.

'For fuck's sake!' Ross slammed his door shut, but stood with his back to it, keeping the distance between them. 'What the hell are you playing at? Will you get dressed and go?' he hissed. 'It's over, Portia. Over.'

Portia placed her hands on her hips, holding the coat open so

151

he had an unobstructed view. She said nothing, watching him closely, a slight smile curling her lip.

Ross looked; he couldn't help it. Her high breasts were round and full, the red nipples kept erect by the tiny silver rings through them, linked by a fine, shimmering silver chain. More jewellery glittered and danced in the thick black bush of her pubic hair, making him suspect that her nipples were not the only part of her anatomy to be pierced. Ross tried very hard to keep his eyes on her face.

'The thought of someone coming in never bothered you in the past, I seem to remember,' Portia smiled provocatively. 'In fact, if I recall correctly, it added a certain delicious *frisson* to our love-making.' She stood up deliberately and turned her back on him, slowly bending over his desk, lifting her coat to reveal her creamy-white bottom, twisting round to look at him invitingly in a classic erotic magazine pose. She was absolutely stunning; all soft white curves against the blackness of the silk, her breasts falling gently from her ribcage, quivering as she breathed, the silver chain between them tinkling on the desktop.

Ross's eyes followed the gentle movement, but he was pleased to find that he had no difficulty in resisting her. 'No, Portia,' he said coldly, 'it was you who used to get such a thrill knowing that someone might walk in on us. I always hated it.'

Portia digested this piece of information for a moment. Something shifted behind her eyes and they narrowed slightly. This was not going to be the pushover she was used to. It was a unique experience to have to ask twice. She moved her bottom enticingly.

'OK, darling, lock the door if it will make you feel better. But I'm ready for you, Ross. I'm so wet; give it to me long and hard, the way you used to. Please, darling?' She swayed her hips and again something glittered alluringly in the blackness of her pubic hair.

Only Portia could wear diamonds in her labia. 'For God's sake, Portia! Put it away. I've told you. I've got work to do.'

It occurred to Portia that he might actually be serious, that he was turning her down. Slowly she straightened up, a hint of doubt registering in her eyes for a second. She walked across the office till she was standing just in front of him, her hard nipples brushing his chest. Although she was tall, she had to bend her head back to look at him. 'Are you really turning me down, Ross?'

'Just go, Portia,' he said wearily. 'I had enough of your games a long time ago.'

Portia looked at him for a long time. 'OK,' she said, surprising him with how easily she had given in. She pulled the coat round her but did not tie the belt, then sat down, blinking obliquely up at him. 'I think I'll go and visit Clarissa.'

'What?' Now she had his full attention.

'Clarissa. She seems to be doing awfully well on the Treasure Hunt, with your help. Maybe she'll give me some tips, even if you won't.' She was watching Ross's reaction carefully. Of course he had to be in on whatever it was Clarissa was up to; he was her referee, after all. She saw the alarm in his eyes and hid a smile.

'There's no point,' he said quickly. 'Leave Clarissa alone. You'll see her on Saturday.'

'There's nothing in the rules to say that we can't get together to discuss the technicalities.' Portia stood up and stepped towards him; she ran a red fingernail gently down the line of his jaw, smiling again when Ross flinched slightly. 'No, I'm here, and I'm bored, thanks to you. I'll just go and pay her a visit.'

'You can't,' said Ross, louder than he intended to. 'She won't be in today.'

Portia gave him a slow smile, carefully re-fastening the belt on her coat. 'It's very strange, the way you have become so protective of Clarissa all of a sudden. You know, Willie Barnes was exactly the same when I spoke to him. It's heartwarming, really. But I think I'll drop in on her anyway.' She reached up and placed a kiss on his lips before leaving, Ross too distracted to prevent her.

Christ, could this day get any worse? he wondered, running his hands through his unruly black hair. Now he was going to have to face Chrissy. And soon. He had to get hold of her before Portia did.

Chrissy had actually managed to get out for a run this time, wearing the same blue satin shorts and skimpy yellow top she had chosen for her previous attempt, when she had allowed herself to be distracted by Dominic. She had decided to go to a small park nearby, rather than attempt a longer run. The short walk there would do as a warm up, and anyway, it would have been foolish to attempt anything too ambitious when she was so out of practice.

On the way, Chrissy thought about Ross. She hadn't heard from him for a few days now, and her feelings were mixed. On the one hand, it was probably for the best; she did not need the complications of Ross's moralistic disapproval and his unpredictable mood swings. On the other hand, she missed him dreadfully.

Arriving at the park. Chrissy put Ross firmly from her mind. She took a quick look round, doing a few stretches. Surprisingly, for the heart of a busy city, it was almost deserted. There was an old woman walking a dog and some young mothers pushing buggies near the pond. As she warmed up, Chrissy noticed a young man walking down the grassy slope towards a large willow tree overhanging the pond. He was carrying books and folders as well as a rug and a polystyrene cup of coffee. She thought that he was probably a student, here for a day's serious studying.

Her route round the edge of the pond and up a hill towards the far gate took her quite close to him and she was aware of his eyes on her as she jogged quickly past, her long legs moving easily, her breasts bouncing freely without the support of a bra. The feeling was not uncomfortable and the friction, causing her nipples to push erect through the fabric of her top, added a pleasant dimension to her run.

The day was beginning to warm up and Chrissy had worked up quite a sweat by the time she passed the student again. This time he smiled at her, his eyes lingering appreciatively on her prominent nipples and the patches of sweat on her yellow top. There was nothing offensive in his look, just admiration, and Chrissy smiled back. Even after she passed him, she could feel his eyes following her. She was aware of how her satin shorts must look, how they would seem to shimmer and flow as she moved, caressing the shifting curves of her buttocks.

154

Part-way through the second lap, she began to tire and forced herself to slow down, reminding herself that she was unused to exercise. Breathing heavily, she decided to turn and retrace her footsteps rather than run the long way round again – maybe if she came back tomorrow she would manage another full circuit, but for today it was too much.

The student did not look up as she approached; she saw that he was engrossed not in his book but the morning newspaper. Slowing her steps slightly, Chrissy watched him as he sipped his coffee. He was older than she had first thought, in his early twenties at least, and pleasant-looking rather than handsome. He had chosen a good spot, fairly well-hidden by the hanging fronds of the willow tree and she had to squint slightly to see him properly. Lying beside him on the rug was his T-shirt – he obviously intended to sunbathe while he studied. His chest was smooth and muscular, completely hairless and the brown discs of his nipples were as hard and puckered as Chrissy's own.

She noticed all this as she passed, unaware that her steps had slowed even further. Her mind was on the Treasure Hunt. How, if she was playing the game properly, she would approach him, slip between the fronds of the willow, remove her top and . . . Here in the park in broad daylight? Who was she kidding? She grinned to herself.

'Chrissy!' So engrossed had she been in her fantasy, Chrissy had not heard anyone come up behind her. She jumped almost out of her skin.

Ross had intended to go straight to Clarissa's, but then he had remembered this park only a few streets away. A few minutes to take a walk and calm down again had seemed like a good idea. The last thing he needed was to go straight to Chrissy with his hackles already up. That was no way to start an apology.

He had calmed down, enjoying the haven of peace the little park offered, watching appreciatively as the female jogger ran round the pond, her long legs moving easily; he had been astounded when he recognised her as Chrissy. At that point, before she got close enough to see him, she seemed to run out of steam. She slowed her pace and rested for a few moments before retracing her steps, moving away from him. Ross hurried after her. God, she was beautiful. He felt a familiar stirring in his groin as he watched her blue satin bottom walk before him. He was close enough to see her turn her head and look, rather speculatively, he thought, at the man sunbathing under the willow tree.

'Chrissy!' He saw her jump and turn to face him, delight springing to her eyes when she recognised him. But Ross looked over her shoulder to the sunbather. 'Not interrupting anything, I hope?' he asked, tightly, then cursed himself and his jealousy. That was not what he had intended to say at all. He saw the light dim in Chrissy's hazel eyes and her shoulders slump slightly.

'Hi, Ross,' she said flatly. 'Nice to see you, too. Is it time for my lecture?' She looked theatrically at her watch. 'I must have forgotten.' Turning she began to walk away.

Ross could have kicked himself. He took a deep breath and called her name again, his voice gentler this time than Chrissy had ever heard it before. She also heard the hesitation and uncertainty in it. Slowly she turned back to face him, her eyes wary.

'Wait, Chrissy, please. Can you forget I just said that? I've come to apologise and invite you out for lunch. I'm sorry.'

There was nothing quite so disarming as a genuine apology and Chrissy could hear the sincerity in his voice. But she was rather confused. 'What exactly are you apologising for?' she asked carefully, her eyes skittering guiltily to the student who had occupied her fantasies a few moments before.

Ross shrugged wretchedly, unable to meet her eyes as he pushed his hair back wildly from his forehead. 'For my behaviour at Orlando's. For everything. For judging you without knowing the facts.'

'But you still don't know the facts.' She was puzzled, but she was not going to let him off the hook too lightly.

'I know. But they're none of my business.' He looked at her now and she was shocked by the deep shadows under his eyes. It was apparent that Ross had not been sleeping too well. He looked devastatingly handsome and rather dangerously so, but there was no doubting his sincerity. There was an intensity in his expression that Chrissy was at a loss to understand, but which had the strange effect of making her legs weaken. A shiver passed through her and she told herself it was just the sweat from her run cooling on her hot skin.

'OK,' she said, backing away from him slightly, 'apology accepted.'

Ross looked as if he was about to say something else but instead, with an angry, helpless gesture, he stepped closer. Swiftly he tangled his fingers in her hair and pulled her to him, capturing her mouth in a kiss that was both hard and intense. For a second Chrissy was taken by surprise; her hand came up as though to push him away, pressing against the hard muscle of his chest. But in the next instant her resistance vanished and she trembled against him, her mouth softening, yielding, as she parted her lips, allowing his tongue to delve inside and taste her sweetness. Feeling the touch of her tongue on his, Ross felt himself harden in immediate response and he ground his lips on hers, bruising the tender flesh in an attempt to assuage the hunger that tore through his body.

He wanted her, God, how he wanted her!

When they finally broke apart, he stared down at her, reading the confusion in her startled eyes and knowing that it was mirrored in his own. Consciously, he loosened his grip, but did not let go of her completely.

Chrissy finally found enough breath to speak. 'Ross, is there any insanity in your family?' she asked shakily.

For a long moment he stared at her, then grinned wickedly. 'Maybe. What about lunch? You never answered me.' His fingers were stroking the sweat-damp skin at the small of her back, making it impossible for her to concentrate.

'OK,' she gasped. 'Then will you tell me what this is all about?'

'Of course.' Ross brushed his lips over her forehead, tasting the sharp tang of salt on her skin and was rewarded by a powerful surge of lust, his cock straining against the thick denim of his jeans. He had to have her, and soon.

'Come on, my car is just around the corner.' He took her by the hand and began to pull her in the direction of the gate, but Chrissy resisted.

'No, wait. I'll have to go home first and take a shower.'

'You can shower at my house,' he said urgently, remembering how she had looked lying in his deep Victorian bath. He wanted to see her like that again.

'Ross.' There was a warning in Chrissy's voice, and she pulled her hand from his grasp. 'I'm going home to have a shower and change. Then I'll have lunch with you.'

Ross looked as if he was about to argue, but then he gave in. The last thing he needed at the moment was another fight. 'OK, but hurry. I'm starving,' he said by way of an excuse, though the look in his eyes suggested that food was the furthest thing from his mind.

It only took Chrissy ten minutes to shower and change, but she needed that time to gather her thoughts. That Ross's apology had been heartfelt and genuine, she was sure. And she also understood that he was apologising for more than his behaviour in the restaurant. But exactly what else was going on, she had no idea; she only knew that she liked it. This Ross, with the feral, lustful gleam in his eye, was the one she definitely preferred.

Having a hunch that food did not actually feature too prominently in Ross's plans for the afternoon, she did not waste too much time choosing clothes, but slipped on a simple short cotton dress then pulled a comb through her damp hair as she ran lightly down the stairs.

Ross was waiting impatiently, sheer strength of will preventing him from following Chrissy upstairs and into the shower. He felt wonderful. He loved Chrissy – he knew that now. It was such a relief not to have to struggle against his own emotions any longer, as if a great weight had been lifted off his shoulders. They would work things out. They had to. He was ready to take a risk again.

Chrissy came down the stairs, warm and damp, smelling of nothing more exotic than soap and shampoo. Ross felt his cock leap to attention, his stomach clench with the need to pull her into his arms and kiss her. She wore no make-up, her skin glowing with a clear translucence no amount of money could buy. Her clothes were practical and flattering, but even fully dressed she did more to raise his blood pressure than Portia had in all her naked splendour earlier that morning.

The thought of Portia jolted him out of him out of his trance. She could be here any minute.

'Let's go,' he said.

In Ross's battered old car, Chrissy was surprised to find that she was a little nervous. Ross seemed different, more at ease, as though he were no longer fighting some internal struggle; though the sexual heat was still there. She could see it in the way he looked at her legs, the way his eyes constantly strayed to her reflection in the mirror. At last she had to say something, just to break the silence. 'Don't you have to work today?'

Ross shot her a quick look. 'What? Oh, you mean the clothes? I was on a building site first thing this morning and this afternoon I had planned to visit one of our hostels. I rarely wear a suit for those kinds of visits. I don't want to stick out like a sore thumb.'

Chrissy turned in her seat and looked at him appraisingly. Was he serious? Wasn't he aware how his appearance jarred with his words? Ross flashed her a quick grin, his teeth perfectly white and even, his black hair gleaming and his blue eyes sparkling. He looked absolutely breathtaking. She frowned slightly. Although he was once again wearing jeans, they were still a designer label, and the blue T-shirt, which brought out the colour of his eyes so beautifully, bore a tiny logo on the pocket so exclusive she could not quite place it. And those teeth. Though undoubtedly his own, they were almost too perfect. No British child could go through the National Health system and emerge with teeth as even and white as that.

'Don't "the homeless" object to you swanning around in an outfit that probably costs more than a month's rent?' she teased.

'What?' Ross looked down at himself, puzzled. 'It's just a pair of jeans.'

'Armani,' she corrected him, 'and that suit the other day, you didn't get that in C&A.'

Ross was amazed at her words. 'I need a good suit for my work,' he said defensively, negotiating his way through the traffic. 'I meet with a lot of businessmen when I'm fund-raising. I can't look scruffy.'

'And the rest?'

159

'My mother buys a lot of my clothes,' he admitted slowly, affronted when Chrissy started giggling. 'But that's because I'm too busy most of the time to go shopping. People give me clothes and things for birthdays and Christmas.'

Chrissy laughed again. 'Your mother buys your clothes? How old are you, Ross Sinclair? Does she buy your underwear as well?'

'No,' he huffed. 'I never wear any.'

Chrissy smiled again, but his words drew her eyes to the crotch of his jeans, where the gentle swelling of his manhood was faintly outlined by the thick denim.

'You can check if you like.'

She realised he was watching her in the mirror, smiling.

'No, thanks.' She found herself blushing. 'I'll take your word for it.'

They drove on for a while, Ross seeming a little distracted by what she had said. Eventually he sighed. 'There's something you should know about me. Then we can have lunch, OK?'

Chrissy wondered what it could be, but nodded silently. Her bare thighs began to stick sweatily to the seat and she shifted her position. Ross too, seemed to be feeling the heat, for he glanced at her long tanned legs as she wriggled to get more comfortable, then quickly rolled his window down fully, a sheen of sweat on his upper lip.

He turned the car and they drove out into the country. Chrissy half-recognised the road to Ross's house and wondered if that was where they were going, but after a while Ross pulled off the road, parking the car beside a field. Wordlessly he climbed out and waited for Chrissy, looking out over the rolling fields as he stood with his back to her. An element of tension had returned to him, reflected in the stiffness of his shoulders. He climbed the fence, turning to help her over.

'Can you manage?'

'No mud this time?' Chrissy asked apprehensively.

'No mud.' He smiled, but there was a tightness about it, as though he found it difficult. Chrissy thought some of the light had gone out of his eyes.

'It says "Private Property".' She scrambled after him.

160

'It does, doesn't it? Come on, it's not far.' He led the way up the hill towards a small wood.

The wood was surprisingly dense and cool after the hot sunshine, but Ross did not linger. He held Chrissy's hand tightly. Fervently she hoped there was not going to be another one of his unpredictable mood-shifts, but this time she recognised his tension was not directed at her. Leaving the trees behind, they burst out into the sunshine. Chrissy blinked a few times, dazzled.

They were on top of a hill, a long, grassy slope rolling downwards. Far below them was a field in which horses grazed, their graceful heads lifted to watch them. Beyond the field was a house, although the word barely did justice to the huge, elegant U-shaped building, standing regal in the sunshine.

'This is my parents' home,' said Ross, his voice sounding angrier than the words seemed to demand.

Twelve

Chrissy had trouble finding her voice. 'Well, that explains the teeth,' she finally managed to blurt.

'What?' Her words forced Ross to look at her; he was totally thrown.

Chrissy smiled and shook her head. 'Nothing. But your work . . . Why did you choose a homeless charity?'

'Just to wind my father up,' he said bitterly, turning back to stare at the distant house, Chrissy looked at him hard and he shrugged. 'Well, that's what he would have you believe anyway. Look at this place. I could occupy ten rooms and no-one would even know I was here.

'I love my work,' he continued, a sadness in his blue eyes that Chrissy had never seen before. 'I genuinely believe I can make a difference, but every day I have to fight against hostility – from the people I work with, those that don't know me anyway – and from my own family who feel that what I do is a personal insult to their lifestyle.'

There was pain in his voice and Chrissy put her hand on his arm. 'I'm sure they are proud of you. And I'm sure that with your level of commitment you must be great at your job.'

Ross covered her hand with his, relaxing slightly. He smiled. 'I *know* I'm great at my job – with my family connections I'm the best bloody fund-raiser they have ever had. Can we sit down for ten minutes? There's something else I need to say to you.'

Ross lay on his side, leaning on one elbow, facing her, his concentration focused on a daisy that grew in the grass between them. Chrissy stretched out on the grass, staring up at the cloudless sky, waiting for whatever it was he had to say.

'I was brought up here, in that house,' Ross said finally, his voice low. 'Most people think I had a very privileged childhood.

And compared to some I did,' he added quickly, 'but . . . Well, the "privileged" seem to live by different rules to the rest of the world. My family, anyway. It took me years to realise not everyone behaved like them.

'My father has had a mistress for almost twenty-five years,' he continued flatly. 'I've lost count of the number of affairs my mother has had. She used to move her lovers into the house when my brother and I were away at school. Often she didn't bother moving them out again during the school holidays. My father didn't seem to mind. And apparently, my brother has moved back home now since his wife kicked him out after finding him in bed with the nanny. Infidelity runs in my family.'

Chrissy looked up at his harsh tone to find him staring fixedly at the house, a mixture of pain and anger in his eyes. Wordlessly she reached out and caught his hand.

The contact seemed to bring Ross back to reality; he frowned slightly, as if he had forgotten that she was there. Then his eyes cleared. He rolled towards her slightly and Chrissy met his gaze, very conscious of his hard, fit body beside her, so close; his clean, spicy, masculine scent filled her senses. Feeling suddenly light-headed, she tried to sit up, but Ross moved quickly, pinning her with his arm and shoulder. He stared down at her, his remarkable eyes almost tender, and it was clear that his thoughts had shifted subtly. There was no doubt that he was very aware of her under him. His voice was low as he spoke.

'I brought you here deliberately, to try and get you to understand my behaviour these last few days. I haven't meant to be so critical of you, but I just can't help it.'

Chrissy listened to his words, her attention fixed on his full, sensuous lower lip as he spoke. She could feel the warmth of his breath on her cheek, the unbearable lightness of his touch as he stroked her hair. She closed her eyes, frightened of her whirling emotions, knowing that she was falling for Ross Sinclair, knowing that she could no more resist him than she could stop breathing. He dropped his mouth to hers and kissed her softly on the lips and it was like no kiss she had ever experienced before, filled with such tenderness, such longing, that she felt her very soul leap in response. When they broke off, he held her tightly, his face buried in the fragrant softness of her hair.

'I mean it, Chrissy. I can't enter into a relationship without commitment. I've seen what it does to people. I can't live like that.'

Chrissy's heart leapt; was he really saying what she thought he was? She snuggled more closely against him. When she spoke her voice was hesitant, muffled. 'I lived with my partner, Marc, for almost four years. One day I came home from work to find him in our bed with another woman. He didn't even have the excuse that I'd come home early,' she said flatly. She was silent, remembering the scene, Marc and Miranda laughing, not bothering to cover their nakedness; Marc even suggesting that she join them. Chrissy had stared, open-mouthed with shock, unable to speak or move until Marc had coolly informed her that Miranda would be moving in with them for a trial period, hoping she would not be so unsophisticated as to object. He did not even try to duck when the blue vase his mother had given them sailed accross the room and caught him on the side of the head, so surprised that his mousy little Chrissy had the spirit to do such a thing, or such a good aim. 'It seems Marc and I had an "open" relationship for about two years, only he forgot to tell me. I've tried commitment, Ross, and it hurts. So this summer, I thought I'd just try fun for a change.'

Ross's grip had tightened on her as she spoke, and Chrissy, acutely tuned to his moods, realised he was angry. 'Bastard! I can tell you that any man who would not be satisfied to have you in his bed is a fool. Did you love him?' he added harshly, as though it were somehow her fault that he was angry.

'Oh, yes, I loved him,' said Chrissy, but for the first time she wondered if that were actually true. She had never doubted her love for Marc before, but neither had she ever felt in his arms the way she did now in Ross's, breathless and uncertain, keenly aware of the hard length of his body as he moved restlessly against her.

Suddenly Ross went very still, his dark brows coming together in a frown as something occurred to him. Without seeming to move at all, his weight shifted subtly. Somehow what had been an intimate caress, his arm resting lightly on her chest, suddenly became a force pinning her on the grass.

'What about Will, Chrissy? I need to know before this goes any further.'

Chrissy looked back at him, her own eyes troubled. How could she put into words that the warm feelings she had when she was with Will were nothing compared to the sudden violent rise in her temperature she experienced just thinking of Ross? 'Will is the nicest man I have ever met,' she said carefully, 'and I like him a lot. But he knows I don't love him. I've never lied to him about that.'

Ross felt relief flood through him. 'Just so you remember,' he said roughly, something primitive entering his expression as he wound his fingers in her hair. 'I don't share.' His mouth came down on hers, possessive and hungry. He kissed her with hot, hard skill, one hand wandering high up the length of her leg, the touch of his fingertips on her skin exquisite. His touch felt more like the caress of an old familiar lover than a new one, so sure and confident. Chrissy jerked her mouth from his to gasp in surprise, quivering under his touch.

Ross's eyes narrowed with triumph and the hot fire of passion. 'I want to be inside you,' he murmured, 'Come back to my place?'

Chrissy, unable to believe he had to ask, and incapable of speech, nodded. Ross pulled her to her feet, not letting go of her hand as he led her swiftly back the way they had come. But in the cool shade of the woods he stopped to kiss her again, his blatant need for her obvious, feeding her own rising passion. She had never before felt so desired. Ross was like a man who had been starved of food and had been suddenly allowed in to the feast. His tongue plundered her mouth and his hand came up to fondle her breast through the soft cotton of her dress; he was frustrated when he could not gain access to her bare flesh.

'I would rip it off you and take you here and now,' he murmured, breathing heavily, 'but I want to take my time. I want this to last forever.'

Her own need as urgent as his, Chrissy slipped her hand between their bodies, flattening her palm against the tight muscles of his stomach. Brazenly, she would have gone lower, wanting to touch the hard, indisputable evidence of his arousal, but Ross caught her hand, a low moan escaping his lips.

'Do that and I won't be responsible,' he murmured. With a supreme effort of will he pushed her away and held her at arms' length, his breathing ragged. 'Come on.' This time he did not touch her again, apart from when his hands circled her slender waist as he helped her over the fence. He lingered for a second, releasing her only reluctantly to open the car door, the look in his eye bringing a hot wild blush to her skin. Neither of them spoke till they pulled up outside his cottage ten minutes later. Ross caught her arm as she climbed out.

'Are you sure about this, Chrissy?' he asked softly. 'Because if you're not, say so now and I'll take you home.' She would never know how hard it was for him to say those words, or the relief that washed through him at her reply.

'I've never been more sure of anything in my life.'

Once through the front door, Ross paused only to kick it shut, his eyes burning with a fierce predatory intent. Chrissy found herself backing slightly under the force of his gaze.

'Take the dress off,' he ordered, his voice hoarse.

'Ross, I . . .'

'Take it off!'

Panic and excitement rushed through her veins at his tone, leaving her dizzy and breathless, and totally unable to resist his demand. Swiftly, before she could become self-conscious, she caught hold of the hem of her dress and pulled it over her head, standing before him wearing only her white panties.

Ross stared at her wordlessly for what seemed like an age, a slow heat smouldering in his eyes, melting through her, turning her insides to liquid.

'Let me see you completely naked.'

Chrissy slipped off her panties. Emotions chased across his face as he noted her willingness to comply, a flare of lust darkening his pale eyes. His gaze seemed almost to penetrate to her very soul, leaving her as exposed and vulnerable emotionally as she was physically. She shivered.

A low rumble came from deep in his throat. 'God, I've dreamed about you like this. You are so, so beautiful.'

With that he reached out and stroked her breasts, almost

reverently, with his fingers. The heavy globes hardened at his touch, swelling against his palms, as he circled each nipple with his thumb, simultaneously easing one ache, but creating another, deeper more urgent ache inside her. Chrissy moaned. Unable to help herself, she looked down. He had teased her nipples to hard points, the rosy tips glowing darkly in his large, male hands.

'You feel so good, Chrissy.' His voice was low and caressing. Now that he had her in his thrall, Ross did not seem to be in quite such a hurry. 'I've thought of nothing but your shaven silken pussy since the restaurant, of how much I wanted to see you naked in the daylight, to explore you properly.' While he was talking, the flat of one hand smoothed down her belly and over her mound, cupping her sex possessively. He groaned deep in his throat as his fingers moved over the velvety soft skin, enclosing her whole sex in his hand, making no attempt to part her outer lips, though she longed for him to do so.

Chrissy made a small sound, somewhere between pleasure and desperation. Ross kissed her neck, mouthing her so softly she could barely tell where her own skin ended and his lips began. She could feel her whole body buzzing, a hot river of pleasure flowing from where his hand cupped her sex, willing him to continue his glorious exploration and bring her the relief her body craved.

Ross could feel her trembling and felt a wave of masculine exultation wash over. He allowed one probing finger to slide boldly inside her, parting the sweet, moist folds. Chrissy jumped as though electrified, involuntarily shuffling her feet, parting her legs slightly, inviting a deeper, even more intimate exploration. At the same time she caught hold of Ross's head in both hands, taking him by surprise as she kissed him hard on the lips, thrusting her lower body against him, uncaring what he would think of her now, desperate for the release only he could give her.

And Ross responded. All pretence, all teasing was abandoned as his tongue delved inside her mouth, wrestling erotically with her own, mimicking the rhythm of his fingers. He felt her tense but only held her lithe body more tightly, his hand flashing across the hard bud of her clitoris as her orgasm spiralled out of

167

control, taking them both by surprise. Chrissy's legs gave way, unable to support her weight; but Ross was there, holding her strongly, stroking her bud till the last trembling spasm had passed, deepening the long, erotic kiss while she sagged against him.

With a low animal sound, he scooped her naked body into his arms, savouring the feeling of her bare bottom against his hand for a second, as he lifted her. The muscles of his shoulders and arms tightened as he held Chrissy close against him, striding for the stairs as if she were no weight at all.

On the landing, his eye was caught by the reflection in the full-length mirror and he swore softly at the sight that met his eyes. The swollen lips of her sex were clearly visible in the long mirror, the skin a deep pink, glistening with the excitement of her recent arousal. His ribcage rose and fell as he drew in deep breaths, not trusting himself to speak.

He made it to the bedroom in half a dozen strides, dropping her gently onto a low futon mattress, causing her breasts to bounce enticingly. Ross, in the process of stripping off his shirt, followed this interesting movement with his eyes but did not pause. Chrissy watched him, anticipation making her mouth dry. She hadn't realised before just how muscular he was, and she gaped at his broad chest, her eyes following the tightly curled black hair as it arrowed down over his abdomen to disappear into the waistband of his jeans. Jeans he was even now undoing.

Chrissy's eyes followed his hands, hungry to see if the huge bulge fulfilled its promise, as purposefully he slipped each silvery stud from its buttonhole, only managing to undo half the buttons before his cock sprang free, his powerful vibrant length rearing up towards his navel. The shaft was long and thickly veined, the skin flushed and dark with need.

A hungry ache stirred deep inside her at the sight of him. Eagerly, wanting to touch him, she reached out, but Ross, kicking his jeans off, was too fast for her.

'No!' Catching her hands in one of his, he pinned them above her head on the bed. This caused Chrissy to arch her back, thrusting her breasts up to meet his waiting mouth. She wriggled in his grasp, the position not entirely comfortable and Ross looked down at her appraisingly, his expression impossible to read. Then he bent his head and buried his face in her breasts, his mouth closing around a nipple; he rasped the sensitised flesh with his tongue before sucking her deep into his mouth. The sweet pulling sensation drew an answering response deep in her womb, and her back arched higher, taut as a bow.

Her hands were still pinned above her head, but he could not totally prevent her from squirming in pleasure. The feel of her lithe body wriggling erotically beneath made him growl his fervour out loud.

Using his knees, he forced her legs apart, lowering himself onto her sweat-slicked body. He moved his hips slightly so his cock slipped into her furrow, separating the lips of her sex but not penetrating her. She could feel the intensity of his need in the tip of his cock, his male energy surging, and the low groan he uttered sent her pulse racing out of control.

'Please.' The word came out as a whisper. Exquisitely she felt the satiny head of his penis push inside her, its thickness meeting initial resistance before nudging past her sweet moist opening. Ross closed his eyes for a second, the pleasure almost unbearable, but still he did not lose the steely control he was exerting over himself.

'Ross, please . . .' she gasped, unable to find the words for what she wanted.

At the sound of his name, a whispered plea, Ross let out a roar, driving deep inside her, allowing only a second or two for her body to adjust to the thickness of him, driving in and out in a fast, powerful rhythm, Chrissy cried out in shock at his sheer size, the way he filled her totally; her cry turned swiftly to a sob of pleasure.

'Chrissy, Chrissy,' Ross's voice was hoarse with need as he moved in and out of her, releasing his hold on her arms as he gathered her to him, groaning as he felt her wrap her arms around him, pulling him even closer, even deeper.

There was nothing gentle about their love-making. It was quick and hot and hard, and her orgasm, when it came, was wild and all-consuming, a searing, shattering pleasure that jolted through her, on and on, spinning her higher and higher as she sobbed his name, unaware that her finger-nails were raking a pattern on his back and buttocks. And then Ross stiffened above her, his head thrown back, the tendons standing out on his neck, till with a judder of terrifying passion he throbbed and spasmed inside her, filling her, claiming her for his own, her name loud on his lips.

He slumped against her, resting inside, his breathing deep and ragged, unwilling to lose the closeness. Chrissy savoured his heavy weight on her, stroking his broad shoulders and back. She revelled in the power and strength she could feel just below the surface, enjoying the solidness, the maleness of him. After a few seconds, concerned that he was suffocating her, Ross shifted his weight onto his elbows, looking down at her, desire undiminished in his hot eyes.

'You have no idea how I've dreamed of this moment, Chrissy.' Tenderly he smoothed the damp hair from her forehead, his voice raw with emotion. He held himself very still, gazing into her eyes for a long time, saying nothing.

Could he know what she was thinking? Could he feel her growing love for him? It was almost as though he could read her thoughts, could see into her very soul, and already knew her better than she knew herself. A blush spread over her skin, her face and breasts glowing a rosy pink under his scrutiny.

He lowered his head and kissed her, an intensely erotic kiss, possessive and gentle. Incredibly, Chrissy felt him swell and harden inside her. A moan bubbled deep in her throat, but found no release; he continued to kiss her in a long, slow, blissful exploration as his cock began to move inside her again, slowly, sensuously.

Chrissy wanted to hold him, to wrap her legs tightly around him, but could not. Her limbs felt so heavy. She was barely aware of anything but his hard body; the clean, masculine smell of him; the sensation of his skin sliding over hers; the mind-drugging sensuousness of that slow erotic kiss – and the sweet fusion as their hips rocked together. Her nerve-endings were going wild, her body flooding with warmth again as she strained towards something bright and wonderful, something that she knew was just within her reach. She could not tell where her body ended and his began. Surely it had never been like this before?

Ross felt cocooned in soft velvet, stroked by a million tiny feathers as he slid in and out, Chrissy's inner muscles tightening, massaging him and surrounding him with pleasure. Pleasure that just went on and on.

Gradually he increased the tempo. Chrissy ceased to be aware of anything, her whole being centred on the man who held her so tenderly in his arms; tiny rippling waves of delight washed over her, chased through her till she clung to him, sobbing into his shoulder, as another orgasm overwhelmed her, an exploding, white hot kaleidoscope of light and love that left her trembling and exhausted in his arms.

Ross groaned deep in his throat, her convulsing inner muscles again triggering his own climax; it was no less intense for being so slow and controlled. His deep agonised, blissful cry filled her ears as he moaned her name, his seed shooting deep inside her.

Chrissy's heart was singing as she rested her head on his shoulder, listening to the slowing thud of his heart, feeling cherished and protected. She was unable to speak, frightened of the emotions that churned inside her, knowing that she would never be able to put into words what she felt at this moment. She loved him. She loved Ross Sinclair with all her heart and being. But still she had to be careful; she had to protect herself. Ross had opened up to her, revealed some of the personal hurt he carried inside; but even in the throes of passion he had not said the words, had not said that he loved her

Chrissy lay beside his warm masculine body. Worn out by their exertion she felt herself drifting off to sleep. Ross drew the duvet over both of them. He lay awake for a long time, lightly stroking her hair.

Entwined in each other's arms they dozed for several hours, through the warm afternoon into early evening. What actually woke Chrissy was a hard object jabbing uncomfortably into her thigh. She shifted her weight sleepily, reluctant to wake completely, but could not escape the persistent prodding. Eventually she was forced to open her eyes; Ross was smiling at her, his face only inches from her own.

'Oh good, you're awake.'

'No thanks to you,' she mumbled, snuggling against him.

'What do you mean. I never touched you!' Eyes twinkling, he raised both hands innocently. His hard penis continued to press into her thigh.

'Oh, no? What do you call that, then?' She jerked her hips slightly, causing him to wince.

With a low growl he rolled on top of her and, giggling, Chrissy opened her legs to receive him. She was already wet, ready to welcome him and with his penis embedded deep inside her, he quickly brought them both to a fast, intense climax. They remained like that, pressed together till the last pulsing shiver of orgasm had passed.

It was Ross who broke the silence. 'I wish I could wake up like that every day,' he murmured gently, kissing the tip of her nose. Breathlessly, Chrissy waited for him to say more; but he was silent, seemingly content just to be with her. The silence was only broken by a deep rumble from Chrissy's stomach. She had not eaten since breakfast and it was now six o'clock.

'I'm starving,' she complained, embarrassed.

'Thank God for that! So am I, but I was afraid of spoiling a "special moment". What do you say we go find something to eat? I was supposed to provide lunch, after all.'

Ross's kitchen proved a disappointment. Some bread with fur growing on it; three eggs; and a suspect piece of bacon. It was quickly agreed that they should go out to eat. Ross suggested they return to Orlando's, the Italian restaurant they had been to the other night.

'You never know,' he murmured in her ear, 'play your cards right and you might get an action replay.'

'You'll be lucky,' said Chrissy, pushing him aside with mock severity. 'I'm afraid my priority is food, right now. You come a very poor second!'

Chrissy wanted to return to Clarissa's to change her clothes, but Ross convinced her they were too hungry for that. After he promised to drive her home very early next day, before he went to work, she agreed, and they set off in his car; Ross was more at ease, more relaxed than she had ever seen him.

At the restaurant the waiter's face blanched when he recognised them. He was busier tonight, several tables were filled, and the last thing he needed was these two sulking and bickering once more. But to his relief they could not have been more different. They held hands; sat close together; touched each other at every opportunity; talked constantly, heads together, murmuring softly. They also, he noticed, consumed vast amounts of food between them. They lingered over coffee then, arms around each other, walked out into the warm evening.

'I feel better for that.' Ross patted his flat belly contentedly as they made their way to the car.

'Me too. But it's just made me sleepy again.' She rested her head on his shoulder.

'Let's go back to my place and you can sleep – eventually.' There was a glint in Ross's eye that sent a very pleasant shiver through her.

They drove in companionable silence for some time. Through lowered eyelashes Chrissy watched Ross, admiring his profile, his relaxed concentration as he wound his way through Edinburgh's traffic. Her skin seemed to tingle with awareness of him, her eyes drawn to his hands on the steering wheel, beautifully manicured, very masculine and able to bring so much pleasure. In fact the memory of those hands on her skin, his warm breath in her ear, sent a tremor thorough her body, a rush of warmth to fill and swell her sex. A dull pulse began to beat between her legs, low and insistent, triggering an answering tingle in her breasts. Looking down she saw her nipples push up against the fabric of her top.

They had left the traffic behind now and were approaching a lay-by, screened from the road by a clump of trees.

'Pull over, Ross.' Her voice was low and throaty and Ross glanced at her in surprise. The urgency of her need must have burned in her eyes, for he cursed softly and immediately steered off the road. Even as he applied the handbrake, Chrissy was reaching hungrily for him, kissing his cheek, while her hands fumbled in his lap, her speed making her clumsy with his button fly.

'Chrissy . . .'

'Sh. Don't talk.' She effectively silenced him with her lips, her busy hands finally freeing his cock to lie soft and pale in her palm. Her eyes were luminous in the gathering twilight, the pupils dilated with desire. Ross tore his eyes away from her reluctantly only to glance nervously into the gathering darkness outside.

'Chrissy, don't you think we should wait till—'

Chrissy made a small, excited sound and bobbed her head down into his lap, where she breathed deeply, drawing the very essence of him deep into her lungs. Ross moaned helplessly, eyes closed, his head rolling back on the seat. Anxiety had kept his penis soft but now, with her warm breath nuzzling his groin, he began to grow and harden.

'Oh God,' he whispered as her hot lips fastened around him, 'Oh God, don't stop. Whatever you do, don't stop. That feels so good.'

Little whimpers of satisfaction bubbling inside her, Chrissy held him in her mouth, feeling him swell in the warmth and moisture till he was so big her lips were pushed apart and she had to clasp her hand around the thick base of his shaft to hold him. Her need now a burning ache, she ran her lips up his length one more time before reluctantly letting him slip from her mouth. Eagerly she pushed her seat back and hitched up her dress. She wore no panties, a fact that made Ross groan loudly, the unmistakable musk of her arousal assaulting his senses.

'Please, Ross,' she moaned, parting her legs as much as the confined space would permit, inviting his caress. His penis was jutting from his opened jeans, hard and virile, and she continued to stroke him with her fingers, raising her dress higher with the other hand to pull and tease her hard nipples. The whole thing was so arousing that Ross was totally unable to resist. Leaning across he touched the slippery folds of her sex, easing his fingers inside.

'God, you're so wet, so ready for me,' he moaned.

'Quick, please, I need you inside me!' Chrissy moved her bottom feverishly, grinding the aching bud of her clitoris against his fingers, conveying her urgency.

But no matter how willing they both were, sex in the front seat of that car was next to impossible. Ross was just too tall, his head banging the roof, his knees bent awkwardly. They would both have laughed if they had not been so frustrated as they tried to arrange their limbs into an acceptable position. Finally Chrissy gave up.

'Wait a minute.' She opened her door and stepped out into the cooling air, her dress still bunched up in her arms, her breasts exposed. In disbelief Ross watched her nipples harden to tiny peaks in the evening air.

'For God's sake, Chrissy! Get back in the car. What if someone sees you?'

'No-one will see us if we're quick. Come on, don't be such a prude.' Laughing at the mingled expression of lust and horror on his face, Chrissy walked round to the front of the car and leaned across the bonnet. She grinned at his startled face through the windscreen and shook her breasts provocatively. 'Not coming to join me?'

No matter how nervous Ross was, his cock was twitching with a need that could not be ignored. Breathing heavily, he got out of the car, making his way to stand behind her as she pressed herself along the hot metal.

'You'll have us both arrested,' he growled, his hands roughly kneading the firm white globes of her upraised buttocks. Chrissy moaned with the heat of his touch, thrusting herself back against him. With a strangled cry Ross plunged deep inside her, sinking his cock right to the hilt in her molten flesh. He pistoned in and out, hard and fast, Chrissy moving with him to meet his thrusts. Their moans of pleasure and the slap of skin on skin were the only sounds that disturbed the near darkness. But when Chrissy came it was with a loud, almost animal cry, echoing through the secluded lay-by and Ross had to pull her upright, pressing his hand lightly over her mouth and his teeth into the back of her neck, holding her very still as his cock pulsed and exploded inside her, his seed spilling forth in sharp shuddering jets.

Immediately he pulled her dress down over her naked bottom, turning her round to kiss her hard. They were both breathing heavily, their eyes glowing, but Chrissy had to laugh as he anxiously tried to refasten his trousers without breaking their kiss.

'You didn't strike me as the nervous type,' she teased.

'I'm not,' said Ross, relaxing as he fastened the last button. 'Except when I'm having sex with a beautiful woman not ten yards from a major bus route. Just you wait till I get you home, you sex-mad bitch.' He would have kissed her again, but another car drove into the lay-by, stopping behind them. Several small children swarmed out to stretch their legs, their parents eyeing Ross and Chrissy suspiciously.

'Lovely evening,' Chrissy called to them and she and Ross climbed giggling into the car, heading quickly homewards.

Thirteen

That night spent in Ross's bed was one that Chrissy would remember for the rest of her life. They made love tenderly, wildly, passionately; indulging themselves in an orgy of sensuous, tumultuous pleasure. Finally, exhausted but fulfilled, they collapsed into deep slumber, their limbs entwined on the damp sheets, as though even in sleep they could not bear to be parted.

But as morning drew near, her sleep became more fitful. It seemed to Chrissy that however she lay, there was often a hard penis pressing hopefully against her, a warm hand moulding her breast. Dreamily, through a sleepy haze, her body moved against him, positioning itself so that his cock could slide into her warm, wet centre. As they drifted in and out of wakefulness, it was as if their bodies continued to pleasure them while their minds were absent. In the darkness, dream and reality merged in a haze of shared sexual delight. Chrissy felt warm and safe and loved as she snuggled in his strong arms.

Eventually she came fully awake to find brilliant sunshine streaming through the window and Ross's tongue gently lapping between her legs.

'Mm,' she sighed, wrapping her thighs around his head, rubbing herself on his ardent lips. She would have thought her body's capacity for pleasure completely drained and was thrilled when the familiar warmth began to radiate from her womb throughout her languid body. Before long she was panting, her limbs, still heavy with sleep, spasming in a muted, gentle, intense wave of pleasure.

Ross crawled up her body to kiss her, tasting of her own sweet juices.

'Morning,' he smiled.

'That was wonderful,' Chrissy stretched luxuriously. 'What a way to start the day.'

'Unfortunately that's as much as we've got time for,' he said. 'Some of us have got to work today, you know, especially after skiving off yesterday. Not that I'll be fit for much, after last night.' He chuckled softly, a pleasant, satisfied, somehow very masculine sound.

'Yes? Well you're not the only one with things to do, Ross Sinclair. First things first, I've got to go and mark you on my Treasure Hunt card under "master craftsman". I may even give you a gold star.' Playfully she slapped his thigh as she sat up and wriggled off the bed, unaware that Ross's body had tensed at her words. She did not see the look of utter disbelief that darkened his handsome features as his eyes followed her retreating back.

In the bathroom Chrissy looked longingly at the bath, but she did not have time. Ross really did have to get to work, so she would wait till he had run her home and then have a shower. In the mirror her eyes were glowing with happiness – the eyes of a woman who had spent the night in the arms of the man she loved. Her gaze was held for a moment by her puffy, much kissed lips, before sliding down to her shoulders and heavy breasts, where tiny marks of passion could be seen on her otherwise flawless skin. Satisfied by the joy she saw reflected, and already missing the warmth of Ross's arms, Chrissy hurried back along the passageway to the bedroom.

Ross was sitting stiffly on the bed with his back to her, pulling on his jeans. He did not turn round.

'Hi. Miss me?' She scrambled over to him and wrapped her arms around his waist, rubbing her face on his shoulder.

Abruptly he stood up, walking to the wardrobe to remove a shirt.

'Ross?' There was something about the rigidity of his stance that made her uneasy. 'Ross, are you OK?'

He meticulously closed the wardrobe door before turning to face her. Chrissy flinched at the icy rage sparking in his blue eyes. 'Did last night mean nothing to you, Chrissy?' His voice was tightly controlled. 'Do I mean nothing to you?'

'What? Of course you do. I . . .' She was totally confused,

bewildered by the deeply-etched lines of hurt and anger on his face.

'Is that all I am to you? Another notch on the bedpost? More points on your stupid Treasure Hunt?'

At last understanding dawned. Chrissy felt relief surge through her and she smiled. 'No, you don't understand . . .'

'No,' he snarled, 'I don't understand. And I never will understand. You are just another spoiled little bitch, using other people for her own amusement – and I'm just another poor sap who was taken in!'

'No, listen, Ross, I can explain,' she tried again, but he was beyond reason.

'You are so wrapped up in yourself, aren't you?' he continued furiously. 'You don't give a shit about anybody else. I suppose I should consider myself lucky to be allowed to take part in your game, glad you consider me worthy of a quick fuck.'

Chrissy was exasperated by his refusal to listen. 'Ross, you are just being stupid—'

'Stupid? Yes, I'm that, all right.'

'For crying out loud, would you just listen to me.' She was getting angry herself now, her own voice raised.

'No! I've listened enough. Now get dressed and I'll take you home. I want you out of my life – as of right now.' His lip was curled with contempt.

'You really are the most insufferable, unreasonable, pig-headed man!'

'Yes. Fine. Now get dressed.'

Furiously Chrissy began to pull on her clothes. It did not take long. She slipped her crumpled dress over her head, not bothering to take the time for underwear. The silence lay heavy between them for a few moments. It was Ross who broke it.

'Wait. I'll get my keys.'

'Don't bother,' she snapped, sliding her feet into her shoes. 'I'll make my own way home.'

'Don't be silly! It's six o'clock in the morning. How are you going to do that?'

'Silly?' she blazed. 'First I'm a whore, now I'm silly. You truly are an arrogant bastard, Ross.' Not waiting to fasten her shoes, she stormed out of the room and down the stairs, pulling open the back door before she realised that she did not have her handbag. It lay on the kitchen table where she had left it the previous night and she snatched it up, cursing tearfully when it flew out of her grasp, spilling the contents all over the floor. Eyes blurred with tears, she picked things up, checking only that she had her house keys and purse. Anything else he was welcome to. She would not stay in this house one moment longer. The back door slammed with a satisfyingly loud bang. Chrissy did not notice her Treasure Hunt card lying just behind the door.

At the front gate, she turned left, with no real idea where she was going. She vaguely remembered seeing a sign to a railway station when they drove back last night, and was relieved when she saw the sign again, showing she was heading in the right direction. Obviously her sub-conscious was a better judge of men than her conscious mind, and had known she would need it.

The quarter-mile walk did not take her long, anger adding speed to her steps. Tears were never far from her eyes, but she did not give in to them, swallowing hard against the lump in her throat. It was only a small station and unmanned, but she managed to buy a ticket from a machine and had only five minutes to wait for the first train of the day. Who the hell would be using a train at this time of the morning? she silently raged.

She was surprised to find that there were actually quite a few people, all businessmen, already on the train. The men huffed slightly at her intrusion, gathering their papers about them, annoyed that their early morning peace had been disturbed by this dishevelled beauty with the wild, tousled hair and short, crumpled dress which rode up to reveal an alarming amount of smooth thigh when she threw herself into a seat. Chrissy glowered furiously at them when she realised she was being watched, albeit surreptitiously; she was tempted to move, to find an empty carriage. But, she asked herself petulantly, why should she? Let them move if they did not like being scowled at. She was sick of men and their moods and fragile feelings.

She was fuming. Ross Sinclair might be a fantastic lover and a potentially wonderful person, but he was also intolerant, narrow-minded, and had no sense of humour to speak of. Well, it was better that she had found all this out before she had done or said anything foolish. Tears were gathering behind her eyes again, but she determinedly blinked them away.

But when the train eventually pulled in to Waverly, Chrissy stayed in her seat, in no hurry to leave. She felt empty, drained. An overwhelming sense of loneliness overtook her, and she could not shake the feeling that everything in her life had changed. Why had she ever thought this Treasure Hunt would be fun?

Back at Clarissa's house, in need of comfort and a friendly voice, she phoned Karen in the Orkneys. Karen was not there, but Chrissy left a message asking her to phone back. It was over an hour later when the phone rang, and for a moment she was not going to answer it, convinced it was Ross, phoning to apologise. But as the answer machine kicked in and she heard Karen's familiar voice, she snatched up the phone.

'Chris? Oh Hi. Thought I'd missed you. What's so urgent?'

'Oh nothing,' said Chrissy, keeping her voice light. 'Nothing's urgent, I just thought it was time I called you.'

Karen was not fooled by her tone. There was a moment's silence. 'OK, Chrissy, what's up? It's this Treasure Hunt, isn't it?' Suddenly a thought occurred to her. 'Oh God, nothing's happened, has it? Nobody's done anything stupid? You're all right, Chrissy, aren't you?'

'Yes, I'm fine,' she hurried to reassure her friend. 'Honestly, I'm OK. And the only person who has done anything stupid is me. You were right. It was a stupid idea. I shouldn't have gone along with it in the first place. It was immature and childish.'

'Immature and childish? Why do I get the feeling those aren't your own words? Did someone call you that? One of your customers?'

'No! Well, yes. Not those exact words, but similar, I suppose.'

'Someone whose opinion matters?' guessed Karen shrewdly. 'Want to tell me about it?'

And of course Chrissy did want to tell her about it. Why else would she have called? Falteringly at first, then in a rush, Chrissy told her all that had happened in the last few days, about Will, but mostly about Ross.

Karen was silent for a moment, her heart aching for the pain she heard in her friend's voice. 'This Ross Sinclair sounds quite a man. It doesn't seem too unreasonable that he wouldn't want the woman he loves to be sleeping with a wide and varied cross-section of the public.'

'Maybe – if he loved me. I was beginning to think he might, although he's never actually said anything. But surely if he had any feelings for me at all, he wouldn't always be so ready to see the worst in me. Do you know, we've fought every single time we've met?'

'Yes, but just think of the great sex when you make up!'

'I don't know if it's worth it, even for that. Anyway, the whole thing is immaterial. He made it quite clear that he never wants to see me again and, to be honest, I don't know if I could stand seeing him, knowing what he thinks of me.'

'What about Will? He sounds too good to be true. There aren't any rules that say you can't fall for the nice guy once in a while.'

Chrissy sighed deeply. 'I could never feel for Will the way I feel – felt,' she hurriedly corrected herself, 'for Ross. Will deserves better. So that's another thing. I'm going to have to call him today and explain.'

'Then what will you do?' Karen's voice was full of sympathy.

'Well, I'll tidy up here and go home later, I suppose. The builders will be finished by now.'

'What about this Hunt Ball you told me about?'

'I won't be going to it. I've had enough. Clarissa's supposed to be back anyway, though I haven't heard from her.'

'But what about all the effort you put into it – although I'm not sure that's exactly the right word? How many points do you have?'

'I'm not sure. Not that many, despite what Ross might think. That's another thing. I've lost my bloody card. To think that this was going to be the best summer of my life!'

'Oh, Chris, I'm sorry you're so miserable.'

'Yes, well, I'll get over it. Now, tell me how your dig is going.'

Chrissy stripped the bed and threw everything into the hamper, replacing the sheets with fresh linen she found in a cupboard on the landing. Although she realised that Clarissa would have someone come in to clean before moving back into her home, it was not in Chrissy's nature to leave a mess for another person to sort out; anyway, she enjoyed it. There was something therapeutic about housework – as long as she didn't have to do it too often. Humming loudly, she moved into the bathroom, picked up the few towels she had used and squirted cleaner into the bath. Resolutely she scrubbed the already gleaming enamel.

After a run, a shower and a decent breakfast, her natural optimism had begun to reassert itself. Even the phone call to Will had not been as difficult as she had anticipated. It was almost as if he had been expecting the call and, typically, made things as easy as possible for Chrissy, though there was no mistaking the sadness in his voice as they said goodbye.

Then Chrissy was ready to get her life back on an even keel once more – without the presence of Ross Sinclair.

Fourteen

Outside Clarissa's house at that moment, Portia was eyeing the front door thoughtfully.

Beside her on the pavement, nibbling distractingly on her ear, was Scott Wilson, the polo player, whom Portia had met the previous day at an impromptu party thrown by a friend. His young athletic body and ever-hard penis had provided a welcome diversion to the tedium that was Edinburgh in July. During the long, imaginative night they had spent together, Scott had let slip the fact that he had a promise of a further session with Clarissa before the Treasure Hunt was over: an interesting piece of information that had brought them to Clarissa's doorstep today.

'I'm not sure exactly how I'm going to play this.' Portia turned to face Scott. 'Just keep quiet and follow my lead.'

Scott, who couldn't care less what Portia was up to, nuzzled her neck as his hand caressed her firm backside. 'Does this mean I get to fuck both of you?'

'Maybe,' Portia pushed him away in irritation. 'Just do as you're told. All right?'

'What if Clarissa really is in the Caribbean? Can I still fuck you again?'

'Be quiet!'

In actual fact, due to a further phone call to Stephanie, Portia knew full well that Clarissa was still away, and planning to stay away for a while yet. What she didn't know, and what she planned to find out, was what exactly was going on and why.

When the doorbell rang Chrissy was in the kitchen. Quickly wiping her hands on a tea-towel, she ran her fingers through her hair, and hurried to answer it.

Standing on her doorstep was a tall, striking-looking woman with jet-black hair who stared at Chrissy rather disconcertingly. Beside her was a man who looked familiar.

'Clarissa, my sweet!' Scott swept her into his arms, kissing her hard on the mouth. Chrissy had to struggle to push him away.

'Luke? Scott?' she asked weakly. 'What are you doing here?'

'Scott,' he said. 'Luke unfortunately has received rather a nasty bang on the head during a match and is a little bit unconscious. Or he certainly was the last time I saw him. But I'm here to hold you to your promise. Remember?' He spun her around and kissed her again. Flustered, Chrissy tried to fend him off, looking over his shoulder to his companion, who had come in to the house and was standing in the hallway, smiling.

Relief and delight rushed through Portia, but she kept her face impassive. This young woman was most definitely not Clarissa Asquith, though she did look rather like her. Now she knew exactly what was going on! Clarissa, cunning bitch, had found a double to play the game for her while she lay sunning herself in the arms of her fat tycoon. It was so clever, so smooth, that Portia had to admire her style. She honestly would not have thought Clarissa had the imagination. This added a sweetly intriguing new dimension to things. Portia was already thinking on her feet.

She smiled, her scarlet lips parting over gleaming, perfect teeth. 'Put her down, Scott. This isn't Clarissa.' How she enjoyed the look of surprise and dismay on Chrissy's face at her words; she had to get this conniving little bitch to the ball tomorrow. It would provide the perfect finale. 'Come along, darling. Why don't we have a little chat?'

She swept past Chrissy, taking charge, and threw herself onto an armchair. She was still smiling, but it wasn't friendliness that Chrissy saw in her dark eyes; it seemed more like gloating – or triumph? Scott, on the other hand, looked as confused as Chrissy felt. Damn. It was so unfair to be caught out when she had already decided to give up.

'Don't look so worried, darling, your secret is safe with us, honestly. We've come to help – haven't we, Scott?' Her voice rang with genuine-sounding laughter and Chrissy began to relax slightly.

'I take it you know Clarissa?'

'Oh yes. Clarissa and I are very good friends. In fact, she sent me to ask you a favour.'

'You've spoken to her?' asked Chrissy. It had bothered her that she was going to give up without being able to explain herself to Clarissa.

'Yes, of course,' lied Portia smoothly, 'we had such a long chat. Unfortunately she won't be back for tomorrow. She wants you to go to the ball and take her place.'

'What? I can't do that. Everyone will know I'm not her. I won't fool anybody!'

'You fooled me,' said Scott encouragingly, unsure what was going on, but not prepared to allow the chance of sex with two beautiful women to slip through his fingers if he could possibly help it.

Chrissy looked at him, natural kindness preventing her from mentioning that Scott did not look like the hardest person in the world to confuse.

'It won't be a problem,' said Portia. 'I'll help. You really look terribly like Clarissa. With me by your side to answer any awkward questions, you'll be fine. You won't have to stay long; just put in an appearance.'

'I'm sorry.' Chrissy shook her head. 'I'm not going to the ball. You couldn't give me Clarissa's number, could you? I really ought to speak to her.'

'But you have to go! You'll be letting Clarissa down dreadfully if you don't.'

Privately, Chrissy felt that Clarissa should have thought of that before deciding not to turn up. 'Sorry, but I've made up my mind. I won't be going.'

'But you have to!' Portia was struggling to keep control of her temper. Who did the little bitch think she was? No-one backed out of Portia's games. 'You're in with such a good chance of winning, you know. You've done awfully well, so far.'

'I doubt it,' smiled Chrissy. 'Anyway, it's immaterial. I don't want to.'

'But you're so close, I know you are. I've heard all sorts of

186

stories. And just think of the good that Ross Sinclair could do with all that money!' She had got a reaction. Was it the mention of Ross or the money? 'Clarissa did say that she would pay a financial incentive if you were to win, didn't she?'

'No, she certainly did not. I didn't enter this for the money.'

Portia smirked at the outrage in Chrissy's voice. So it was Ross. The silly little cow had the hots for Mr Purer-Than-Thou. This was almost too easy. Already her mind was working on how she could pay Ross back for rejecting her. 'Ross will be so disappointed,' she sighed. 'You know how dedicated he is to his charitable work. He's probably got most of the prize money allocated already; you know what he's like. He'll have to disappoint so many people. Poor Ross – people are always letting him down. Still, if you have really made up your mind . . .'

'Wait a minute.' Chrissy recognised that she was being manipulated, but allowed herself to be swayed. She had to think; it was difficult with this woman watching her so keenly, and Scott sitting beside her on the arm of the settee familiarly stroking the back of her neck, distracting her and playfully resisting all her attempts to push him away.

What if it was true and she actually was in with a chance of winning? Perhaps she should reconsider. After all, what more could she lose? Ross couldn't have a lower opinion of her now if he tried. And if the money would really help some homeless people, it seemed churlish not to continue with the hunt.

'I've lost my card. I can't prove that I have any points at all. Scott!' His hand had slipped round her shoulders and was lightly rubbing the side of her breast. Chrissy glanced quickly at the other woman but, remarkably, she was ignoring Scott, her attention all on Chrissy.

Sensing victory, Portia immediately became very business-like, rustling through her bag. 'It's OK. I have a copy. Tell me what you've done so far and I'm sure Ross will vouch for you.'

Don't count on it, thought Chrissy, but she picked up the card and began to run through it, adding ticks as she went. When she had finished she slid it across to Portia who barely looked at her score.

'Excellent. If you and Scott can add a few points today, I'm sure you'll win.'

'What do you mean, add a few?' Chrissy looked uncertainly from Portia to the suddenly hopeful Scott and back again. 'Who exactly are you, anyway?'

'I'm sorry,' gushed Portia, happy now that she seemed to have the upper hand. 'My name is . . . Alice. Alice Goldie. I'm an old friend of Clarissa's. She asked me to come and pass on her message and try and persuade you to stand in for her tomorrow, one last time. Please say you will, then I can run along and let you and Scott . . . get on with it.' She shot Scott a warning look when she realised he was going to protest at her leaving. She could not really expect Chrissy to go upstairs with Scott while she sat down here and made herself a nice cup of tea.

'You did promise,' said Scott, edging closer to Chrissy and whispering in her ear, 'remember? I get to tie you up and spank you. I've thought of nothing else all week.'

Chrissy could not help smiling at his earnest expression. A shiver of excitement passed through her at the image conjured up by his words. Her life had been just so weird in these last few days.

She was neither stupid nor naive; she knew that there was more going on here than met the eye, but what the hell? Did she care? One last fling before she returned to boring normality. This was exactly the sort of casual, uncommitted behaviour Ross was continually accusing her of anyway. Why make him a liar? What did she have to lose?

'OK, I'll do it. But nothing too outrageous,' she warned Scott.

Ten minutes later she was waiting in Clarissa's spare bedroom, wondering what she had let herself in for. Alice had left, promising to see her on Saturday night at the Ball, and Scott had gone to the car with her to fetch something.

Chrissy knew nothing of the whispered conversation they had had, or the fact that Scott left the front door unlocked on his return. Already her stomach muscles were clenched in a tight excited knot, anticipation quickening her pulse.

Growing impatient with waiting, Chrissy decided to undress. There was no point being coy; she had agreed quite blatantly to have sex with Scott. He was likeable and attractive, but the very cold-blooded efficiency of the decision sent a tremor of excitement tingling through her body. Quickly stripping off her outer clothes, Chrissy loosened her bra and allowed her breasts to tumble free. Her nipples were hardening, reflecting how eager she actually was for this new experience. Her panties came next and she stood naked and shivering, not entirely from the cold, in the empty room.

A full-size mirror reflected back her wide, apprehensive eyes. For a second she surveyed her own body, drawing comfort from the familiar curves, reassured by the sight of her high, firm breasts, flat, almost concave stomach and smooth bare pubic lips, which were already starting to swell with anticipation. She winked at her reflection and squared her shoulders, inadvertently pushing her breasts forward.

This was how Scott found her as he burst into the room. 'Oh, wow, you look fantastic! God, what a body! I'd forgotten just how totally gorgeous you were, Clarissa – or whatever you're name really is.'

'Just call me Clarissa; it's simpler.'

'Here, look what I've brought.' He held up his hand; a pair of silver handcuffs dangled from his fingers.

'What? No way!' If he thought he was going to handcuff her he could think again. That was going further than Chrissy had intended.

'No, it's OK.' Scott saw the horror on her face and hurried to reassure her. 'They're not real. Honest. Look,' Stepping closer, seeming almost unaffected by her nakedness in his eagerness to demonstrate his toy, Scott showed Chrissy the tiny release lever in the handcuffs. 'They're stage props, honest. I just thought they'd add a touch of authenticity. Atmosphere, you know?'

Suspiciously Chrissy tried the lever a few times, till she was sure she believed him and was satisfied she could work them. 'You can use them, I suppose. But that's as weird as it gets, OK.'

Scott nodded. 'I can spank you, though?' he asked eagerly as he fastened a handcuff around her wrist.

Chrissy nodded, not quite trusting herself to speak, excited more than she understood why by the image of helplessness and sexual vulnerability Scott's eager lust was producing in her mind.

'Great. Just wait till Luke hears about this, the poor bastard! Is that comfortable?' He had fastened both wrists together behind her back, the position causing her breasts to jut forward.

'Yes, fine.' This was rather bizarre. He seemed deeply concerned for her comfort but had made no attempt to touch her sexually.

'How about a blindfold?' he asked mildly. 'I think it may sort of add to the atmosphere as well.'

'OK.' She tried to shrug but found it difficult with her hands so constricted.

Quickly he pulled a black mask from his pocket and tied it over her eyes, not too tightly. Chrissy only had a second to wonder about how he happened to have it on him. Immediately the bedroom disappeared from her view, she felt his hands on her breasts, lovingly stroking the nipples to hard peaks. She groaned with pleasure at the sudden intimacy. Scott was whispering in her ear, his breath playing softly over the sensitive skin.

'I won't gag you. I want to hear you moan with delight when I touch you. I want to share everything with you.' Chrissy heard a zip sliding down and knew he had taken his penis out of his trousers. He stood behind her and she could feel it pressing deliciously into the cleft of her buttocks as his hands continued to cup and hold her breasts, his lips nuzzling into her neck. She felt the heat rising inside her; she wanted to press back against his unyielding body but could not, concerned about keeping her balance, disorientated by the handcuffs and blindfold.

She moaned again, and suddenly he was gone, leaving the skin of her back tingling with goosebumps where he had touched her.

For a long moment Chrissy waited, anticipating his return. When he still did not reappear she began to get restless. Somewhere in the silent house a clock ticked loudly. All at once it to occurred to Chrissy just how helpless and vulnerable she was. What exactly did she know about Scott?

'Scott?' she called tentatively, 'Scott, I'm getting bored with this.' A noise told her that he was back in the room and she swung round, hoping to face him. This time when he came to her he was naked. When he spanned her buttocks with his hands and pulled her sharply against him, Chrissy could feel the throbbing heat of his cock pressing into her lower belly. His lips fastened on her breasts, sucking hungrily, his teeth drawing tugs of delight from deep inside her. Chrissy trembled and gasped, glad of his strong hands supporting her.

The darkness of the blindfold heightened her other senses; she was incredibly aware of the feel of his skin against her; burning, turning her body to a molten river of need. Scott was slightly shorter than Chrissy and for a moment she envisaged him sliding his rigid penis along her furrow, embedding it deeply inside her. The very thought of it sent a fierce shiver of pleasure through her.

Suddenly Scott bent down and hoisted her over his shoulder, his arm holding the back of her knees.

Chrissy felt dizzy and disorientated as she was swung through the air, the wind knocked out of her for a second. Just as she got enough breath back to complain, she was moving again as Scott carried her to the bed, where he sat down and dropped her over his knee. Although this felt slightly less dangerous than when he was standing, it wasn't particularly comfortable and Chrissy squirmed on his knee, unable to put her hands down for balance.

'Scott! What the hell—'

A hand came down with a resounding slap on her upraised bottom.

'Scott!'

'Put you over my knee and spank you. That was the agreement.' His hand came down again. And again. Chrissy struggled furiously, but he held her firmly with one hand on the small of her back as the other continued to rise and fall on her reddening buttocks. At first she was so outraged that she forgot how easily she could release herself from the handcuffs, even in this position. She was aware of the hair-roughened skin of his thighs rasping on the softness of her belly as she wriggled on his knee. Her hair had fallen over her head, trailing the carpet, and her breasts swung forward from her ribcage. Her nipples had hardened to rigid cones, swollen with blood and excitement; they bumped against his calf with each stinging blow.

The feel of his hand hitting her bottom was smarting rather than truly painful. A warm glow began to creep beneath the pain, spreading over her burning flesh, upwards and outwards throughout her body, a shiver rippling visibly through her. Though clenching her flaming buttocks tightly, Chrissy was shamed by a sudden rush of moisture escaping from her vagina and trickling down the inside of her thighs. Humiliated, but still wildly excited, she stopped struggling, her breath coming in panting sobs.

Scott too was breathing heavily, the hard length of his cock now fiercely jabbing her belly. He stopped the spanking and began to massage her fiery buttocks instead.

'Do you like that? Your arse is aflame, so hot and accessible to me.' He continued the massage, his fingers kneading her bottom, sometimes quite roughly, separating her cheeks, leaving her feeling exposed and vulnerable.

Chrissy did feel hot. A liquid heat seemed to be surging through her veins, flowing into her sex, feeding a desire that was almost an overpowering force. She moaned loudly in frustration. What he was doing shouldn't feel as good as it did. He should let her up now; they could—'Aaagh.' The moan turned into a sharp cry of surprise and pleasure as Scott's mouth came down on her burning skin, his lips nipping gently over her glowing cheeks, before he glided lower. He brushed the swollen flesh of her sex, separating each fold with his tongue and opening her like the petals of a flower, exposing her even more intimately to his gaze.

Chrissy was distracted momentarily by a noise to her left. A soft click; it was familiar, but she couldn't quite place it or concentrate because of what Scott was doing to her. It felt so wonderful, so delicious. His mouth left her to be replaced by his hand again, stroking, touching. When a finger slipped inside her, she gave a tiny jump and would have fallen off his knee had it not been for the firm, gentle hand on her back. Chrissy was moaning steadily now. Her feet had found a purchase on the floor and she was straining up to meet his hand, oblivious to the other discomforts of her position, knowing only that she must have relief soon or she would explode.

Scott was in no hurry. Again and again he dipped his fingers into her honeyed well, drawing out her moisture, soothing it over her cheeks and the crease of her bottom. Chrissy squirmed at the erotic bliss of his touch, beyond shame now, parting her legs slightly, desperately inviting further intimacy. But she stiffened in shock when she felt the nudge of his thumb, sliding along her cleft, smoothing her silky fluid into the puckered rose of her anus.

'Scott! You can't . . . Scott!'

'Shh, relax.' His voice was soft, smooth as treacle as he gently worked his thumb round and around, and then, ever so slowly, inside her sensitive, forbidden orifice, the fingers of his other hand once again swirling inside her warm centre, stroking, sliding repeatedly over the desperate bud of her clitoris.

'Aaaah.' The shock of being probed so deeply and in such a doubly intimate fashion was too much. Chrissy writhed and sobbed in his lap, her own ecstatic wriggling only adding to the pleasure his hands were giving her, almost painful in its intensity. With her head drawn back in rapture and muscles straining against her bonds, a long cry that was almost a scream escaped from her lips, and she spun wildly on the edge of consciousness.

Even afterwards, Scott kept up a gentle rubbing, bringing her slowly back to earth, wringing every last drop of pleasure from her panting, pleasure-seared body. Only when she finally stilled did he carefully slide out from under her, holding her strongly in his arms as he lowered her face-down onto the bed, her knees and feet on the floor. In the next instant Chrissy let out another loud groan of sheer pleasure as his cock slid confidently inside her, meeting no resistance, her body already open and welcoming, desperate for the intense pleasure his total possession of her inner being would bring. His penis wonderfully sheathed in her hot silkiness, Scott paused for a second, savouring the sight before him.

'There's a mirror here,' he whispered, and she could hear how his voice trembled slightly. 'I can see you in it. You look absolutely magnificent, so beautiful.' Suddenly he pulled out, then thrust straight back into her, hard and fast, and she felt herself spiralling once again towards orgasm, her world exploding into brightness, a thousand shining stars glowing and shattering behind her eyes. On another level she was aware of Scott withdrawing his penis and heard his sharp cry as hot jets of semen splashed onto her upturned buttocks.

Again she heard the clicking noise, strangely familiar.

Breathing heavily, Scott wiped her skin with tissues, then lifted her easily onto the bed. Chrissy was reminded of just how fit a sportsman he really was. Still dazedly recovering from her second powerful orgasm, she was only dimly aware of him loosening the handcuffs and refastening her arms to the head-board above. Her feet were being tied too, spread wide apart to the posts at the foot of the bed.

'Hey,' she protested, but only weakly. She felt warm and relaxed and wonderful. Whatever Scott was planning now, she was sure she would love it. To feel herself held open and blatantly displayed like this as she was kept captive, however willingly, was very arousing. She moaned softly, her head moving on the pillow, giving her the idea of removing the blindfold. With a little concentration, she was able to loosen the material enough that it slipped over her forehead and dropped onto the pillow. Chrissy blinked in the sudden light, but nothing had prepared her for the sight that met her eyes.

'Hello, darling.'

Alice and Scott were standing watching her. Scott was naked and near the head of the bed, his long thin cock erect again and only inches from her face – so close in fact that she could see the shiny anticipatory drop of moisture forming on its fiery tip. He was smiling at her happily, but his eyes were hungry. Alice was at the foot of the bed. Chrissy had to twist her head to see her properly, but even then could not quite believe what she was seeing.

Alice was also naked. She was standing with her hands on her hips, a lascivious smile on her crimson lips. High and full, her large breasts seemed to point at Chrissy, the nipples as deep a red as her lips, linked by a silver chain through her nipple rings. A glossy jungle of black hair sprouted from between her legs, curling over her thighs and lower belly. In her hand she held a polaroid camera. Grinning, she lifted the camera and captured Chrissy's expression of shock on film: identifying the clicking.

194

Although Chrissy had seen plenty of naked women in her life, she had never been sexually aroused by any of them. But it was obvious from the way Alice's eyes were fastened on the glistening lips of Chrissy's open sex that she had no such inhibitions. Her interest was blatantly sexual. There was something so primitive in her dark eyes that Chrissy immediately began to squirm and struggle against her bonds, shocked at the growing response she recognised in her own body.

She swallowed hard, unable to take her eyes from the other woman's fettered breasts. 'Look, this wasn't part of the deal. What do you think you're doing?'

Portia moved forward and climbed onto the bed, kneeling between Chrissy's outstretched legs. She was right, this hadn't been part of the deal. What Portia had intended to do was to humiliate the little tramp, take some incriminating photos of her with Scott, and embarrass the hell out of her tomorrow night at the ball. And send some to Ross, of course. She was almost sure there was something between these two.

She had not intended to get so turned on by Chrissy's body and the obvious pleasure she had taken from Scott that she couldn't resist joining in. She smiled and licked her lips.

'Why, darling, you look positively delicious lying there, so pink and tempting, spread open for me to enjoy. Good enough to eat. After all, why should Scott have all the fun?' She leant forward and laid one red-tipped hand flat on Chrissy's breast, feeling the puckered tip of her nipple rise against her palm. She smiled again. 'Your heart is racing. I don't think you are quite as unmoved as you would have me believe.'

Slowly Portia slid her hand down, dragging it lightly over Chrissy's soft skin, massaging her taut belly for a few moments till she felt the tension release. Her gaze did not waver from Chrissy's face. 'See,' she crooned, 'see how nice it feels. I promise you, it's just going to get better and better.'

Scott was watching, fascinated. It excited him tremendously to see the two women together, Chrissy bound and helpless. His mouth was dry with anticipation, waiting for the moment when it would be right to join them.

Chrissy continued to squirm. A white-hot heat seared through her wherever Alice's fingers touched and, unconsciously, she arched her back in pleasure. She was bound tightly, a prisoner, helpless. She was not responsible for what was happening; there was nothing she could do to make her stop. This wasn't her fault!

Alice seemed to know exactly what she was thinking. She smiled in secret satisfaction. 'You can stop me any time you want, you know; just take off the handcuffs,' she whispered, and Chrissy felt her breath, cool against the burning lips of her vagina, as Alice brushed a kiss over her spread sex. She felt her body respond, swept along in a tingling rush of pleasure and knew that if Alice stopped now, she would die.

Portia smiled like a cat when Chrissy stayed silent. She stifled her own moan of pleasure. It was perfectly obvious that darling Chrissy had no experience of loving another woman. Well, no matter – Portia was going to thoroughly enjoy initiating her. With a small sigh she gently prised Chrissy's labia even further apart with her fingers and at the same time darted her tongue delicately over the erect little bud of her clitoris.

The response was exactly as she had expected.

Hit by a bolt of pure pleasure, Chrissy whimpered and tried to draw her legs up, to wrap her thighs around Alice's head, but was prevented by her bonds. Writhing and moaning in frustration, she arched her back as much as she could, one instinct still urging her to pull away but another, more powerful and much more primitive instinct striving to encourage Alice's tongue to greater efforts, greater depths.

Chrissy felt a touch on her cheek and turned her face to find Scott's cock nudging at her lips. Eagerly, without hesitation, she took him deeply into her mouth. Her tongue lashed the underside of his shaft, as he moved in and out of her softly gripping lips, his breath coming in short grunts.

Between her legs Alice's tongue continued to swirl and lick and probe, delving deep inside to drink the sweet nectar it found there, flicking incessantly backwards and forwards over the hard nub of her clitoris till Chrissy felt she would die with pleasure. As it became obvious that Chrissy's orgasm was imminent, Portia spoke imperiously to Scott, 'Get away. I want to see her face when she comes.'

Scott slipped reluctantly from her lips and, kneeling beside her, began to rub his hand quickly up and down his shaft, still slick and shiny with her saliva.

The increasing rhythm and pressure of Alice's tongue drew Chrissy ever onwards and she could feel the sharp, hot waves of orgasm gathering in the tip of her clitoris, waiting to burst forth and engulf her, making her grind her sex more urgently against the other woman's mouth. Sensing her imminent orgasm, Portia took the hard little bead between her teeth, nibbling with infinite tenderness, till Chrissy screamed, her whole body arching off the bed, rigid with mind-blowing pleasure that just seemed to go on and on. Her eyes flew open as she felt the hot sticky spurts of Scott's semen land on her heaving breasts, adding to her pleasure as he massaged his sticky seed into her sweat slick skin.

Then she was lost again as wave after wave of orgasmic release swept through her, setting her body alight till she thought she would die.

She did black out; she knew it must have happened because when she next opened her eyes she was alone. Shakily she sat up, realising she had been released from her bonds, feeling deliciously perverted and sexually replete. The fact that Alice and Scott were gone helped; she did not have the embarrassment of facing them.

On the pillow beside her were some polaroid photos, her Hunt card and a note. The photos were totally explicit, some of them taken by Portia while Chrissy was still blindfolded, some apparently taken later, by Scott. Each one sent a rush of warmth to her cheeks, and also unbelievably to her swollen, sated sex.

There she was: bound, naked and blindfolded, bent over Scott's knee, while his fingers were clearly shown probing inside her. In another, she was face-down on the bed, Scott's creamy come glistening on the cheeks of her bottom, her face contorted in delight. And in another she lay in an attitude of wild abandon while Alice sank her tongue between her thighs. Well, the 'nude photography' box on her Hunt card could be well and truly ticked off now.

Reluctantly, because she found them such a turn-on, Chrissy tore the photos into tiny pieces. Exciting though they were, she would not like them to fall into the wrong hands.

197

Her card, she noticed had been marked up to date. The photographs were there, plus bondage, spanking and lesbian. A flush spread over her as she read the words. Who would have thought that she would ever have ticked those boxes, or enjoyed the experiences so much? The note said simply, *'See you at the Hunt Ball!'*.

Fifteen

By Saturday afternoon Ross had replaced the faulty lock on the bathroom door, mended a leaking pipe, ripped up some rotten floorboards and was now knocking down a brick wall at the back of his property. It was a sturdy, well-made wall and there was nothing actually wrong with it, but he knocked it down anyway, enjoying the satisfying thud of the heavy sledge hammer as he swung it against the brick.

He had been like this since Chrissy had left on Thursday morning. When he went in to the office he cleared mountains of work which then had to be checked surreptitiously by his colleagues for careless errors. He paced the floor when there was no work, yelled down the phone and then apologised repeatedly to anyone who suffered the sharp end of his tongue. In the afternoon, to everyone's relief, he went home early to work manically on his cottage, achieving more in two days than he had in the previous two weeks.

But still he was restless – still he thought of Chrissy. Had he been too harsh? Yes, he damn well had. His quick temper had got the better of him once again, and he'd blown it. A normal man would have laughed off her comment for the joke it – hopefully – was meant to be, and she would still be here with him now.

Well, too bad. He hammered viciously at the wall. If Chrissy had had any feelings for him she would not have gone off so quickly, would she? She had made no excuses at all, no attempt to talk him round. That alone said a great deal about what she actually felt. No, it was better that it ended now, before either of them got more involved, in too deep. He gave the wall another savage whack.

A noise disturbed him and looking up he found Will, his

hands stuffed in his jeans pockets, watching him.

'Ross,' Will said, by way of greeting.

Ross acknowledged him with a nod and continued working. Will watched silently for a while, then went to the toolshed, helped himself to a pickaxe and joined him, his strong arms swinging in unison with Ross's. Soon the wall had been reduced to a satisfying pile of rubble. Sweat was running freely down Ross's bare, dusty chest; Will too looked hot as they surveyed their handiwork.

'You've done a good job. What are you going to put here?'

'Don't know,' Ross said belligerently. 'Maybe another wall.'

Will merely nodded. 'I could do with a drink.'

'Me, too.'

In the kitchen he helped himself to two cans of cold beer, passing one to Will and pressing the other to his forehead for a second before snapping it open and drinking deeply. He leaned back on a worktop while Will sat at the table.

'It's the Treasure Hunt ball this evening,' said Will.

'So?'

'You're not going?'

'Why would I do that?'

'Chrissy's going.'

Ross paused, beer can half-way to his lips, then continued drinking. 'Where did you hear that? From Chrissy?'

'No, not from Chrissy. She dumped me.'

Ross could barely hide the elation he felt at these words. At least she had been telling the truth this time. 'Too bad,' he said.

'Isn't it?' said Will drily. Then, more seriously, 'You've got to go to her, Ross.'

'Why?'

'She loves you.'

'Yeah? She's got a funny way of showing it.'

'She loves you,' Will repeated quietly.

'Shut up, Will. You don't know anything about it.' Ross crushed his empty beer can in his hand and threw it angrily at the wall. Will stared at him silently.

'Fuck.' Ross felt stupid. Crossing the floor to where the can lay, he bent down and noticed a piece of card behind the kitchen door. Hesitating just for a moment, he picked them both up, tossed the can in the bin and the card on the table, then headed to the fridge to collect another two beers. He was going to get extremely drunk tonight; Will was welcome to join him if he wanted.

He sat at the table, pushing a can of beer towards Will. The card lay between them.

'What's that?'

Ross had of course recognised it immediately. 'Treasure Hunt card. The reason I won't be seeing Chrissy. The bitch must have left it here to taunt me.'

'Don't call her that.' Will spoke quietly, but there was a dangerous edge to his voice. Ross was immediately ashamed of himself anyway. He opened the can of beer. Unable to help himself, he smoothed the card carefully with the flat of his hands. 'Well used,' he muttered bitterly as it curled back on itself. Derisively his eyes raked down the columns of different categories. She hadn't wasted her time!

But then, with his beer can poised half-way to his lips, Ross stopped and read the card more carefully. He read it again for a third time, with a rising sense of panic. Carefully he laid his drink down. Oh shit, he'd really done it this time.

'What is it?' asked Will, seeing Ross's face blanch.

Ross ignored him, staring wordlessly at the card. There was no category for 'Master Craftsman'. She really had been joking! And he had launched into his moral tirade once again. Shit – no wonder she had walked out. Groaning loudly, Ross dropped his head into his hands. Why was he always such a fool? There was no way she would accept another apology from him – what the hell was he going to do now!

He looked up bleakly at Will. 'Why am I such an arsehole?'

Chrissy was very pleased with her choice of dress for the evening. She had found it, still boxed and wrapped carefully in leaves of tissue, among half a dozen others in Clarissa's massive walk-in wardrobe. She did not feel guilty borrowing it, even though it had obviously never been worn – if she was going to be Clarissa one last time, then she may as well do it in style.

And this dress definitely had style. It was a simple sheath of shimmering silk, the colour of old gold, which fell in a fluid line from thin shoulder-straps. When she stood still, it revealed nothing; it was modest and demure, skimming her body all the way to her ankles. But when she moved even slightly, it seemed to flow like liquid gold, clinging to every dip and curve, sensuously accentuating her glorious figure. Of course it was impossible to wear anything at all underneath it.

She had dressed her hair carefully, piling the honey-coloured tresses high on her head, apart from a few artful tendrils which framed her face. Applying a little more make-up than usual, she achieved a look of wide-eyed innocence that made her smile when she remembered what her attendance at this ball signified. Her own gold-drop earrings and a pair of satin shoes finished off the outfit perfectly. She looked and felt like a million dollars.

A postcard had arrived from Clarissa that morning, post-marked London. It merely said that she and John had decided to go abroad; there was no mention of when she would be back or that she wanted Chrissy to go to the Hunt Ball for her. Chrissy was beginning to suspect that this behaviour was rather typical of Clarissa: thoughtless and inconsiderate. Well, it didn't matter. After tonight she need have no other contact with her, though a strange sense of duty and of seeing things through to the end made her decide to go to the ball anyway.

The Treasure Hunt ball was being held at a private club, behind Prince's Street. Chrissy had no trouble finding it. Before going in, she stopped at a bar a few doors down to brace herself with two large vodkas in quick succession, ignoring the amazed stares of the other customers when they saw her silken splendour and elaborately arranged hair.

What a difference it would have made if she had someone to go in with; Ross, for instance. Quickly she pushed the thought away. She had deliberately not allowed herself to think of Ross. He was out of her life, and soon Clarissa would be, too. This was to be her last performance. Squaring her shoulders, savour-ing the way the movement made the thin silk flow over her nipples, she entered the room where the Hunt ball was in progress.

It was rather an anti-climax. The music did not stop playing; people did not turn to stare; and no-one leapt up to denounce her as an impostor. In fact it looked like any other pleasant, lively party. Chrissy let out the breath she had not been aware of holding, and helped herself to a glass from a passing waiter.

Champagne. Of course. Quickly she drained her glass, enjoying the warm glow that it gave her, the way the bubbles tickled her nose, and had another. As she sipped from the glass she looked around. It was very similar to the party where she had met Scott and Luke. And Ross, of course, but she was not going to think about that. Downing the drink and collecting another, she began to mingle, chatting with people she half-recognised, before moving on. Suddenly she was swept off her feet in a massive bear hug.

'Clarissa! You look great! I only came tonight because I knew you'd be here.' It was Phil, the lawyer whose inability to recognise Clarissa the previous week had been responsible for this whole strange affair. 'That dress is absolutely stunning! Here, have a drink. Have you spoken to Portia yet? Do you know who's won?' The whole time he was talking, he was familiarly stroking her near-naked bottom. Pleased to meet someone she knew, Chrissy nonetheless deftly removed his hand and accepted another glass of champagne.

'No, I haven't met her yet. I've only just arrived.'

'Come on, then! What are we waiting for? Let's get the judging over and announce the winner.' He laughed, then pulled her close and growled in her ear. 'Although if you find you are short of a point or two, I don't mind nipping upstairs for ten minutes. I'd hate to see Portia win again. No? Well, OK then, she's over here.' He led her to a table that Chrissy had not noticed before, where a striking, black-haired woman in an extremely short and expensive-looking black dress was sitting alone. Chrissy was pleased to see another known face, if a little embarrassed when she recalled the events of their last meeting.

'Alice, am I glad to see you.'

The woman smiled without warmth and took a long draw on her cigarette.

'Alice? Who's Alice?' Phil did not stop for an answer. 'Come on, Portia, who's going to announce the winner? Do we have to wait for Ross and Bas?'

Portia? Chrissy's legs almost gave way, and it was not just the effect of the alcohol she had consumed. She stared at the woman, her mind spinning, unable to think of a single sensible thing to say. What the hell was going on?

Suddenly and inexplicably, the situation struck her as very funny, and to keep herself from giggling, she quickly drained her glass. Phil looked from one to the other in confusion, feeling that he was missing something. Portia spoke first.

'Piss off, Philip. Clarissa and I have things to talk about.'

'But I . . .'

'I said piss off! Go and get us a drink – and don't come back for at least ten minutes,' snapped Portia. He looked as if he was about to argue, but Chrissy flashed him a grateful smile and he slunk off reluctantly.

'Well.' Portia smiled malevolently. 'I wonder if dear Philip would be so eager to please if he knew what a fraud you really are.'

'Oh, I don't know,' Chrissy felt deliciously warm and happy, 'I shouldn't think he'd be the least bit bothered really.'

'What do you mean? You deceived him. Of course he'll be angry!'

'You deceived me and I'm not angry.' Chrissy unsuccessfully stifled a giggle. 'Or is it all right for you to be Alice but not all right for me to be Clarissa?'

'That was different,' hissed Portia. 'I was just trying to find out what sort of game you were up to.'

Chrissy hiccupped loudly. 'Deceit and sex. Lots and lots of lovely sex – same game as you, I should think.'

'This is not funny!'

'It is a bit. Just a little bit. You have to admit it.' Laughter bubbled inside Chrissy again at the look on Portia's face. She really was taking this rather seriously. Chrissy looked around for Phil. Maybe if Portia had another glass of champagne she would lighten up a little bit.

'Will it still be hysterically funny if I send Scott for the photographs we took yesterday? We kept some, you know. I'm sure people here would be glad to see them,' snapped Portia, more and more annoyed.

'No,' admitted Chrissy, 'that probably wouldn't be funny. That would be very embarassing.' She pouted for an moment, then grinned. 'But just as embarrassing for you, I suppose. From what I remember, I'm masked in all the photos except the ones Scott took of you and me together. We'll both be disqualified for trying to score points off each other!' For some reason Chrissy found this hilarious, and began to laugh again.

'Right,' snarled Portia. This was not going according to plan. Why wasn't the little bitch more scared, begging her not to denounce her? 'I'll soon wipe that smile off your face. I'm going to make you take this seriously!'

Leaping to her feet she rapped her hand loudly on the table. 'Hello everyone, can you please listen up just for a moment?' Chrissy blinked in amazement. Portia's voice had switched from a snarl to a husky drawl almost instantly. Now, she was laughing pleasantly.

'You all know why you are here tonight. To have a good time of course, but also to hear the results of the little competition Clarissa and I have been involved in. I'm afraid I have something to tell you that you are not going to like very much.' She paused dramatically and looked around. Despite what she had said earlier Chrissy held her breath. She hoped that people would see the funny side of things, but you never knew.

'Actually, Clarissa and I have exactly fifteen points apiece,' Portia lied, making up a number. 'That makes it a draw!' There were good natured shouts of 'fix' and 'cheat' from the crowd, but it was obvious that she had not quite finished. 'So what we have decided to do is to have a tie break. Isn't that right, Clarissa?' Everyone turned to look at Chrissy and all she could do was smile back. What the hell was Portia up to?

'It's going to be a very interesting tie-breaker, and it will provide a little bit of extra entertainment for this evening. Clarissa and I are both looking forward to it very much, aren't we, Clarissa?'

For the first time, through her pleasant alcoholic haze, Chrissy remembered some of the warnings she had been given about Portia in the past. She smiled again, but a little more warily this time.

'Good. Here's what we plan to do. We want all the men in the room to form two orderly lines. And any women who want to join in, of course.' She turned and winked broadly at Chrissy who was paying real attention now. 'Clarissa and I will be stationed on these two chaise-longues. What will happen is that each of you will approach us in turn, and we must give you an orgasm, any way we can. Or you can give us one, if you prefer. The one who has given or received most orgasms in, say, one hour, will be the winner! Of course everyone is allowed to call support and encouragement to their chosen candidate while waiting in the queue, and you can even join both queues if you prefer. OK?'

A loud cheer went up at her words. Obviously little events like this were not unheard of when Portia was involved. Chrissy was struck dumb.

'Well, I know which line I'm going to be waiting in.' It was Phil with Chrissy's drink in his hand.

'What? I . . . I don't think . . .'

'Sound's hot, doesn't it?' Phil was standing very close to her, lightly stroking the back of her neck. He was staring openly down her cleavage.

'Stop that.' Chrissy pushed his hand away. She had to think. Her head felt fuzzy, though, and she couldn't concentrate. 'Stop it, Phil; I mean it.'

She got unsteadily to her feet, beginning to wish that she had not had quite so much to drink. Phil's hand slipped round her waist to support her and he pulled her against him so she could feel the hard pressure of his groin.

'Boy, are we going to have a good time!' He nuzzled her neck.

'That's enough!' said Chrissy sharply, pushing at his chest with the flat of her hand. This wasn't real. It could not be happening. People just didn't do things like this, did they? She looked around and blinked in horror when she saw Portia, her slim body surrounded by several laughing men who were jostling to see who could undress her first. When she saw Chrissy watching, she smirked, blowing her a kiss from her scarlet lips.

'Hey, who said you get to be first?' A florid-faced man whom Chrissy vaguely recognised shoved Phil good-naturedly out of the way. He dropped into an empty seat and pulled a startled Chrissy into his lap. 'You should have introduced yourself properly last week, Clarissa, at that other party.' He leered. 'We could have had lots of fun then, instead of fighting. Not that I can blame Ross for wanting to keep you to himself. Are you going to keep that dress on? I think you should.' Drunkenly he began to maul her breasts through the thin fabric. Chrissy slapped his hand away.

'Let go of me!' She twisted sharply and almost made it out of his grasp, but he was too strong.

'Oh, do that again, Clarissa, please. That gorgeous arse of yours feel so good squashing my cock.'

Portia, her hand already inside the trousers of one of her admirers, smiled sweetly across at her. 'What's wrong, Clarissa? You agreed to play the game, didn't you? You can pass Hugo over here when you're finished with him.'

'I did not agree to this game.' Chrissy found her voice. 'This is disgusting! You must be mad if you think I'll go along with this.' She continued to struggle futilely against Hugo, identifying him now as the man who was arguing with Ross the first night they met. Waves of nausea washed over her. Whether this was caused by the alcohol she had consumed or her distaste for what was going on around her, she did not know. She only knew that she wanted to leave – right now. Everyone seemed amused at her overreaction.

'Come on, Clarissa, be a sport. It won't be the first time, will it?' Hugo tried to kiss her face, but she turned her head sharply.

Suddenly a hand closed on her wrist and jerked her out of his lap. She was pulled with such momentum that her head spun dizzily for a second. Blinking rapidly to clear her vision Chrissy was astonished to see Ross standing over her captor. There was something so chilling in his icy blue eyes, so incongruous in his dusty T-shirt and jeans amidst the formal splendour of the ballroom, that the room quickly lapsed into silence.

A muscle ticked wildly in the side of Ross's jaw, but he did not look at Chrissy. 'She said to let her go.' He spoke quietly, but his voice carried through the silent room. Only Hugo, goggling drunkenly, did not notice the menace in his stance.

'Get in line, Ross. She's gasping for it! As you should know better than most – but you've got to wait your turn.'

'You . . .' Ross's hand closed on the other man's shirt collar and he yanked him to his feet, into the onrushing path of his clenched fist. There was a loud smack and Ross held his stunned victim upright for a moment before allowing him to fall back into his chair, blood streaming from his nose. The whole thing happened so quickly, Chrissy could only stand and stare.

'Hey, steady on, Ross, you can't do that. It was just a bit of fun. You can't do that!' Phil was flabbergasted, staring from Ross back to Hugo, who held his hands to his face in disbelief trying to stem the blood.

'Can't I?' Ross's fists were still clenched as he turned his gaze on Phil, his eyes bright with a rage that made the other man take an involuntary step back.

'Well, well well,' drawled Portia, stepping forward, uncaring that she was dressed only in a strapless bra and a thong. 'Can't you just taste the testosterone in the air? I never thought you had it in you, Ross. I wish I'd seen this side of you before.'

'Shut your stupid mouth, Portia.'

'Oh, such a forceful man. You're making me soooo wet.'

Ross ignored her, and turned to Chrissy. 'Are you coming?'

'Yes, of course.' Still unable to believe he was here, or how handsome and dangerous he looked, his rage directed for once at somebody else, Chrissy stepped close to him.

'Where are you going, Clarissa darling? You're not going to forfeit the game, are you?' Portia's voice dripped with concern.

'You're mad, Portia. You're all mad if you think I'd go along with this. Get out of my way.'

'Hang on a minute, I've got a little present for you, Ross. I'm sure you'll find it an interesting memento. Scott! Bring me those photos.' Scott, who was watching the whole thing with an expression of wry amusement on his face, patted his pockets loosely.

'Photos? Gosh, I seem to have lost them,' he drawled, more prepared to face Portia's wrath at the moment than Ross's. This did not seem the time to tell her that he had flushed the photos down the toilet even before leaving Clarissa's house the day before, thinking Portia was likely to pull a stunt like this and wanting nothing to do with it. He winked at Chrissy.

Portia shot him a savage look before turning back to Chrissy. 'But what about the Treasure Hunt? What about the ten thousand pounds?'

Chrissy was aware that Ross had paused on his way to the door to listen to her reply. 'Stuff the Treasure Hunt and the money,' she said, her voice loud and clear. 'You are all bloody insane!'

'Looks like I win again, darlings.' She heard Portia's voice trill. 'Now, why don't we continue where we left off? Scott? Come here, darling; there's something I really need to say to you.' The doors swung shut.

Out on the pavement, Ross pulled her by the arm to where he had parked his car. Wordlessly he opened the door for her then climbed into the driver's seat. Chrissy was still a little confused and shaky. Belatedly she began to wonder exactly what Ross had been doing at the ball, why he had so suddenly and so handily arrived to save her. He had offered no explanation and he looked no less angry now than he had inside. Surreptitiously she eyed his tense profile, his stiff shoulders.

'Where to?' he asked tersely.

Without having to think about it Chrissy gave him her home address. She was finished with Clarissa and everything about her. It was time to go home. Ross drove in silence for some time.

'I've never done anything like that before,' he said finally, his voice flat and grim. 'Hit someone, I mean.'

'I believe you.'

'I mean it. I've never done anything like that.'

'I *believe* you.'

He was silent again for a while. 'I think I've broken something in my hand. It's bloody sore.'

'Serves you right. I could have handled it.'

'I believe you.' He managed a wry smile.

They pulled up outside the address Chrissy had given him. 'Where's this?'

'My place.'

Awkwardly, they sat in the car, each staring straight ahead out of the window.

'Chrissy . . .'

Chrissy braced herself for the lecture that she surely knew was coming. Her chin came up in an unconscious gesture. 'Let's go inside. We can't sit here in the car, arguing.'

Her words were like a blow to Ross. Well, why should she make it easy for him?

Wordlessly, she led him into her house and up the two flights of stairs that led to her loft. In other circumstances Ross would have been interested in the renovation work that was going on in the house, but for the moment he found himself distracted by the sway of Chrissy's hips as she climbed the stairs ahead of him. That dress, the way the light caught the gold silk, accentuating every dip and curve, kept his attention focused firmly on her body and his own semi-arousal, allowing him to put off thoughts of the unpleasant scene that no doubt lay ahead. Somehow he just had to persuade her to give him another chance.

Chrissy walked stiffly ahead of him into her home. She was perilously close to tears and could not afford to let him see how vulnerable she was at the moment. 'I'll put the kettle on. Sorry, I don't have anything else to drink. And you'll have to take it black. I've no milk.' She pulled mugs out of the cupboard above and turned straight into Ross's arms.

'Chrissy, I need to talk to you.' His voice was surprisingly gentle. Startled, she looked up at him, saw the uncertainty in his eyes. To her horror she was overcome with a surge of misery and longing, and she immediately burst into tears, hating herself, but unable to stop.

'Ross? Oh Ross, it was horrible. You were right. They wanted me to . . . They wanted me to . . .'

'Sh.' Guilt stabbed through him as he held her tightly. He should never have let her go to the damn ball alone. He knew, better than most, what Portia was capable of. Unconsciously he tightened his grip on her. Chrissy pressed her face into his chest, sobbing wildly, breathing in the comforting, familiar scent that she had missed so much.

'Chrissy, darling, are you all right? I should have been there. I'm sorry. Are you sure you're OK?' His voice was gentle as he stroked her hair.

Unable to trust herself to speak, Chrissy nodded, then, as her head started to spin again, wished that she hadn't. 'I am now. I feel awful.' Very much regretting the alcohol she had consumed, she was still aware that he had offered no explanation for his presence. If it was to be an 'I told you so' lecture, then it would just about finish her off. She decided to get her apology over with first.

She pulled away from him, but could not look him in the eye. 'You knew it was going to end like this and you tried to warn me,' she sniffed. 'I'm sorry. You were right. I should have listened to you.'

Ross stared at her in disbelief – she thought that he was here to gloat. Well, it served him right that she had such a low opinion of him. 'I wish you wouldn't say that,' he said awkwardly, drying her tears with his handkerchief. 'I haven't been right about much where you are concerned. I . . . I've come to apologise. Yet again. Will you ever forgive me, Chrissy? I've made such a fool of myself.'

'*You* have? Think how much of a fool I've been.' Chrissy managed a watery smile, desperately hoping her mascara was not running down her face.

To Ross, she had never looked more beautiful. He pulled her closer. 'I love you, Chrissy. Please say you forgive me.'

Chrissy's heart leapt at his words, but she stared at him in confusion. 'But . . .'

'I love you. I've loved you from the first night I saw you. God, I've been so eaten up with jealousy, these past few days.' All the time he was talking he was dropping soft kisses on her upturned face. Chrissy felt the yearning in her body's immediate response, and struggled to maintain her control. She had to be sure.

'Ross?' Her voice was a whisper. Instantly he froze, gazing almost fearfully at her. Chrissy looked deeply into those clear blue eyes, eyes that had haunted her dreams for so many nights now, and thrilled at what she saw there, the love and desire shining from within. Knowing that his desire was for her made her inner flesh leap, the familiar liquid response of arousal flooding through her sex. He loved her!

Tears sparkled in her eyes once again, but this time Ross kissed them away. When she opened her mouth to speak he caught her lips with his own, kissing her softly. It was like no kiss he had ever experienced before. When she felt the brush of his tongue against her teeth she opened her mouth to him, revelling in the way their bodies moulded, a hot spark of desire igniting low in her belly. Taken by surprise by the strength of her reaction, Ross deepened his kiss, aware of the hardening in his groin where their bodies pressed close.

'Do you forgive me?' he whispered, his voice hoarse with emotion.

In reply Chrissy stepped away from him silently, slipped the straps of her dress over her shoulders and allowed the gold silk to shimmer to the floor, so she stood naked before him. Ross's gaze was hot on her skin, and he stared for a long time.

'God, you are so lovely,' he groaned. 'I've missed you so much.' He reached slowly for her, tenderly touching her breasts. Chrissy looked down, watching as his strong hands stroked the honey-toned softness of each breast; she saw how the dark tips of her nipples rose against his palms. She moaned. She wanted him so badly, but did not want this moment of intense closeness and anticipation ever to end.

Her moans seemed to act like a spur to Ross's own arousal. Part of him was aware that she had not responded to his declaration of love, but if that was how it was to be, then fine. She would grow to love him; he would see to that. He would see to it that she would never want another man again. Almost roughly he grabbed her bare bottom and pressed her hard against him.

'Do you have any idea how much I want you?' he growled. 'I want you now, no conditions attached. I only ask that you give me a chance. I never want to be without you again.' His voice was thick with emotion and the whole time he talked he was massaging her buttocks, brushing soft feathery kisses over her face and throat.

Chrissy could not trust herself to speak. This was more wonderful that anything she could have imagined – Ross loved her, wanted to be with her. Wordlessly, her actions speaking for her, she loosened his trousers, reaching inside to free his straining cock. He gave a ragged gasp when she released him, his manhood rearing up between them as he kicked off the rest of his clothes. In wonder, Chrissy wrapped her fingers around his penis, a visible thrill running through her as she felt him swell with pent-up, tumultuous, desire.

Suddenly Ross caught her by the hand and pulled her towards

the bed, pressing her down on the covers. He leaned over her for a second, his eyes so dark with desire he looked almost like a stranger, making Chrissy shiver under the intensity of his gaze, the emotion she saw there almost overwhelming. He began to kiss her and this time there was nothing tender in his kisses. His tongue plundered her mouth savagely, their lips and teeth clashing with a bruising ardour. When he traced a line over her throat and collar-bone to take her breast into his mouth, he left a burning trail of white-hot kisses on her skin where his lips and teeth had passed. As he nipped and sucked hard on each nipple in turn, Chrissy writhed in his arms, the pull of his mouth on her an exquisite agony that sent hot darts of pleasure to her very core.

He continued his almost rough tasting of her breasts while one hand slipped between her legs to check her readiness for him. Discovering how wet she was, he groaned loudly, his own desire mounting rapidly. With a growing sense of urgency he lowered himself, his hard body completely covering her. The moist parted lips of her sex cradled his penis in a welcoming kiss that made them both tremble in anticipation. The tension within him was mounting, his breath coming in deep ragged gasps, but he paused for a moment to gaze at her in wonder.

'I've dreamt of nothing but this moment for two days. I want to stay like this forever, knowing that I'm just about to be inside you.' The look in his eyes was so full of love and tenderness that Chrissy felt her own eyes fill with tears again.

She reached up and clasped her hands around his neck, kissing him fervently. 'I love you,' she whispered.

For a moment he went very still, as if he could not believe his ears, then, with their gazes still locked, he moved his hips slightly so that his hard penis slid inside her in one long smooth stroke, sheathing him in her soft warm velvet. He rested inside her for a second, savouring the way her inner walls clasped him snugly.

'Do you really mean that?'

'Yes. Oh yes, I love you.' They stared at each other, frightened by the strength of the emotions that churned through them.

Then suddenly they both started to laugh. Chrissy pulled his face down to meet hers again, kissing him joyfully, as Ross began to move his hips in a rapturous rhythm. She felt herself rising on the crest of a gigantic wave; it felt so good to finally say those words, to know that he shared her feelings. Her legs wrapped tightly around his waist as they rode the wave together.

Every time his plunging penis dragged the protective hood from her swollen clitoris, Chrissy cried out her pleasure. Every tightening of her powerful inner muscles stroked his erection till he thought he would die just with the thrill of being inside her. The wave continued to rise, the pleasure continued to grow. Now Chrissy could hear a low keening animal noise and had no idea whether she was making it or if he was. Her back arched as she tried to pull him even deeper inside her, taking his massive length easily.

He said her name softly, unable to believe that she was truly here in his arms, and Chrissy's eyes flew open and locked with his again. The look that passed between them was enough to push them both over the edge as they raced headlong together along a tunnel that had no beginning, no end – just a whirling vortex of pleasure that went on and on and on. Chrissy twisted and bucked, calling his name again and again as she was filled with him, filled by the seed of his love and desire. Nothing that had happened to her in the last few days had prepared her for this. She wept in his arms, shaking with the violent emotion of an experience so mind-blowing in its intensity that she knew it could never be matched with any other man.

When at last the waves of pleasure ebbed away and he gently lowered her back onto the bed, Ross's eyes, too, had a suspicious sheen. He held her close, as if by maintaining contact he could ensure that he would never lose her again. They lay like this for a long time.

Chrissy was the first to speak. 'I'm sorry that I lost you all the money,' she whispered.

'What money?' He seemed engrossed in his task of kissing a line down the curve of her back over the swell of her bottom.

'The £10,000. The Treasure Hunt money.'

Ross stopped what he was doing for a moment to look at her hard. 'Let's agree never to talk about that. It's in the past. I never want to hear Clarissa or Portia's name again. Anyway,' he continued, his attention distracted by the tiny dimples on her lower back, 'I get the money either way.' He swirled his tongue over the dimple.

'You what?' Chrissy spun round and sat up, almost knocking him off the bed. 'You get the money anyway? What the hell does that mean?'

'Didn't you know?' Ross laughed at the look of disbelief on her face. 'Down and Out gets the money whoever wins. Clarissa or Portia. That was the deal. Ow.' He raised his hands to protect himself as Chrissy smashed a pillow down on his head.

'Didn't you think to mention that earlier? Bastard.' She hit him again, as hard as she could.

Ross caught her arms and pinned her to the bed. His eyes sparkled with amusement. 'Would it have made any difference?'

'No, but it would have been nice to know. Know I didn't have to feel guilty about letting you down.' She wriggled from beneath him, and rolled him over till she was straddling his flat tummy, her breasts swinging inches from his face.

'Are we fighting?' asked Ross, his eyes on the full round globes.

'You're damn right we're fighting.'

'Great. This kind of fighting, I enjoy.' He nuzzled her breast joyfully with his lips and Chrissy moaned, dropping her pillow. 'We can fight like this every day.'

And as she felt his hard length of his penis pressing against her once more, Chrissy could only agree.

A Message from the Publisher

Headline Liaison is a new concept in erotic fiction: a list of books designed for the reading pleasure of both men and women, to be read alone – or together with your lover. As such, we would be most interested to hear from our readers.

Did you read the book with your partner? Did it fire your imagination? Did it turn you on – or off? Did you like the story, the characters, the setting? What did you think of the cover presentation? In short, what's your opinion? If you care to offer it, please write to:

> The Editor
> Headline Liaison
> 338 Euston Road
> London NW1 3BH

Or maybe you think you could do better if you wrote an erotic novel yourself. We are always on the look-out for new authors. If you'd like to try your hand at writing a book for possible inclusion in the Liaison list, here are our basic guidelines: We are looking for novels of approximately 80,000 words in which the erotic content should aim to please both men and women and should not describe illegal sexual activity (pedophilia, for example). The novel should contain sympathetic and interesting characters, pace, atmosphere and an intriguing plotline.

If you'd like to have a go, please submit to the Editor a sample of at least 10,000 words, clearly typed on one side of the paper only, together with a short resume of the storyline. Should you wish your material returned to you please include a stamped addressed envelope. If we like it sufficiently, we will offer you a contract for publication.

Dangerous Desires

J. J. DUKE

*In response to his command, Nadine began
to undress. She was wearing her working
clothes, a black skirt and a white silk blouse.
As she unzipped the skirt she tried to keep
her mind in neutral. She didn't do this kind
of thing. As far as she could remember, she
had never gone to bed with a man only
hours after she'd met him . . .*

There's something about painter John
Sewell that Nadine Davies can't resist.
Though she's bowled over by his looks
and his talent, she knows he's arrogant
and unfaithful. It can't be love and it's
nothing like friendship. He makes her
feel emotions she's never felt before.

And there's another man, too. A man
like Sewell who makes her do things
she'd never dreamed of – and she
adores it. She's under their spell, in
thrall to their dangerous desires . . .

0 7472 5093 6